Witches Were For Hanging

Patricia Crowther

R.J. Stewart
Books
P.O. Box 802
Arcata, CA 95518

Witches Were
For Hanging
by
Patricia Crowther

**From an original concept
by
Arnold Crowther**

2007 Edition
R.J. Stewart Books

ISBN: 978-0-9791402-5-9

R.J. Stewart
Books

P.O. Box 802
Arcata, CA 95518
www.rjstewart.net

About the author:

Patricia Crowther was born and educated in Sheffield. In 1960, she was initiated into the Craft of the Wise by Gerald Brosseau Gardner and is also heir to a secondary hereditary tradition of witchcraft from the North of Scotland.

The Author is an ordained High Priestess of the Great Goddess and a *doyenne* of the Craft. Now being over 70, she is known as a Grand Mother of the Craft. Over the last forty years and more, she has been a leading spokesperson for the Old Religion through her lectures, books and regular television and radio interviews.

For Ian, with love. And for all those
Children of the Goddess - Past, Present
and Future

CHAPTER 1

Death was very close to the small rodent which sniffed the night air. Its bright eyes surveyed the woodland scene, utterly oblivious of any danger. The owl poised itself, about to swoop on its prey, then suddenly, both creatures froze, as the ground reverberated to the sound of rhythmic thuds coming nearer with every passing second. The bird uttered a screech and flapped off into the wood, but the mouse trembled and twitched, temporarily unable to move. A twig cracked under the weight of a heavy boot, breaking the spell, and the small, brown thing darted into the undergrowth to live another day. Thus, fate moves through apparently unrelated incidents. Without knowing it, the traveller had saved a tiny life from extinction.

A scudding cloud eclipsed the waxing moon and the man heaved a sigh of relief. He kept to the side of the path, within the dark shadows cast by the overhanging trees, occasionally glancing behind him. Rough gusts of wind shook the foliage, snatching off small branches, and the far-off scream of a night animal, caught in a snare, caused his breath to quicken, momentarily.

A shaft of moonlight gleamed through a break in the trees and disclosed the man to be in his middle years. An open, honest face was made arresting by a pair of amazingly blue eyes, and even the sombre clothing failed to conceal the rippling muscles of this, six foot tall, son-of-the-soil.

Robert Maxwell was, indeed, a farmer. His father, a widower, had died suddenly from a heart attack, some years before, and now the running of the farm, Greycoats, was his own affair. He managed fairly well with the help of three hard-working 'hands', but he had plans to take a wife in the near future and the thought gave a sudden lift to his steps. It was the one bright star on his horizon.

The Civil War had made everyone nervous and jumpy, and although the noise of conflict, between the King's Men and Parliament, was merely the rumble of distant thunder in Essex, it nevertheless was a very worrying time. Many lives had already been lost and these included the bright, hopeful young men from the nearby town of Belford. Most of them, not knowing one end of a musket from the other, had been delegated to the ranks of pikemen. Some, Robert Maxwell had grown up with and bore the title of 'friend'. Their hot young blood had flowed to the sympathy's of one side or the other and that had been enough. Now, that same blood had become a libation to the earth, in the way a cause will always rob a country of its brightest hopes.

Both sides had suffered increasingly from shortage of money and man-power and the battle of Marston Moor, in the previous year, had been undecisive even though Parliament had won a slight advantage. It resulted in men demanding to be sent home through lack of payment and weariness. Mutinies and desertion had been the order of the day, with many hundreds tramping southward, penniless and hungry.

With so many farms left in the hands of women and youths, it was easy for the men, beyond reach of military discipline, to steal or beg money and food from them. The forces of law and order were under-manned and ill-equipped so were not a serious obstacle or deterrent.

Up to now, Maxwell had been lucky, in that he had not received any visits from erstwhile soldiers, but it was early days and for this reason he disliked leaving his farm unattended. Another month or so would see the deserters safely to their homes and the end of one worry.

Then, again, there was Naseby which was much nearer home. It was scarcely a month since the Royalists had been defeated there. Still, a victory might take Cromwell's men further afield; it was not likely that the King could hold out much longer.

He sighed as he thought of England's troubles. Robert Maxwell was not a coward but he detested violence of any kind. It was simply not in him to kill another individual. He was aware of being in the minority and knew he was often the subject of local gossip, because of it. Nevertheless, he had considerable courage and a physical strength which brooked no argument. One day he might have to face an enemy of a different hue. Who or what that enemy would be was not yet clear, but for a certainty, he knew it would come to pass.

The now thinning trees at the edge of the forest, disclosed a solitary farm-house. Maxwell again looked around him before opening the small gate. He avoided the path of limestone chippings and walked soundlessly on the soft turf. His hand was upon the iron knocker when a small, inky shadow detached itself from the surrounding darkness. The black cat mewed plaintively, twisting round the stocking-clad legs.

"Where did you come from, puss?" His strong, capable hand stroked the silky coat. "I know you don't live here. You had better be off to where you belong." The cat ignored him; weaving between sturdy calves. "I'm sorry, but you cannot come in. It's too dangerous - shoo!" Maxwell lifted the feline and gently tossed it back into the shadows. "Now, go back home." The cat did not re-appear and with a sigh of

3

relief he grasped the knocker again and tapped lightly upon the door.

Mistress Agnes Nokes, a widow in her fifties, sat sewing in the living-room of Elm-tree farm with her two daughters, Meg and Bess. She was still an attractive woman and had been extremely comely in her youth. Her grey hair was dressed tidily in a bun and surmounted with a stiff, white coif. A dress of blue cotton matched her clear eyes which lifted from time to time to rest fondly on her daughters.

Bess, the senior of the two, was nearing her thirtieth year and endowed with a well-rounded figure. She was no beauty, but her neatness of dress and abundant red-gold hair, escaping from beneath a white cap, gave her a certain distinction. Since her father's death, ten years before, Bess had taken over the responsibility of their small-holding; feeding the animals and looking after the crops. That evening, she was busily engaged in cleaning the household silver, a frown on her usually placid countenance.

Her sister had seen only eighteen summers and was a less robust girl, yet her's was the stronger character of the two sisters. Meg's pale-gold hair fell around her shoulders and her thin hands showed a tracery of blue veins as she helped her mother separate the skeins of coloured silks. Her beautiful violet eyes held a far-away expression in them, most of the time, which greatly annoyed her more down-to-earth sister. Bess could see no sense in day-dreaming when there was a farm to run and always something to do. Still, they managed to agree on most things and were a happy family.

The peace of the room was broken by a tap on the door. "Who can that be at such an hour?" asked Mistress Nokes. "Go and see who it is Bess, my dear."

4

Her daughter hurried to the door, released the bolt and slowly opened it a few inches. "It's Robert," she squeaked, excitedly.

"Let him in quickly."

Bess released the door and Robert slipped into the room. His movements were surprisingly graceful, considering his burly frame. He greeted Mistress Nokes, kissed Meg on her cheek and taking Bess in his arms, he whirled her off her feet to her cries of delight.

"I hope no one saw you coming here," Agnes looked at the man, anxiously.

"Have no fear, Agnes, I took good care to keep out of sight as I came along."

"Well now, sit ye down, Robert. Meg, fetch him a tankard of ale."

Robert lowered his large frame into an accommodating chair while Meg put aside the silks and disappeared into the kitchen.

Bess leaned over him. "Is all prepared for Saturday's meeting, darling?"

"Aye! I have informed all the others, sweetheart, and they will all be there, but I'm afraid I have some bad news for you. It's about Jane . . . come, sit on my knee." He caught her hand and Bess was soon nestling on his lap.

"What about Jane?" asked Meg, framed in the doorway, a brimming tankard in her hand.

"Is she sick?" queried Bess.

"Would to Old Hornie she was. Thanks Meg." Robert took a swig of the ale. "It's far worse than that. She's been accused of witchcraft by Matthew Hopkins and his mob."

In the shocked silence that followed, a falling log in the grate, sounded unnaturally loud.

5

"Where is she now?" Meg's voice came out of the stillness.

"They've taken her to prison. She lies in a stinking cell, closely guarded."

Mistress Nokes put her head in her hands. "Oh, bless her, Hopkins will make sure she does not escape; every woman executed means twenty silver shillings to him. This town has not been safe since the witchfinders arrived here. We all go in fear of our lives and never know, from one day to the next, when *our* turn will come."

"Aye, that's true enough." Bess nodded. "My heart aches for poor Jane, but I suppose we can consider ourselves lucky to have kept the coven together all this time. Jane's the first one to be caught."

Meg's violet eyes filled with tears and she began to weep bitterly.

"How can you talk so of poor Jane," she sobbed. "We'll never see her again."

"Maybe on the gallows." Robert's knuckles showed white as he tightened his grip on the tankard. "Hopkins will make sure she receives the maximum penalty."

Bess suddenly jumped off his knee. "But what if she denounces us all as witches? The judges always make their victims reveal who their accomplices are, as you well know!"

Meg looked disdainfully at her sister, her pretty face swollen with weeping. "You make me sick, worrying about your own skin. Jane would never give us away - she would rather die first."

"She'll do that right enough," Robert smiled grimly. "Once you're accused of witchcraft you're as good as dead."

"That is so," said Mistress Nokes, nodding her head. "We can't possibly save her now, but we must not let her get into

6

the hands of the torturers, they would force her to confess everything and also our consciences would not allow her to suffer. How long has she been in prison?''

''Three days,'' answered Robert.

''I dread to think what she's had to put up with from those filthy gaolers. The wretches would rape any female who fell into their hands - especially a virgin!'' She poked the fire savagely.

It was one of Mistress Nokes' foibles that she always had a flame in the hearth - even in summer!

''They even brag about their loathsome deeds in the local inns,'' growled Robert. ''Why only yesterday a turnkey was pompously declaring how he had seduced sixteen condemned witches in one week!''

''They make me want to vomit,'' snarled Meg. ''They should all be strung up.'' She kicked a convenient stool.

''All this will not help Jane,'' chided her mother. ''We must see that poison reaches her before she is taken to the torture chamber. It will save her from much pain and suffering - and also protect the Craft.''

''You can't do that Mother!'' screamed Meg, rounding on the old lady. ''Jane is too young to die.''

Mistress Nokes stood up and put her arms round the weeping girl.

''I know it sounds callous and cold my dear, but she cannot escape death, and poison is the easiest way out.''

Meg wiped her eyes on her apron and hugged her mother:

''I know you are right, but it all sounds so terrible. What are we to do?''

''I'll try to deliver it to her first thing in the morning,'' Robert smiled at her reassuringly.

"No!" snapped Bess. "I'll deliver it. It will be much easier for a woman to get past the guards, than it would be for a man."

Robert took her hands within his own:

"I don't like it. What if a gaoler attacked you? I could not bear to take such a risk."

"I'm afraid we'll all have to take risks in the future - I feel it in my bones. It's like a darkness drawing ever nearer." Mistress Nokes shivered and drew her shawl more closely around her shoulders. "If only it was like the old days, when the followers of the Old Gods were allowed to worship without being molested. Even the priests and churchmen used to attend the Great Sabbats." She gazed into the fire, her mind slipping back into the past. "Both the old and the new faiths tolerated each other and worked side by side. Now, they have taken our sacred groves and hills and built churches upon them, hoping to lure us away from our gods."

The others listened to her with rapt attention; always fascinated when Mistress Nokes spoke of bygone times.

"The early church did not think our gods would be such diehards; they hoped the people would soon forget them."

"That's true," Robert smiled wryly, "but the folks were not ready to desert their gods as easily as that. They became rivals to the established church, so the priests call us heretics and say our Horned God is the Devil."

"Such balderdash!" snapped Bess. "Surely, one must be a Christian first, in order to become a heretic?"

"Correct!" Robert grinned at her. "But now we are compelled to attend church or be fined! The Puritans think we are *all* Christians, although many of us only pay lip-service to the new faith."

The conversation seemed to cheer Meg up a bit and she smiled, mischievously:

"I wish I had lived in those days. I have heard that the squires often supplied the feasts and as many as three oxen and a dozen sheep were roasted on the spits, and the dancing went on until dawn. But, all this talk of food makes me feel quite hungry; I'll go and find something to eat for us all." And she disappeared into the kitchen.

"Meg is right," sighed her mother. "The Old Religion was, and still is, a joyous one - and that is the real reason why the Puritans hate us. Now, we are forced to worship in secret and we will have to be even more careful in the future." Her hands gripped the arms of her chair as she looked anxiously around at the surroundings she loved. "May the Old Ones guide us in these times of peril."

Bess paced round the room, restlessly:

"But, why have we become such outcasts and our religion condemned as Satanism?"

"Don't you understand, child?" Mistress Nokes banged the arm of her chair with a clenched fist. "*We* are the scapegoats, now. Human beings will not take the blame for their own faults, and now they have found an easy way out. It is much simpler to say 'my crops have been bewitched,' than to admit it is due to their own neglect. An incompetent leech can also blame the death of a patient on witchcraft."

Her daughter's face coloured in anger and frustration:

"I'm sick to death of the lies that are told about us and the way we have to live, like moles, creeping in the dark to attend our rites. It's terrifying." She shivered, in spite of the warmth of the room.

Meg returned with a laden tray:

9

"Come on, let's eat. I'm starving." She cut into a large fruit cake and helped herself to a piece of cheese. "Mmm . . . lovely!"

Everyone helped themselves to the food, and for a while, the room was silent. Meg seated herself on a stool near to the fire. The reflection from the flames, leaped and danced over her delicate features, making her look like a nymph of the woodlands. She gazed pensively into the gleaming logs:

"Remember Jane's grandmother?" she mused. "Just because she wouldn't allow old Giles to have one of her goats, he went to the authorities and told them she had killed *his* goat by putting the 'Evil Eye' upon it."

"How could a blind old woman do that?" scoffed Bess. "She could barely hobble around her cottage."

"That made no difference," replied Meg. "No one cared about *her*. All the neighbours swore that she had dealings with the Devil and changed into a cat before going off to the Sabbat."

"Young Oliver was to blame for that," interrupted her mother. "He swore, under oath, that he saw her leave her home in the shape of a cat, while, presumably, the cat took over her body and slept in her bed until she returned."

They all hooted with laughter.

"How can folk believe such nonsense - especially when it comes from a mere boy?" cried Meg.

"These days, people are ready to believe anything about witches," replied Robert. "If a lie is told again and again, folk begin to believe it's the truth. In fact, you begin to believe it, yourself! It's terrible to think that the fantasies of a child can bring torture and death to an innocent old woman."

"An old dame who owns a cat and lives alone is definitely in

10

danger, these days," added Mistress Nokes.

"I love cats," said Meg, softly, "but now I'm frightened even to stop and stroke one! If our dear Tib-tab had not died two years ago, the locals would have sworn that Mother had a familiar." The others giggled.

"There was a stray cat outside the door when I came in," exclaimed Robert, "but I drove it away."

"I should think so, too!" Bess poked him in the ribs. "We don't want cats here, we can't take any chances. You dare not even trust your own children once the witchfinders get at them."

Meg ran into the kitchen, then suddenly appeared with a large, white sheet draped over her head. She proceeded to amuse them by parading round the room, moaning softly and wringing her hands. Then, she stopped abruptly in front of Robert and pointed a long, slender finger at him.

"There was one, John Darrell, who brought forward a boy, William Somers of Nottingham, I believe; to accuse thirteen women of bewitching him." She flung out an arm, dramatically. "The man would have received a sovereign for each woman!"

"It's a paying game right enough," growled Robert.

"Just think," mused Bess, "thousands of people - men, women and children, have already been burned to death on the Continent."

Meg returned to her seat and held a white hand above the fire: "I suppose we must be thankful that England does not burn witches. Even a little burn hurts dreadfully."

"I can't see it's any worse than hanging," argued Bess. "You can at least inhale the smoke and suffocate before the flames reach you."

She stood up and yawned. "Let's talk no more of such

miseries. We are holding the festival on Saturday, when we must work magic for good crops. For a few hours we shall escape the horrors of this world and worship the gods we love."

Robert stretched his huge frame:

"I must away now and let you get some rest. The hour is very late and Sally will be wanting her stable and a feed. I left her tied up, hidden safely in the forest."

He bade them farewell and embraced Bess. "Take care when you go to the gaol tomorrow my love. I shall not know a moment's rest until you are safely back. Blessed Be!"

"Blessed Be!" chorused the others, as Bess led him to the door.

"Open it cautiously," called her mother. "You never know who may be watching. I've felt I have been spied upon ever since our last meeting."

The others turned and stared at her, and Meg, the empty tray in her hands, sat down suddenly, making the crockery rattle loudly. It was Robert who found his voice:

"By whom?"

"I don't rightly know. I just felt I was being followed when I walked home."

"You never told me, Mother," said Bess, her voice sharp with anxiety.

"Nor me," echoed Meg. Her errand to the kitchen temporarily forgotten, she replaced the tray on the table, frowning.

"Oh dear, I didn't want to worry you, girls. Maybe I imagined it. I'm just a silly old woman." She waved them away. "Goodbye Robert. Take care."

Bess could not resist a last kiss on the doorstep, and the black cat slid into the warmth of the room.

12

"Look!" shouted Meg. "That cat's come in!" She snatched up a convenient broom. "Get out - oh get out, do! We cannot have you in here."

The cat fled behind the settle, spitting defiantly at the offending weapon which hit the floor with a resounding 'thwack' just behind it.

"Let it be, Meg," commanded her mother. "It looks lost and hungry poor thing."

Bess, now thoroughly alarmed, closed the door. "But it cannot stay here, we dare not have a cat in this house - especially a *black* cat!"

Mistress Nokes coaxed the animal out and lifted it into her arms.

"We of the Old Faith are taught to love animals. I'm not turning a stray cat away, particularly when it needs food. Fetch some milk for it, Meg."

Her daughter threw down the broom in disgust and clucking indignantly, walked over to the dresser where she poured some milk into a wooden bowl.

"Place it near the fire, dear."

"Are you sure it doesn't want a cushion to sit on, too?" asked Meg, sarcastically. Her mother ignored the remark and put the cat down beside the bowl. It drank the contents, greedily.

"Poor thing. I wonder when you were last fed."

Bess flushed with anger:

"That cat can only bring evil to this house." She pointed an accusing finger at the feline. "Turn it out *at once*!"

Mistress Nokes continued to ignore her daughters and took the animal into her arms again:

"You are very thin. I wonder to whom you belonged?"

13

"Maybe some fool of an old woman who was hanged for a witch just because she *would* keep a cat!" sneered Bess as she slammed home the bolt of the door and stormed out of the room.

CHAPTER 2

The next morning, Bess set off down the lane on her way to the town's gaol. The sky was cloudless and there was no breeze to invigorate the land from the sun's heat. It was going to be a very hot day! A sky-lark sang joyfully somewhere in the vault of heaven, but there was no joy in the heart of Bess Nokes as she thought of Jane, lying in a damp and musty cell. She breathed a prayer to the gods that her mission might be successful.

Forty minutes of brisk walking brought her to the outskirts of Belford. The town sat just beyond the fringes of the Tendring Hundred, that pear-shaped area of Essex which lay on the coast between the Colne and Stour rivers. The latter claimed the privilege of being the river from which Edward the Third sailed in the Cog Thomas, to fight and emerge victorious, in the battle of Sluys.

Because of its position, Belford gained much from both inland and sea-going communities. The smacks and hoys, laden with fish from Harwich, sailed or rowed continuously up the Stour to deposit their sea-harvest on the quay-side at Clayton - a tiny port, half a mile from the town. And provided the weather aided the farmers, Belford would groan under the weight of land produce, too, for most of the year.

Again, due to its position, the town, in earlier times, had often been protected from the marauding companies of Dane and Saxon invaders, who had assuaged their blood-lust on the more easterly settlements, including Dovercourt and West Orwell. Belford had watched helplessly as they became transmuted into funeral pyres.

15

Many of the town's youth had sailed in Elizabeth's ships to bombard and rout the Spanish Armada in the Channel. And Belford had lit its victory beacon on Maiden Tor, joining hundreds of other, similar boon-fires, throughout England.

Now, in the summer of 1645, it was the town's market day and the place was packed. Laden carts mingled with droves of sheep and cattle, all making their way to the centre of the town.

'How I hate crowds,' thought Bess, as she pushed her way through the jostling throng of people. The hot air was full of shouts and the cries of stall-holders proclaiming their wares. She was startled when a man lurched out of an inn and blundered into her; his round face, red, and glistening with sweat. Bess eluded his grasp and gritted her teeth. She must not be put off by such things when her friend was in danger and in need of help.

Taking a route through the maze of narrow streets and alleys, she soon came within sight of the gaol. A great, stone structure, it served also as an armoury and stood atop a slight rise on the perimeter of the town, like an outcast - a leper. It seemed descriptive of all those unfortunate prisoners who had perished within its walls . . . a forbidding memorial.

Bess shivered as she neared the grim building and stopped for a moment in the shelter of a doorway, her heart pounding at the enormity of her quest. Again, she pulled herself together and checked to see that she had not forgotten anything. No, she had brought the necessary things. A silver-knobbed walking stick and a bundle tied up in a coloured kerchief. She started off again and began to hobble, using the stick for support. Quite soon, she was limping through the great archway of the prison.

16

There was only one guard on duty and for this she was thankful. He stood picking his teeth with a piece of bone. Bess sensed him eyeing her up and down, and as she approached him, he spoke:

"What ails thee, lass?"

"It's nothing serious. I twisted my ankle yesterday and it still pains me."

He spat on the cobbles. "That's bad. I knows how painful a sprain can be. But, what is your business here?"

"I've brought my father's dinner, sir. He's one of the turnkeys. Will you be so kind as to take it to him?"

The man shook his head and answered as she had hoped he would.

"Nay, that's impossible, lass. I dare not go off duty here - we're one short, already." He rubbed an unshaven chin, "I suppose *you* could take it to him," he said, slowly.

"Could I?" Bess gazed up at him innocently and asked if he was hungry.

"I've not had a bite to eat since the cock crowed and I'll not get anything until I goes off duty in two hours time."

"Then, *do* have some of this." Bess untied the cloth as she spoke and handed the guard one of the savoury-looking cooked chickens that it contained.

"Bye! You're a generous lass and no mistake. God bless you for your kindness," he said, tearing at the white meat and stuffing it greedily into his mouth.

"Now go and finish your errand and don't be too long about it, mind."

Relief flooded through Bess as she hobbled through the archway. She had surmounted her first obstacle with very little difficulty.

A burly gaoler leaned up against one of the cell doors, his ugly face made more repulsive by a week's growth of dark stubble. He scratched himself and yawned, hugely, as another man came down the passage towards him.

"How's your new witch, Jonathan?" grinned the newcomer, a tall, lantern-jawed individual. Jonathan's face registered disgust:

"A pox on yon hell-cat! Here, just look at them scratches," he bared a hairy arm for the other man to see. His companion gave a harsh guffaw: "Been up to our little tricks again, 'ave we?" he chuckled.

"And why not?" Jonathan snarled. "Don't we all take the women we fancy before the torturers get at 'em? Why should fine flesh be wasted? Tell me that! We might as well enjoy them while they're in good shape - aye - and give 'em a bit of pleasure into the bargain. They're no good for it after they've been broken on the ladder or pressed in the boot, as you well know."

"Aye," the other agreed. "I'd hate to be in *their* hands, the stinking butchers. Only yesterday, one of them was bragging he could make the Pope, himself, confess to witchcraft, if he could get him on the rack."

He walked over to the nearest cell and peered through the grill:

"God's grace, you've a beauty in there. The ones I've got are as ugly as sin, with dugs like empty leather bags! It makes me spew to look at 'em. You'd think they'd convict some pretty wenches so that I could have a ride now and then." He spat, contemptuously.

"They tell me you don't do so bad, Tom," grinned Jonathan, scratching his head. "The trouble is, I'm too particular who I gets into. I'm not like you - as long as it's female, you couldn't care less."

"That's as maybe," the other, leered. "But, look at that old crone you had last week - must 'ave bin seventy if she was a day! Don't tell me you didn't tumble her," he grinned evilly.

"What if I did?" Jonathan folded his arms, arrogantly. "At least she was easy; not like this bitch," he indicated the cell door. "I can't even feel her bubs without her fighting like a fiend from Hell. She must have the Devil in her to get a man of my strength down. I've tried to poke her ever since she came, but I can't get near it. They do say as how she is a virgin, too."

"And they do say as how you've taken more maidenheads than any other gaoler here. You're losing your grip me lad."

Tom grinned, enjoying the other's discomfort.

"Oh yes? Well, there's another one I'll 'ave before this night's out."

Jonathan cocked a dirty thumb at the cell and Tom chuckled:

"Well, you'll have to be pretty quick about it. She's for the torture chamber at sundown." He straightened his jacket. "I'd better go and see how the old hags are getting on. I never know when they might turn into wolves and leap through the bars." He laughed hollowly at his own joke and strolled off.

Jonathan watched him through narrowed eyes until he was out of sight, then he went over to the cell and unlocked the door.

Jane lay on a heap of rotting straw. She was a pretty girl, just past her twentieth year. Her fair hair hung in a tangled mass and her dress - through previous encounters with Jonathan - was torn and dirty. She uttered a pitiful cry when he

19

entered - her eyes staring in her thin face. "Get out and leave me alone!"

Jonathan smirked at her:

"That's no way to speak to the only man who can give you a bit of comfort in your last hours."

Jane clenched her hands in the straw:

"Get out I say, or I'll kill you," she shouted.

"*You* kill *me*? I like that!" Jonathan chortled. "And how, may I ask? Will your master strike me dead with fire and brimstone?" He adopted a wheedling tone. "Come on - I like a wench with some guts."

As he approached, Jane pressed herself back against the wall, her eyes flashing with terror.

"Get away, or I'll scratch your eyes out," she panted.

But Jonathan still came on - intent on his goal. He wiped the sweat from his forehead, mechanically. "Surely you don't want to die without knowing a man? I'm strong and virile - I can satisfy any female." He breathed unevenly.

"You stinking, foul creature," Jane shrieked. "Leave me alone and get out!"

Jonathan was now thoroughly aroused:

"Your hot temper only makes me want you more. Come lass, give me a kiss." The remnants of his control finally vanished and he rushed at Jane; lifted her up and pressed her body against the rough stone wall. She could smell his fetid breath and the stench of stale sweat and she fought like a demon; kicking out with her bare feet.

Her efforts had little or no effect on Jonathan's great bulk. He seized one of her breasts and squeezed it until she screamed in agony, and as he leaned over her, she buried her small, white teeth into a hairy forearm. He yelled and reeled back:

20

"You bastard," he gritted. "I'll have you if it's the last thing I do." The gaoler caught the neck of her dress and ripped it down to the waist. The sight of her shapely figure fired his ardour afresh and he made another effort to grab her, but Jane struck out with her nails and achieved her objective. Her tormentor shrieked - his hands covering his injured face.

"You bloody bitch! You've blinded me."

He wiped away the blood that trickled down his cheeks and was relieved to find he could still see.

"You whore from Hell!" he roared. "Why should I want *you* after you've given yourself to demons? Go and lay with your fiends, you would only soil my body."

Jane's final defence had certainly dampened Jonathan's lust and he lumbered out of the room. "May the torturers tear your heart out!" he growled as he slammed and locked the door behind him.

As he turned, he saw Bess standing in the passage. Her unexpected presence temporarily stunned the gaoler.

"And who in God's name are you?" he asked.

"The guard outside is my brother," she said, quietly. "He let me in."

The man's bloodshot gaze slithered slowly over her. She was better looking than he had realised. He rubbed his features with a grubby rag.

"Dick never told me he had such a comely wench for a sister."

Bess smiled at him coyly and Jonathan began to feel a bit better.

"What have you there, lass?" He pointed to the bundle that Bess was carrying. She untied the cloth, "Food. Would you like some?"

21

She held out the second chicken. He grabbed it without answering, and breaking off a leg, sank his teeth into the succulent morsel.

As he shoved the meat into his mouth, he asked Bess what she wanted; touching her under the chin with a greasy forefinger.

"I would like to see the witch that you have in your care - the young one who was brought here three days ago," she stated, evenly.

"And what would a fair maid like you want with a stinking whore like her?" he asked, chomping noisily.

"I want to spit in her eye and beat her with this stick," Bess said, venomously; waving the weapon in front of Jonathan's startled face.

"You must not soil those pretty hands on that foul creature. The torturers will revenge you for whatever ill she has done."

"But I must have personal revenge," cried Bess. "She bewitched my husband and took away his manhood."

The gaoler grunted as he slowly picked his teeth - his mind digesting her words.

"You have indeed been wronged," he murmured. "So, you can't get any satisfaction from your man?" His eyes narrowed, craftily. "You have certainly come to the right place."

He threw the stripped carcass onto the floor; wiped his mouth on his sleeve, and belched loudly.

"Give us a kiss and I'll see what I can do for you. I would enjoy seeing you thrash her."

Bess hoped she would not show her feelings of repulsion as she allowed Jonathan to pull her towards him. His fat hands felt at her breasts and buttocks and his greasy mouth covered her lips. Bess felt her gorge rise but she dared not resist him.

After what seemed an age to her, the man straightened himself and sighed:

"That was better than yon black witch," he breathed, as he let her go. "It's a pity your brother knows where you are, we could have enjoyed ourselves. A bit of the other would have done you good. You must be longing for it with a man in that condition." The gaoler's coarse laughter echoed hollowly through the stone passage.

Bess forced a smile and stroked his unshaven cheek:

"Now, can I see the witch?" she pleaded.

"Aye . . . if you give me another kiss afterwards, mind." He squeezed her arm playfully and grinned at her.

"Very well, now open the door." Bess knew she must do anything in order to get into her friend's cell for a few minutes. "You can't stay long."

"Long enough for what *I* have to do."

Jonathan unlocked the door and held it open for Bess to enter. Then he followed her inside, anxious to see the fun.

Jane looked up from her bed of straw, but gave no sign of recognition. Bess walked quickly over to her and spat in her face.

"A pox on you - stinking witch," she cried. "You have brought shame upon me and my man. May you burn in Hell!"

She raised the cane and began to beat Jane, unmercifully. The unfortunate girl's screams resounded harshly in the bare cell, but Jonathan leaned against the wall, enjoying the spectacle - utterly impervious to the victim's pain.

"That'll learn ye. It's about time someone gave ye a bloody good thrashing," he chortled.

Then Bess broke the cane in half; threw the pieces at Jane

and rushed out of the cell. Jonathan hurried after her and quickly locked the door on his prisoner.

Jane rolled in agony, moaning softly. After a time, she realised that something hard was pressing into her back. She turned over and her hand closed on a piece of the cane, thrown there by her friend. She gazed at the silver knob. It gleamed and glittered in a ray of sunlight which had forced its way through the small, barred window, high up in the wall.

'What a beautiful thing to have come to me in this dark, dismal place,' she thought. It shone like the full moon and she was content merely to look at it for a while. Then, the sun-beam slowly faded, "Like my luck," she murmured.

She began to examine the knob and found that it unscrewed in the centre to disclose a small cavity. Feeling inside it, her trembling fingers closed on a tiny, glass phial.

"Oh, thank you for this deliverance, Bess," she whispered, and easing her bruised body up, she knelt, holding the phial between her slim hands. "Oh, great God and gentle Goddess, I thank Thee for Thy great mercy. Thou hast truly brought Thy rays - of silver and gold - the Moon and the Sun - into my darkness. Receive me into Thy Summerlands, so that I may be rested and purified. And when I once more return to this world, may I be reborn among my own people and find my way back to the Circle. Let it be in less troublesome times, when we can worship Thee, freely, without fear of persecution. Brothers and sisters of the Craft, I bid thee fare-well!"

Swiftly, she put the phial to her lips and swallowed its contents. Her body - heavy with the sleep of death - slid onto the flagstones and her soul passed to a happier abode. Silence fell in that lonely place, interrupted, momentarily, by an inquisitive rat, which pattered over Jane's outstretched arm, on its endless quest for nourishment.

Outside, in the passage, Bess was trying to deal with the amorous gaoler.
"Please don't bother me any more. I *must* go."
She gave him a push, but his body held her fast against the cold wall.
"Trying to make me think you're a good little girl, eh?" he sneered.
His foul breath caught in her nostrils making her want to vomit.
"What about my brother?" she asked, desperately averting her face.
"That's alright me pidgeon, he can't leave his post. We've got plenty of time."
He pressed closer, and, catching her flaming tresses in a huge fist, pulled her head round and forced his tongue into her mouth. This was more than Bess could bear, and she struggled, furiously. Then, lifting her foot she kicked at him with all her strength. He grunted with pain, but still held her fast, pulling her bodice open and lowering his head to her white flesh. He bit her nipple and she screamed in agony - her head flaying from side to side.
"Shut up, you bitch," he hissed. "I'll not be thwarted twice in one day." He mauled her generous breasts and grinned. "Very nice too! I like a well endowed woman, there's something to get yer 'ands on. Better than yon flat-chested witch."
Eventually, he dragged her further up the passage and propelled her roughly into an empty cell. "Get down on that

straw and keep yer mouth shut or I'll use me fist to ye.''
Jonathan gave her a push and Bess toppled onto the mouldering sacks. She knew it was useless to try and escape, he was already pinning her down with his body. Her mind flew to her lover. 'Forgive me, Robert, you warned me, but I never thought it could happen to me.'

The gaoler was taking off her clothes. She could smell his rank odour and sensed his sexual excitement. His breathing was clearly audible.

'The Gods help me,' she thought. 'Not that!'
Jonathan's hands were strong on her legs - forcing them apart. His kisses were wet and sickening to her. Slowly, he drew her towards him and Bess felt his manhood, hard, against her thighs. Something deep inside her body, suddenly recoiled and scurried away - hurt - into the inner core of her being. The gaoler pushed his hands under her buttocks and a second later his throbbing flesh tore into her body. Bess screamed with the intensity of the pain, and in her subsequent agony, lost consciousness. She had achieved her goal and paid in full!

The door of Jane's cell swung open and Jonathan entered carrying a bowl of skilly. His eyes fell upon the still figure in the straw.

''Still brooding over yer hiding, eh?'' He pushed her with his foot. ''Get up and eat yer vitals.''
A fly walked over Jane's cheek.
'''ere, what's up?''
Hurriedly, he put down the bowl and raised Jane's head; the yellow hair caressing his hand. Jonathan drew back, now thoroughly alarmed. 'Crack', the girl's head met the stones

as it fell from his nerveless fingers. "Jesu - dead!" The gaoler gazed into space, his mind as blank as the walls of the cell. "Christ!" he said.

"So, she finally fell for your charms, eh?"

Jonathan swung round to meet Tom's curious eyes.

"She's dead."

The other laughed. "That's the trouble, you're too rough with 'em. You'll have a sore fork tonight."

"I didn't do it," stammered Jonathan. "She was dead when I came in."

"Come off it. I heard the screaming - enough to wake the dead it was."

"That wasn't her. It was someone else," Jonathan protested, his mind reeling.

"A pretty tale . . . there's no one else here. Don't tell me you lay with demons," grinned Tom.

Jonathan gesticulated wildly. "I tell you I didn't kill her."

"Tell that to the torturers. They'll have something to say about this, I wouldn't like to be in *your* shoes." He slapped the other man on the back. "Still, never mind, perhaps they'll let you take her place on the rack."

Beads of perspiration glistened on Jonathan's forehead. He had to quickly think up some excuse for allowing a witch to escape the gallows.

"I tell you it was no fault of mine. I can't fight the Devil! He came through the bars in the shape of a cat, and then changed into a hideous monster with horns and claws. You can see the scratches on me face. He did that when I tried to save her." Jonathan warmed to his theme. "He was surrounded by a ring of fire that kept me back. I had to watch as he struck her down. It was her soul, he wanted."

27

Tom laughed, sarcastically. "Thou art a brave fellow. I would never have dared to tackle the Fiend, himself."

He peered curiously at the still figure on the ground, then spotted something gleaming against Jane's left foot. He picked up the phial and sniffed it. "This smells very much like poison to me. How did it get here? Did she pay you to buy it for her?" he sneered. "All that nonsense about the Devil - a fine cock-and-bull story."

Tom began searching in the straw, while Jonathan looked on, helplessly.

"Hello, what's this?" He picked up the silver knob and examined it carefully. "Brought into the prison in the top of a walking stick. What say you to this, then?"

Jonathan found his voice. "So that's what that cow wanted with the witch," he muttered, and realising that the game was up, decided to throw himself on the mercy of Tom. "I've bin the object of a foul plot. You're my friend and you've got to help me. They can't discover this," he pleaded, his eyes starting from his head.

"They don't have to, if I confirm your story. Those witchfinders are very thick, they'll believe anything about their victims."

"Then . . . you'll help me?" Jonathan almost cringed before him.

Tom attempted to look dignified. "I have always been a god-fearing man and I detest lies."

"But, you're my friend," gibbered Jonathan, becoming more agitated with every passing second.

"Aye, but suppose they don't believe our story? I'll be blamed as much as you. They'd flay us alive!"

Jonathan's insides quaked. "They'll believe it if you stick by

28

me. Remember how you convinced them when that young girl hung herself with strips of cloth torn from her own clothing?'' He dug a thick finger into his friend's chest, ''But we know that she really died through being raped by you - don't we?''

Tom shrugged and moved away. ''I had to think that one up, myself. *You* didn't help me.''

Jonathan, in a blue funk, was not a pretty sight. ''I'll give you half the money I've saved up if you'll help me . . . you've *got* to help me.''

Tom looked at him in disgust. ''You don't put much value on your life, do you?''

But, Jonathan, the last vestige of composure gone, grabbed his friend's coat. ''I'll give you all I have,'' he whimpered.

Tom grinned, ''That's better,'' and he knocked the grasping hands away. ''Bring me the money tonight and I swear you'll go a free man. Nay, more than that! You'll most likely receive praise for your brave fight with the Devil!''

The gaoler grovelled, ''I'll bring you the money - I swear it!''

''Of course you will. You're too scared for your own neck to do otherwise. You're the biggest coward in Christendom!'' He spat on the floor and sauntered off, banging the door behind him. As soon as he had gone, Jonathan made a dive for the privy.

CHAPTER 3

Mistress Nokes waited impatiently for Bess to return from the prison. She couldn't settle down to her housework until she knew that her daughter was safe. She continually muttered prayers to the Goddess; imploring Her to allow the mission to be a success.

Meg was outside cleaning the hen-house and her mother could hear the indignant clucking of the birds - disturbed from their afternoon siesta. It was now some six hours since Bess had set out.

Becoming more and more anxious, Mistress Nokes went out into the sun-drenched garden. It always looked its best in July. Roses climbed up the trellis round the door, while blue, yellow and purple flowers fought for supremacy in the borders. The huge lavender bushes - one on either side of the path - gave forth a fragrant aroma and she crushed the grey-blue flowers between her fingers; her eyes on the gate.

The black cat lay on the top of the low wall, which separated the garden from the lane. It gazed at her through slitted eyes and stretched languorously. She walked over and picked it up. "We used to believe that black cats were lucky until the witchfinders linked them with the Devil. I hope you bring us luck today and my Bess is able to outwit those gaolers."

The cat licked her cheek with a rough, pink tongue, as if it understood. Then, hearing footsteps, she turned and saw Bess in the lane. "So, you *are* lucky after all," she whispered, replacing the sleepy feline.

Bess ran into Mistress Nokes' outstretched arms. "Oh, Mother, I do wish you would send that animal away. It's an

31

ill-omen.''

''Nonsense, dear,'' her mother chided. ''It has brought us luck! Are you not back, safely?''

Bess pulled away from her mother's embrace and ran quickly into the house. Mistress Nokes followed at a more sedate pace and questioned her daughter from the doorway. ''What's amiss? You're talking like a Puritan. Don't tell me you are beginning to believe in familiars and all that nonsense.'' She stood for a moment until her eyes became accustomed to the interior of the house, then suddenly realised that Bess was slumped across the table, sobbing bitterly.

''Why, what's wrong, child? Were you not able to deliver the poison to Jane?'' She softly stroked the auburn hair.

''Aye, she's got it right enough.'' The voice came, muffled from beneath the folded arms.

''Then, what ails thee, dearest?''

Bess slowly raised a tear-stained face. ''Oh Mother, something dreadful has happened. It was not my fault. I could not stop him - he was so strong! It was all so horrible! What am I to do? What will Robert say?''

Agnes put her arm round her daughter's bruised body. ''Be of good cheer,'' she forced a smile to her lips. ''I half expected this to happen with those lechers.'' She kissed Bess. ''You are still alive, thank the Gods, and you have done your duty to your sister witch. As for Robert, he need never know, but I'm sure he would not blame you - he will understand.''

''Oh Mother, I hope you are right.''

''Of course I am! Now, I'll make you a hot posset and put some of my special herbs in it - you'll soon feel better.'' She smiled reassuringly and went into the kitchen.

Bess dragged her aching body onto the settle. How lovely

it was to be safe again in her beloved home. In no time at all, her mother was saying: "Now, drink this, there's a good girl."

For a moment, it seemed to Bess as though she was a child again. She felt slightly better, already; the day's trials beginning to feel like a dreadful nightmare. Did it really happen? As her hands closed round the comforting warmth of the mug, she began to talk of her terrible experience. The older woman listened intently and when Bess had finished, she patted her hands:

"Let us thank the Gods that we were able to save poor Jane from the torture chamber. She would never have stood up to their butchery. And as for that gaoler . . . I think something should be done about him. Would you like a little air, now?"

Bess nodded and Mistress Nokes led her outside.

They were inspecting the herb garden, when a young lad sauntered up the lane. He picked up a stone and hurled it at the sleeping cat, which emitted a screech and leapt into the bushes.

"It's that young ruffian again," cried Mistress Nokes.

Bess rushed through the gate and started to chase the attacker, and, unfortunately for him, he stumbled in his haste to get away and Bess caught him by the scruff of the neck and hauled him into the garden.

"Go inside and leave the boy to me," said her mother, icily.

Bess, trembling from the encounter, was glad to obey. She really *did* feel unwell.

Mistress Nokes grasped the youngster by the shoulders and proceeded to shake him until the teeth chattered in his head.

"Have you not been taught to be kind to animals?" she asked, her fingers digging into his flesh.

"That's no ordinary animal," he shouted. "That's a demon from Hell! I've seen it in the woods and it always vanishes when I go near it. Let me go!" He struggled furiously, but Mistress Nokes held him fast.

"Don't talk such rubbish, you young fool! Any animal would run away from the likes of you - such a cruel, cruel boy!"

"I tell you it's the Devil! If you don't believe me, you must be a witch!"

Her face whitened at this accusation. "Say that again and I'll box your ears," she cried, rapidly losing control of her temper.

"Leave me alone you old hag," yelled the lad - struggling and kicking. "You *are* a witch!"

Such insolence and hostility from a mere child and following so closely upon her daughter's troubles, was the last straw, and her hand met his cheek with a resounding crack!

"That will teach you to have more respect for your elders," she panted.

"You'll pay for that!" The boy fairly danced with rage, his hand clutching a fast, reddening face.

"Away with you! I want no more of your idle chatter!" Mistress Nokes thrust him away and followed him to the gate.

Once out in the lane, he turned - squinting in the sun-light. "You're the one who will hear more about this," he cried.

She hung over the gate and waved him away. "Keep your threats to yourself and get off home." She was suddenly tired and very shaken as she watched him slink off towards the town. Then, he looked back, pointing with a grubby finger. "I'll see you hang for what you've done to me," he yelled, defiantly.

Agnes walked slowly back into the house and sank gratefully into her chair. "Well, well, what a day." She was still agitated and upset.

Bess came and knelt at her feet, her voice, pleading:

"I told you not to encourage that animal."

"Very well, my dear, I will do as you say. If I don't feed it maybe it will go away. Think no more on it, my child." She leaned back and closed her eyes. Bess, gazed lovingly at her, then left the room on tiptoe.

In the early evening, Robert arrived. He took Bess in his arms. "Darling, I was so pleased you were able to deliver the poison to Jane. The news of her death has spread like wildfire. Rumour has it that she was slain by the Devil! Everyone is praising the gaoler, who is said to have tried to save her from his clutches!"

At the mention of the gaoler, Bess burst into tears and Robert, full of remorse, tried to comfort her.

"Do not cry, darling," he exclaimed, between kisses.

"But . . ." she began.

"Never mind, dearest, I know exactly what has happened to you."

Bess and her mother stared at him. "You know?" came in unison.

"For sure! Was I not gifted with the second-sight? It works very well when something happens to one so dear to me."

Bess looked up at him with brimming eyes. "Don't you mind, Robert?"

"Of course I mind. I would willingly strangle that fiend with my own hands, but it was no fault of yours. I blame myself for allowing you to go on such a dangerous errand. You were lucky to return, at all!"

"You mean it will make no difference to us?" asked Bess, wonderingly.

"How can it, when I love you so much? Besides, many women have known more than one man before they wed."

"That is true," agreed Mistress Nokes. "These days, very few girls have not known the pleasures of the flesh - and some are not unwilling victims."

"Oh Robert, I do love you," sighed Bess, hugging him tightly.

"I think the sooner you two are wed, the better," smiled her mother.

Robert looked at her in surprise. "Then, I have your consent to marry Bess?"

"With all my heart, Robert. And when the coven meets on Saturday, I will announce the good tidings and see that you are joined together by our ancient rite of Handfasting."

"Thank you, Mother dear," Bess ran and kissed her, "there is nothing I want more than to become Robert's wife."

Just then, Meg came in through the back door. Her hair was tied up in a kerchief and she had bits of straw adhering to her skirt:

"Thank goodness that's done," she said, walking into the room. "I must have fallen asleep in the orchard . . ." she stared at their faces. "What's happened? Has someone found a fortune?"

Robert winked at Agnes, "You could say that," he laughed.

"Stop fooling and tell me about Jane. Did you manage to pass the phial to her?" Meg's attention was riveted on her sister's face.

Bess nodded, reassuringly, "Yes, dear, don't worry. Jane is beyond all suffering now. I will tell you about it, later." Her face clouded suddenly as she remembered the awful begin-

36

ning to the day.

"But, what's the matter? You look troubled, Bess."

"Please, Meg, I'll tell you later." Bess gave her a hug.
"Now, there is something much more cheerful to tell you . .
." she paused for effect, "Robert and I are to be wed!"

Meg clapped her hands and whirled Bess round the room.
"Oh, how lovely! I'm so pleased for you both, and we can
do with a man about the house." She laughed mischievously
and kissed Robert on the cheek.

"I'll have none of *your* sauce, Mistress," Robert grinned,
pretending to box Meg's ears, and there ensued some horse-
play between the three of them until Mistress Nokes intervened:

"That will do - that will do!" she cried above the din. "Goodness me, it's worse than the May Day celebrations."

Robert whispered to the girls and they collapsed, giggling.
Mistress Nokes suddenly realised the similarities between the
May Day revelries and the present occasion. She, too, chuck-
led, then remembered what she had wanted to say.

"We must have a toast. Fetch some ale, Meg."

Her daughter dashed from the room, her skirt still trailing bits
of straw.

"I wonder what *she's* been up to this afternoon," Bess tittered, giving Robert a sly nudge.

"Now, stop this at once," her mother pretended to look shocked.
"I never heard such talk."

Meg returned with four brimming tankards of frothy beer.
"What did you say?" She looked at them, expectantly.

"Never mind," answered Mistress Nokes, smiling at Robert.
"Now . . . allow me," she held up her tankard. "To a long
and happy life, and may the Gods be good to you both!"

37

"Aye! I'll drink to that," agreed Robert.

Four arms were raised and four pewter mugs kissed above the shining table, as they pledged the toast. The gaiety continued, unabated, until Meg realised how hungry she felt.

"Gracious! I have not eaten anything since noon! Can we have that pie you made, Mother?"

"Of course, child, go and fetch it and bring some chutney and the ginger cake. We have not had the time nor the inclination to eat much this day."

They were soon tucking into a well deserved repast. Agnes was an excellent cook - as were her daughters. When they had finished, Bess cleared the table and a comfortable peace settled over the house. Each of them, silent, thinking their own private thoughts. At length, Meg lit the lamps and drew the curtains, mentally wishing Jane well, on her journey to the Summerlands. Her mother's voice broke into her thoughts:

"Now, children, we must think about punishing that villain."

"What villain?" Meg swung round from the window.

"Why, the gaoler who ill-treated your sister, today."

The girl let out a cry and ran over to Bess. "You don't have to tell me what happened, I can guess. I'd like to murder him."

Bess comforted her. "Shush, now, it's all done with."

"Amen to that," said Robert.

"Fear not, Meg. He'll get what he deserves," promised Mistress Nokes, smiling grimly.

"What *do* you mean?" queried Bess.

There was a long pause before she received a reply, then:

"All these gaolers believe in evil witchcraft, or black magic, as they call it. We, witches, have been accused of working it for so long, that tonight, I intend to try it out."

38

There was a shocked silence, then Meg spoke:

"Is not that against the teachings of the Craft? Are we not taught 'perfect love and perfect trust and ye harm none'?"

"Aye," her mother nodded, "but *this* man is *evil* and the law cannot touch him, so I see no reason why we should not take the said law into our own hands."

"But, how do you know it will work?" questioned Robert.

"I don't! But the Old Religion has always had teeth and claws - otherwise it would have died out long ago. What do you think happens to the traitors of the Craft? They are found in a hedgerow - their throats cut with their own athames, and quite right, too! These dissemblers broke the oath of secrecy they took, in the presence of the Gods, at their initiation! They also have the blood of their fellow witches on their hands. Should they be allowed to live?"

Agnes stood up and glared at them, the firelight dancing behind her.

'She looks quite different,' thought Meg, 'she must have been a marvellous High Priestess in her day.'

"Well?" barked her mother; irritated by their apparent inability to reply.

Robert found his voice and answered her with another question:

"Do you believe in black magic, then?"

Mistress Nokes rounded on him. "You should know very well that magic, the name people choose to call the power we evoke, is a *neutral* force. It depends upon the operator as to whether it be beneficial or not. He or she decide how to use it!"

"But, Mother," interrupted Bess, "you told me that if it be used for evil purposes, it will return to the operator *three-fold,* and far worse things will happen to *that* person.''

''Yes, I know that,'' her mother countered, ''but this man has done wicked things to you, and to others. Surely, we have a right to punish him?''

''I suppose if he *knew* about it, or *thought* someone was hexing him, it would work,'' Meg mused, thoughtfully. ''His guilty conscience would make it work.''

''Exactly!'' cried Agnes. ''Now - you see what I mean?''

''Then there cannot be any harm in trying it, I suppose.'' Meg looked at the others for confirmation. ''I'd do anything to get rid of that wicked man - wouldn't you?''

They all nodded, grimly.

''Robert, can you stay for a few more hours?'' asked Agnes.

''Nothing could stop me. I can't wait to get started.'' He clenched his fists, ''By God, it will be a pleasure to do it!''

At the appointed hour, the four witches sat round the table. The celebrations, temporarily forgotten, a very different atmosphere now prevailed. Three pairs of eyes were focused on Mistress Nokes as she softened a dollop of beeswax between her fingers. The windows were shuttered and the only light came from a black candle which burned in a brass candlestick, set upon the table. Next to it stood a small bowl of water and a wooden box containing a quantity of pins.

At a nod from her mother, Meg stood up and proceeded to draw a circle around them with her black-handled knife. This done, she picked up a small incense burner and lit the charcoal, therein. A few swings in the air, and it was glowing and hot. Then, from a little leather bag at her waist, she took some herbs and sprinkled them upon the charcoal. Soon, the room was filled with a bitter, slightly disturbing aroma; the grey-blue smoke rising steadily from the burner and hanging over the table like a shroud.

"It's assofoedita," hissed Meg, as Bess and Robert grimaced at the odour it produced.

The old lady muttered as her fingers manipulated the wax, then she raised her arm as a signal, and the witches began to clap their hands; keeping a slow, but steady rhythm.

Presently, they commenced to chant. The words appeared to be in an unknown language - if words they were! The ambience of the room slowly changed, as the minds of the witches zeroed in on the objective of the rite. The force of their wills was projected and given impetus by the hand-clapping and chanting. They were locked together through their magical intent. The room receded - they were functioning almost entirely upon the level of pure thought. Their minds, probing - meshing - throbbing, with the effort of complete concentration.

Under the capable fingers of Mistress Nokes the wax began to take shape and slowly approached that of a human form. There was no indication as to its sex until the witch rolled a small pellet of wax and stuck it to the thighs of the mommet. Abruptly, the smoke condensed into a single pillar hovering above the table, and presently, the figure was raised and held within it.

At once, the chanting ceased - the eyes of the witches piercing the image - their wills coalescing into one, final, united effort. Then, Mistress Nokes slowly lowered the figure and spoke:

"I baptise thee with this holy water and name thee, Jonathan Pitchfork." With these words she solemnly sprinkled the image with water from the bowl. This done, she laid it down and motioned for the wooden box to be brought over to her. Robert obeyed - his face, a mask - small beads of perspiration standing on his forehead.

The sorceress took a pin from the box and plunged it into the heart of the mommet:

"May you die soon - by the light of the Moon," she intoned, venomously.

The others joined in and chanted the words over and over again, while Mistress Nokes held each pin in the candle flame before pushing it home into the wax image. "Die! Die! Die!" The words almost forced their way from her mouth - so great was her determination. "Die! Die! Die!" repeated the witches in unison.

Finally, she leaned back, exhausted. "Close the Circle, Meg." She sighed and closed her eyes. "Now, we have to deliver this mommet to Jonathan Pitchfork."

Robert stood up, swaying slightly. A lot of power had gone from him, as it usually did in magical operations. Strangely, for such a strong man, his energy, his vital élan, had been sapped - drawn off him. Still, he knew it would return in an hour or so. He gathered his wits and breathed deeply:

"I can deliver it tomorrow morning. I know where he lives and I can sneak into his cottage and leave it, when his wife is out of the way."

"Bless you, Bob," Mistress Nokes smiled up at him, wanly, "now I think it is time we all retired to our beds. I feel very, very tired after all that work."

Robert bent over and kissed her.

"Stay a minute or two," she whispered. He nodded.

When the door had closed behind her daughters, she turned and motioned him to a seat by the dying embers of the fire.

"Thank you for staying. What I am about to say will only take a few moments, and it's this. I've noticed how drained you are after a rite."

Robert shrugged. "It's nothing," he protested.

But Mistress Nokes thought otherwise. "Now, listen to me. I have watched you - oh yes I have, and I know we are tapping your life-force, even though we do not intend to - at least, not as much as we appear to do. It is a funny thing with magic," she opined, "there are some aspects of it that cannot be controlled. But, when you are married to Bess, I am sure you will find that your troubles disappear. Why? Because you will have a partner who can give you more stability on an etheric level. She will both give and take energy from you, but she will definitely help to maintain a balance - a polarity.

People really do not understand the sexual side of marriage," she continued. "It is crucial, in a magical sense, and also on more subtle levels. That is why it is so important to marry the *right* person. In other words - your other half! The black to your white - the Moon to your Sun ..."

Robert had listened intently to her words:

"You mean I can mate with Bess on a spiritual level as well as upon the physical?" he asked, his large, well-formed hands clasped between his knees, his face - intent.

"I do, and what's more, you can become very strong as a perfect couple. Bess will give you control, and also act as a valve, so that you will not expend too much life-force when making magic. I will explain more at another time, but, suffice to say, your birth-charts reveal aspects which marry extremely well, as do your sun signs - your Libra and my daughter's Taurus." She yawned behind her hand. "Now, I really must go to bed . . . you have the image?"

Robert patted his jacket, "Yes, it's safe with me."

In a few moments he had left Elm-tree farm and set off for Greycoats, the wax figure concealed on his person and his mind buzzing with unanswered questions.

The following morning, Robert set off for Jonathan's cottage. It was a cramped, two-roomed hovel in dire need of repair. Empty bottles and other odds and ends were strewn around the unkempt garden, betraying its owners habits.

Safely hidden behind some trees, Robert saw Mistress Pitchfork leave the dwelling and walk down to an improvised hut which passed for a hen-house. As soon as she was out of sight, he walked quietly into the cottage and laid the wax figure on the table.

The inside of the place was no improvement on the outside! Plaster had fallen from the walls and lay in small heaps on the floor. Dirty dishes were piled on the table and there was not a single piece of furniture in that dingy room, which did not require some kind of repair. The only comfort was a wood fire that blazed in the blackened hearth. A cockroach suddenly deserted its hiding-place by the window and scuttled across the bare boards.

"Ugh," breathed Robert, "what a cess-pit." He was glad to leave the musty room and with an eye on the hen-house, he slipped away.

Jonathan was full of himself. Despite his loss of savings, he felt it had been well worth it, for in the eyes of the authorities and the townsfolk, he was now a hero. People greeted him in the street instead of avoiding him and he had made up his mind to wash himself every day in order to sustain his position as a respectable citizen.

He walked jauntily up to his cottage and stepped into the living-room feeling happier than he had for years. He threw his coat onto a stool and helped himself to some ale. Sitting down, he pushed the dirty dishes out of the way and his eyes fell on the mommet. When he realised what he was looking at, the tankard slipped from his nerveless fingers, spilling the brown liquid over the table. The next moment he was on his feet - the chair crashing onto its side. Jonathan was literally transfixed by the image; his eyes widening in terror - his face, ashen.

He was still staring at it when the door opened and a small, thin, bird-like woman came in, holding a basket of eggs in her arms.

"What ails thee?" she asked, her sharp eyes missing nothing of her husband's appearance.

"Who put *that*, there?" Jonathan pointed at the image with a stubby finger.

"I don't know. What is it?" she peered at the white object, curiously.

"Someone's trying to destroy me," he muttered, still staring at the dreadful sight.

"Nonsense! You must be mad!" her thin voice cracked in the small room.

"I tell you I'm doomed! They're working black magic against me."

Her laugh, like the startled whinny of a frightened horse, broke the spell and he turned on her savagely. "Shut your big mouth. What do *you* know of such things?"

She was familiar with his anger and it disturbed her not at all.

"I know you talk a lot of insane rubbish. It's just a lump of wax and pins." She turned away, losing interest, and began putting more logs upon the fire.

"It's a witch doll," he protested vehemently, "I've got pains in me stomach, already."

"It's a wonder you haven't got pains somewhere else, the number of women you've had." She glared up at him, a log in her claw-like hands; the fire-light gleaming on her ravaged face.

Jonathan looked at his wife in feigned surprise. "Women? What do you mean?"

She threw the wood onto the flames and turned on him, her long, pent-up hatred now revealed on her features. "You know what I mean, you stinking wretch! It's a miracle you've escaped the Spanish sickness considering the filthy hags you've ridden." She spat out the words.

"What are you talking about?" Jonathan's features registered a hurt martyrdom.

"You know well what I'm talking about. I've known for a long time that you've been unfaithful to me. You think your foul secrets are safely shut up in yon prison, but you are not to know that you talk in your sleep," she ended, triumphantly.

"Talk in my sleep?" he asked, in astonishment.

"Yes, you do!" she snapped. "And who is Jane?" she leered. "The one with the pretty dugs and the body of an angel. You know - those dugs you want to kiss. Ugh, you make me want to vomit!"

"I . . . I, don't know a Jane," stammered her husband. But she ignored his weak denial.

"And what of all those other witches you've 'ad, belly to belly?"

46

"I've not had other women . . . am I not a good husband to you?" he pleaded.

"If you're a good 'un, Old Nick's a saint! You lecherous beast. You lay wi' me after you've dipped yer yard in their 'oles. It's a wonder I aint got the pox."

She ranted on at him, the anger held within for so many years, spilling out - a torrent - now completely out of control.

"Shut yer foul mouth, woman. You know not what you're saying."

Jonathan prowled round the room like a trapped animal, kicking at any convenient obstacle.

"Oh yes I do! I've seen the scratches on yer flesh, left by those hags who have fought to save their bodies from your lust. Even the whores of Hell spurn you." She screamed at him, her thin body heaving with emotion.

Jonathan shouted, "Will you shut up?" A vein throbbed in his neck; he was torn between fear and rage, now.

She brought her face close to his, defiantly. "I won't shut up! I've bottled this up long enough. Every time you take me, I think of the stinking bodies you've bin lying with. I've finished with you, once and for all. Get out of here . . . now! I never want to set eyes on you again! And as for this rubbish . . . there!" She picked up the wax image and hurled it into the heart of the fire.

He grasped at his throat. "God, what have you done? You've burned it . . . it will kill me!" He staggered like a dying man.

"I hope it does! You're not fit to live, anyway!"

Her husband rushed over and tried to grab the figure from the greedy flames, but it was too late. The melting wax bubbled and seethed and he burnt his hand, badly.

47

His wife pointed a skinny finger at him. "Look at him, like a little babby," she cried, scornfully. "Scared stiff of a piece of wax!"

His fear, and now the pain from his hand, was too much for Jonathan. He suddenly turned on the unfortunate woman and seized her by the throat.

"You're a witch," he bellowed. "Yes, that's what you are - a stinking witch! You want me dead, and by burning that doll, you know I'll die."

His spouse screamed hysterically. "Ha, ha, I'm a witch and I want you dead . . . well . . . perhaps I do!"

"You rotten bitch, you'll die before I do!" His fingers tightened their grip on her throat.

Fear rose in her like a black cloud and she started to thresh about; her hands clawing helplessly at his face and body - her eyes, huge, and filled with terror.

Jonathan's thumbs pressed relentlessly into her thin neck. "I'll kill you, first, you scum!"

He was quite unable to control his actions, now. A thick, red haze had formed in front of his vision. He was - at that moment - a mad man.

The woman's tongue protruded; her eyes rolled back in her head and she lay limp in his hands. Slowly, he relaxed his grip and she sank to the floor like an old rag doll. Jonathan gazed down at the still figure, then prodded it with his boot.

"Come on, get up, woman." Very slowly, his mind came to the realisation of what he had done. "Christ! I've killed her." He lumbered round the small room like a man possessed. 'Escape,' he thought, 'anywhere,' and made for the door.

The neighbours had heard the noise and already there was a

small knot of people, outside. Jonathan stood for a second, framed in the doorway. "Get out of my way," he roared, pushing through the curious crowd.

"Seize him," shouted someone, "Don't let him get away!" Hands clutched at him and the press of bodies impeded his escape. Now, they held him fast - he was trapped!

Some folk had gone inside the cottage to investigate. One of them, an old man, came out. "He's killed her," he shrilled; his white beard shaking in outraged disbelief. The crowd, stilled, on the words - Jonathan Pitchfork had murdered his wife! The local hero had suddenly turned into the local villain!

A woman's voice broke the silence. "Let's lynch 'im!" Jonathan's insides turned to water and he whimpered in terror.

"The law will do that," called a man. "Take him to the gaol, he can hang with the witches!"

The crowd yelled its approval and dragged him away screaming for mercy. Children pelted him with refuse and he was eventually thrown into one of his own cells.

Next day, he was found dead. Knowing the way murderers were treated, Jonathan had hung himself from the window grid, with his own belt. Bess was revenged. The wax image had done its work!

CHAPTER 4

The inn-keeper of the Black Swan hummed cheerfully to himself as he polished the mugs and tankards. It must have been the glorious weather which lifted his spirits, because the inn was empty save for one man who sat in a corner of the common-room.

The customer's face, above the broad, white collar, had a cunning look and was adorned by a square-cropped beard. Streaks of premature grey showed in his dark hair and his skin carried a pallor which suggested a degree of ill-health.

Of slight build, he had a fastidious air, revealed by well-kept hands and neat clothing. The man's tall, Puritan's hat lay on the table before him as he busied himself making notes in a small book.

Outside, a boy, whistling and scuffing his shoes on the cobbles, made his way, jauntily, towards the inn. He looked up at the crude painting of a black swan, hanging over the doorway; paused for a moment, then stepped inside.

The sudden gloom made him blink, but eventually he spotted the burly figure of the inn-keeper.

"Is Master Hopkins about?"

"Aye, that he is," replied the man, "but what would a young stripling like you be wanting with the Witchfinder General?"

"That's *my* business," returned the boy, impudently. "I don't tell my secrets to strangers."

"Cheeky young varmint! Have you no manners?" The inn-keeper slapped down his cloth - piqued at the lad's insolence.

"I didn't come here for a lecture on manners," sneered the newcomer, "I just asked if Master Hopkins was here."

The man choked, "Why, you little . . ." and he raised his hand with the intention of cuffing the lad. But, as he stepped forward, a voice halted him in mid-stride.

"I heard my name mentioned. Is someone looking for me?"

The inn-keeper gaped and before he could do anything, the boy brushed passed him. "I am!" he answered, snatching off his cap and standing to attention. He had a confidence rarely seen in one so young. "Are you really Matthew Hopkins?"

"The very same," replied the man who had set himself up as a witchfinder.

This individual, who acknowledged his identity in such quiet tones, had become, in a comparatively short space of time, a law unto himself - a feared and respected member of society - metering out torture and death in the once peaceful county of Essex.

Matthew Hopkins' knowledge of witchcraft was confined to the works of King James I; Potts' account of the *Lancashire Witches* and Barnard's *Guide to Jurymen*. For his first 'discovery', he had picked on a one-legged old woman called Elizabeth Clarke; roused her neighbours to denounce others as witches; devised methods of torture to obtain confessions, without leaving any visible signs of torture, and found six victims.

He had seized on one passage from King James' *Demonology*, as a sibboleth for detecting witches - "*Witchcraft meant keeping imps and familiars, which the women suckled by the aid of special teats concealed in various parts of their bodies. These imps, who appeared in the form of various animals, would change their shape into that of a man and have carnal copulation with their mistresses.*" On this ridiculous charge, the old beldame, Elizabeth Clarke and other convicted women, were hanged.

With his success at smelling-out 'witches', this one-time Ipswich lawyer, dubbed himself, 'Witchfinder General'. And for his own convenience, Hopkins called any wart, protuberance, or spot which was insensible to pain and did not bleed - a 'Witch Mark'. He declared that they could easily be found by pricking the victim's body with long pins. The possession of such a mark could convict a person of witchcraft.

The boy stood silently in front of Hopkins; admiring the man who could take life so effortlessly and thinking what a great man he must be. His hero's voice interrupted his thoughts: "Well, boy, speak up! What's your name?"

"Joseph, sir."

"Do they call you Joe, for short?" Something which could have been a smile, flickered across the witchfinder's face.

"Certainly not. My father does not allow it. He is a god-fearing man and believes it is an insult to the Holy Book, to shorten biblical names."

"Your father is quite right," agreed Hopkins, soothingly, taking a swig of his ale. "Now, Joseph, what would you be wanting with me - have you discovered some witches?"

"Maybe I have and maybe I haven't. What do I get if I tell you?"

"That all depends," the man gave him a sideways glance, "let me know who it is and then I will be better able to judge," he finished, triumphantly.

"Oh no." Joseph shook his head. "Let me see your money first."

Hopkins was taken aback at the lad's temerity, but he knew that flies are not caught with vinegar and decided to play along.

"You mean you do not trust me?"

"No, I don't." Joseph was quaking inwardly but kept his face expressionless. He knew he must not show this man any fear or the game would be up, and he, Joseph, taken for an idiot. He might even be accused of something, himself! His belly writhed at the thought, but determination and greed were still strong in him and he stood his ground.

Hopkins allowed his lip to curl, slightly. "I must say you are a very outspoken young lad. Shall we say a penny for your information?"

At these words, Joseph's courage crept back. "Make it a shilling and I'll tell you."

"You drive a hard bargain, but if the information is correct it will be worth it. Now . . . speak!"

"Not until I have the money."

Hopkins decided it would be best to appear benevolent, and called over to the inn-keeper. "Bring a fruit posset for my young friend, here." He took a shilling from his purse and handed it to Joseph. "Here, boy, sit down and tell me what you know."

The lad spat on the coin and took a seat at the table. Then, glancing around him, furtively, he leaned over and whispered: "It's Mistress Nokes."

Hopkins looked at him askance. "Mistress Nokes, a witch? Nonsense boy! She is a fine woman and much respected in the town - or so I've heard tell."

"I tell you, she's a witch. I followed her at the last full moon and saw her attending the Sabbath. The Devil was there, complete with horns and they carried on foul orgies until the cock crowed."

"Impossible!"

"I'll swear on the bible, it's true!" Joseph's face was red with excitement. "Besides that, she keeps a demon in the form of a cat. I threw a stone at it and she put a curse on me. I've been vomiting pins, ever since."

Hopkins' hand tightened on his tankard. "You swear this is true?"

"I've said so, haven't I? It's true right enough and I've brought these to prove it."

Just then, the drink was put on their table and Joseph waited impatiently until the inn-keeper had retired, before bringing a handful of rusty pins out of his pocket.

He held them on a grubby palm and Hopkins gazed at them, stirring uneasily in his seat. "And you vomited these?"

"Aye, I did that, and it almost killed me," replied Joseph, vehemently.

The witchfinder took another look. "I just cannot believe it."

"I'll swear by the blood of Christ, it's true!" insisted the lad.

"Mistress Nokes - a witch?" Hopkins pulled gently at his beard, unable to come to terms with the statement.

He sat without speaking for some time, then inclined his head:

"You seem a pretty shrewd business man, would you like to earn a crown?"

Joseph's eyes, popped, and he slopped the apple-juice over the table:

"Aye! I would that, sir," he cried.

"Then you must do some spying for me. Find out where Mistress Nokes goes to when she leaves her house, at night."

"I'll do that!" he paused, "But I want the payment first."

Hopkins threw him a coin in disgust. "Make sure you do not

55

let her out of your sight and report to me at once, if you see anything strange. Now, be off with you.''

Joseph gulped down the remainder of his drink and ran out of the inn, leaving the witchfinder wondering at his words. ''Mistress Nokes, a witch. I would never have believed it,'' he muttered.

He was still mulling the matter over, when his assistant, John Stearne, entered the Black Swan. A burly man of middle height; his pale, freckled countenance was graced by a short, fair beard, and when he spoke, the burr in his voice betrayed his native Suffolk.

He tapped Hopkins on the shoulder. ''Are we working today?''

''Aye, we'll be off now. Have you got your bell?''

Stearne rang it belligerently.

''That will do,'' grunted his companion, ''do you want to deafen me?''

The two men left the inn and started walking towards the centre of the town.

''This mode of travelling is tiresome,'' grumbled Hopkins. ''When I receive three pounds for every witch convicted, I'll buy myself a horse and carriage, like the Scottish witchfinder, John Kincaid.''

''And a lot of good it did him,'' leered Stearne.

The other, frowned. ''That was his own fault. He became too greedy and was not satisfied with the fourteen women he convicted at Newcastle; he would have annihilated the whole of the Northern female population if he had had his way.''

Stearne hawked and spat. ''Aye! It's through the likes of him that a lot of folk are beginning to believe we are frauds. We'll have to be more careful or they'll find out that we are!

56

I don't want to end up like him - gallows meat."

When they arrived in the square, Stearne began ringing his bell and soon they were surrounded by a crowd of the townsfolk. Hopkins raised his arms for attention:
"All citizens who would bring in a complaint against any woman for a witch, should be sent for, and the victim, tried, by the person appointed."
In a short space of time, four women were dragged forward by their accusers, who swore they had been working evil against them.

Hopkins, strutting imperiously, led them into the town's Assembly Hall, which was used, variously, as a law court, corn mart and militia headquarters. The witchfinder and his assistant were followed by as many of the throng as were able to congregate inside the hall.

Meg, on her way to market, stopped, to see if she could recognise any of the victims. One of the accused women was Margaret Wall, whom she knew quite well. Although, Margaret, and the others, were not adherents of the Craft, they had been selected because their neighbours disliked them for some reason - or so she thought.

Heedless of any danger to herself, Meg edged her way into the packed building. The witchfinders were pushing the women towards a platform that had been erected in the middle of the hall and they were now joined by Hopkins' other associates.

"These women, accused of witchcraft, must endure the process of pricking, to find out if they possess any witchmarks and are truly the vassals of Satan," shouted Hopkins.

Two of his assistants, Mary Summerset and Francis Mill, knew exactly what to do. They seized each woman in turn and tore off their clothing until they stood naked before the sea of curious eyes.

The men in the crowd, laughed and jeered, calling out bawdy remarks about the helpless and terrified women. Meg's quick temper flared up. She could not bear to see her friend so degraded and without quite knowing how it happened, she found herself pushing through the mob until she was standing in front of the platform.

"Stop!" Meg heard her own voice resounding in her ears. "That woman is as innocent of witchcraft as a new-born babe." She suddenly realised the danger of her situation. 'In the Gods names, what am I doing?' she thought. But, determined to make the best of her folly, Meg straightened her cap and smoothed her gown, holding her head, high.

Hopkins looked down at her from the dais, his thin lips drawn back - irritated by the interruption.

"So, you would presume to know more than I - the Witchfinder General?"

Meg held her ground. "I'm sure she is no witch!"

The crowd was divided. Some booed and others cheered and a voice rang out. "If she can recognise a witch, she must be a witch, herself!"

"Aye! Aye! That's true!" came from all sides. "Put her through the test!"

A large woman near the front, gave tongue. "Prick 'er and see! I bet she's covered with witch-marks."

A spotty-faced youth was pushed forward by his mother. "I . . . I . . . I've seen her with the . . . the . . . girl who died in prison," he stammered, then scuttled back into the press of bodies.

'You slimy toad,' thought Meg. Her eyes, full of loathing,

glared at his retreating back.

Hopkins was extremely annoyed at this unexpected turn of events and a small vein throbbed in his neck. There was no evidence that the girl had any connections with witchcraft; no one had brought any testimony against her. But his dilemma was solved for him by some in the crowd, who suddenly grabbed Meg and hoisted her, struggling and kicking, onto the platform.

The witchfinder decided that discretion was the better part of valour and cleared his dry throat:

"What is your name, child?"

"Meg," she returned, acidly.

"Meg - who?"

"Meg Nokes. We are a respectable family as everyone knows," she declared, proudly.

At the mention of the name, 'Nokes', Matthew Hopkins re-membered Joseph's information. Was he facing the daughter of a witch? If he was, then she, too, might be one. However, it would be very dangerous for him, if such was not the case. After all, her mother was, up to now, held in high esteem by many of the 'big-wigs' in Belford and one false step could lead to his downfall. He must have more time to think.

Some of the women in the hall felt sorry for Meg and spoke up:

"Aye, we know her. It is true what she says. The whole family are good Christians and attend services at St. John's every Sunday."

The mob stirred. There was a rough element present that desired some excitement.

"Don't listen to such rubbish. She's a witch right enough," they yelled. "Strip her and let's see what she looks like, this 'respectable' lass.''

Sounds of agreement came from all over the hall.

Hopkins raised his hand. "Very well, very well. I'll deal with her later," he shouted above the din, "let us try these other women, first."

His words infuriated the crowd. "Leave them old dames and get on with the lass," they yelled.

For the space of a breath he hesitated, then his guile prevailed. "No!" he roared. "We'll prick the others, first."

But the blood of the mob was up and they heckled, booed and stamped in frustration. Hopkins attempted to control them but no one listened to him. 'Something must be done to pacify them, God's Death, but what?' His cold eyes flickered over the crowd as he racked his brain for an answer. Then, again, he held up his hand.

"Very well! I will do as you wish," he said, and beckoned to a large, muscular woman. "Take her into that anti-room and prick her," he commanded.

"No! No! No!" they screamed. "Do it here! Do it here!"

But Hopkins was determined now and pushed Meg towards his assistant who dragged her off amid cat-calls and jeers.

"Go on then, take off your clothes," Mary Summerset demanded, locking the door and leaning arrogantly against it.

Meg, seeing there was no escape, began to slowly undress. Although she was comfortable 'sky-clad', as the witches called it, this was a very different state of affairs and by the time she had dropped the last garment, her face glowed like a cherry.

The witch-pricker was accustomed to seeing bare bodies and over the years had become blasé about her work, but when Meg stood before her with her lovely, slim body and long blonde tresses, her emotions, which had long been buried, stirred. "How pretty you are," she said. Slowly, and partly against her will, Mary approached the girl and put her hands on Meg's shoulders. Meg was unaware of any sexual implication in the action. She had been through so much during the last hour, that this unexpected gesture of warmth from another human being, seemed like a haven of protection.

She looked up at the older woman with gratitude, mingled with another, alien feeling - a kind of burning within her, which she was in no fit state to analyse. She shivered, suddenly, as Mary put strong arms around her.

"Oh, oh, what . . .?"

"There, there," Mary smiled, a big, good-natured smile. "You poor child," she murmured, "I will save you from them."

Meg was glad to rest against her. She was utterly shattered both in mind and body. She felt Mary's sturdy form surprisingly soft and warm. 'Like a mother,' she thought, absent-mindedly.

The woman's hands gently stroked Meg's back, reassuringly. Then, it happened! A flame exploded deep within Meg, possessing her entirely and giving her an overwhelming desire to surrender to this tender embrace. She gasped and gave a little cry. Her head lifted and her violet eyes were filled with newly awakened passion. Mary gazed down at her, then bent and kissed her.

The girl started to tremble as she felt Mary's hands caressing her firm, young breasts. The woman kissed her again - hard and long, and Meg's limbs suddenly relaxed. She would have fallen, but for the arms holding her.

Mary's voice came to her from a long distance, "Please forgive me. You are so sweet."

Meg frowned, puzzled. "Why must I forgive you?"

Mary laughed softly and covered her with kisses.

This woman, playing a man's part in a man's world, had long considered herself beyond the kind of feelings that had so recently awakened in her. The idea that most men were vicious, greedy and cruel, had been her opinion for many years; they were not worth considering. And her work had made her like them - or so she had thought. Now, Meg had become the catalyst, melting away the hard shell and finding a different person, within. She felt a new emotion now - compassion - and another - love?

She quickly realised that she must save this girl from the accusation of witchcraft, even if her reasons for so doing were somewhat selfish. She could be forgiven in such circumstances. Putting Meg gently away from her she told her to dress. "I will tell Hopkins that you have no witch-marks on your body," she said.

When Meg was ready, she followed Mary back into the hall and both of them mounted the platform. Mary stared straight ahead.

"This girl is innocent. I have pricked her and can find no witch-marks."

The crowd went wild. "She's a witch, right enough!" came from all parts of the hall.

Meg had re-entered Hell. Her face paled, but she summoned her courage once more. "I'm no witch!" she cried glaring at the upturned faces.

"That remains to be seen!" A woman pointed an accusing finger at her, "How do we know what happened in that room? Prick her in front of us. We want justice done here."

Voices were raised in assent and Hopkins pulled nervously at his beard. Were they never to be satisfied? He wanted to get away from the place, the situation was rapidly getting out of hand. This hysterical mob, already inflamed by the sight of the other naked women, couldn't be controlled much longer. They seemed determined that the girl should suffer along with the others. It was the first time he had had such trouble with a crowd. He sighed, then gave the order for Meg to be pricked.

Two assistants held her while Hopkins handed Mary a bodkin.

"I'll not do it," she whispered under her breath.

"You will, or I'll accuse you of helping a witch," grated Hopkins through clenched teeth.

There was nothing Mary could do but carry out his orders. If she refused to obey him and he made good his threat, both Meg and she could finish on the gallows and that would never do.

She took the pin and lifted Meg's skirts.

"No!" they screamed. "Strip her, first!"

Two burly men stepped forward and obeyed the command. The crowd cheered when they saw Meg standing naked before them. Reluctantly, Mary approached her again.

"Shave 'er first," yelled a fat man near the dais.

"Aye! Shave her," cried the rest.

It was the custom of witchfinders to shave the bodies of their victims before pricking them, in case their hair concealed marks that were supposed to have been made by Satan, or alternatively, concealed teats with which they suckled their familiars.

Forthwith, the two men threw Meg to the floor and held her down while another man picked up a bowl of soap and water and a brush and proceeded to lather her pubic hair.

Pandemonium broke out as the man concluded his task with a razor.

"The Gods pity me," whispered Meg, the tears coursing down her cheeks. The sight aroused the young men in the hall who started kissing their girls and fumbling in their bodices. Hopkins sidled over to Mary. "Now prick her and let's be done with it," he hissed.

The witchpricker's lips tightened, but she plunged the pin into Meg's flesh and was rewarded with a scream as the blood flowed down the white limbs.

"See, she bleeds!" shouted Mary, triumphantly. "The girl is innocent!"

This time, Stearne intervened. "Try another place," he suggested. Again, she jabbed at Meg and again the blood followed the bodkin.

"I tell you she's innocent," cried Mary, her self-control ebbing. But still the crowd stamped and howled for more. Hopkins wished he was miles away. Any influence he might have had on his audience had completely vanished.

"This has gone too far. Turn the pin and be done with it," he growled. Mary glared at him, trembling with rage. "No! This girl is innocent!"

His voice was soft, as the fur of a pouncing cat is soft. "I care not! Finish it I tell you and let's be gone from here."

Mary's face flamed with wrath - now, she did not care what she said. "I will not!"

The Witchfinder General caught at her arm with fingers of steel.

"Then, I shall tell them what kind of a woman you really are and that you wish to keep the doxy for your own pleasure. They'll lynch you, of course." His face was grey, the sweat trickling into his beard.

Mary realised that all her attempts to save Meg had failed, so with a swift, dexterous movement, she turned the bodkin and thrust it between the girl's thighs. Meg remained silent, sobbing quietly on the rough boards. But Hopkins grabbed the pin from Mary's hand and held it aloft in triumph. "See! She has found the mark! The spot is insensitive. The wench feels no pain, there."

The crowd screamed with delight. "She's a witch! She's a witch! The whore of Satan will hang!"

The witchfinders were unaware that the Rev. John Gaule had watched the entire proceedings from the gallery. He had been, like the Vicar of Bray, an outspoken Royalist, but now leaned heavily towards the Commonwealth and paid court to its leading men.

Although an ardent believer in witchcraft, he abhorred the witchfinders and their callous methods. He had once written - *"Every old woman with a wrinkled face, a furry brow, a hairy lip, a gobber tooth, a squint eye, a squeaking voice or a scolding tongue - having a ragged coat on her back, a skull-cap on her head, a spindle in her hand, and a dog or cat by her side, is not only suspected, but pronounced for a witch."* And of all the witchfinders, Gaule detested Hopkins the most, as he knew him for a bloodthirsty fanatic.

The vicar's quick eye had detected how Mary Summerset had turned the bodkin, and he was down the stairs and striding on the platform before Meg's guilt had been proclaimed.

Hopkins scarcely knew what was happening, as Gaule grabbed his wrist and pressed his own hand against the blunt end of the pin.

"Look!" he called to the mob. "That woman has deceived you. She turned the pin round, *before* she pricked this girl. No wonder she did not cry out - it is blunt and can cause no injury! The girl is no witch!"

The people muttered amongst themselves and shuffled in frustration. "Try it again!" someone called.

Gaule knew that the only way to save Meg was to have her pricked in the same place, with the *sharp* end of the instrument. Hopkins dared not refuse the minister's request, and this time, Meg gave an agonised cry and her blood gushed forth anew. Even the most dim-witted in the audience, realised that she had felt the pain of the needle.

"See! This girl is no witch!" announced the vicar. "I demand her release at once!" His mane of white hair seemed to quiver with a life of its own, as he shook his fist at all and sundry.

As if by magic, but really because they feared Gaule, the mob quickly shifted it's attention from Meg, to Mary!

"Shame!" cried an old woman. "That fat cow was trying to cause the death of an innocent lass. It wouldn't surprise me if *she* was a witch, herself!"

"Aye! That's true," called another female. "Maybe she is. Try her and see!"

Meg still lay on the platform; her ordeal had been too great and she had fainted. The vicar swiftly wrapped her in his cloak; picked her up in his arms and left the hall without a backward glance. He took Meg home in his carriage and delivered her to a very anxious Mistress Nokes.

Hopkins simply could not believe his ill-luck. Just about everything had gone wrong and his plans had been completely ruined. Gaule had snatched one of his victims and Mary had

66

been clumsy enough to expose the bodkin trick - at least, to the keen eyes of the vicar. He turned on her. "Have you been up to your little games in that room? Is this your revenge because the lass refused to play them?"

She glowered at him. "Why do you say that?"

"Because I know you so well. You cannot keep your hands off a pretty wench," he sneered.

"You liar," she snarled.

Luckily, the mob heard none of this exchange. Traders were selling refreshments and they were busy regaling themselves with cider and hot pies.

Stearne ambled over to Hopkins to find out what was going to happen next, as he was becoming bored with the whole proceedings. But just then, someone called out, "Try that pricker for a witch!" and Mary blanched, visibly.

"We'd better do it," Hopkins muttered grimly, "or they'll lynch us all."

Stearne opened his mouth; thought better of it and closed it again. "Go on, man, get on with it." The witchfinder gave him a nudge and Stearne reluctantly walked off to speak to his men.

They did not want telling twice! None of them had any liking for Mary and considered her to be domineering. As one, they descended on her and despite her fierce struggles, ripped off her clothes with practised ease. The crowd cheered and more bawdy remarks were heard when her nakedness was revealed.

"So, she *is* a woman after all," screeched someone, "I thought she was a man dressed up."

"She couldn't be a man with those dugs," cackled an old woman, "she's got udders like my she-goat!"

They screamed with laughter as the witchpricker hit out with her fists and kicked like a demon. She bit and scratched, but they held her fast.

One of the women took an egg from her basket and threw it. Her aim was excellent. It hit Mary and the yolk trickled slowly down her stomach. "Right between her milk cans," yelled the woman's friend.

They enjoyed every minute of the spectacle. It was the first time anyone had seen a witchfinder treated like this.

"Shave that bush off her crotch," called a dwarf, from his perch on a stool at the side of the dais.

"Aye! Get rid o' that forest, it's thick enough for the Devil, himself, to hide in. There should be a few marks in there," agreed a fat man.

A one-eyed crone at the back, piped up. "Let *me* pull it out - the way she treated yon poor wench."

Stearne motioned to his men and they threw Mary down. Then he picked up the razor. His eyes held a strange glitter, like the beginning of emptiness. He too, hated Mary, whose sarcastic remarks had so often belittled him in front of Hopkins. What an opportunity to even the score!

Hopkins moved to hand him the bowl and brush, but Stearne waved them away. "Hold her fast," he ordered and proceeded to depilate Mary with the dry razor. She screamed and begged him to stop, but he merely grunted - utterly engrossed in his task.

At the end, he stood up, his face a mixture of satisfaction and something akin to shame. He wiped his brow with his sleeve - strange - he would have given a lot to be able to get away and vomit. But it was not yet finished. "Now - use the pin," grated Hopkins.

Stearne cursed, inwardly. 'What is the matter with me? Am I going soft on the job?' Almost unwillingly, he drove the sharp point into Mary's body and was answered by a shriek, as she strained to get away. Again and again he plunged into the soft flesh and was rewarded in a similar vein. One of the men put a huge hand over her mouth, but withdrew it with a yelp as her teeth ground into his palm.

The people were furious when they saw the blood flowing. This was surely proof that the woman had no dealings with the Devil! Stearne looked across at Hopkins for a lead. Both men were in a dilemma as to what to do. If only there was some spot on Mary's body that would not yield blood. If they free'd her now, she would certainly go to the authorities and expose them. Then, too, there was Gaule to reckon with - he would substantiate her statements.

The heat and stench in the hall were becoming too much, even for Stearne. He had received no instructions from his master, who would not meet his eye. Hopkins had apparently seen something very interesting on a piece of parchment he was reading. 'The turd was ignoring the situation - what to do?' In desperation he began to lather Mary's head, but before he could complete the operation, a voice rang out:
"Try under her arms. That's a good place."
Stearne groaned, but the men had raised the witchpricker's arms above her head, so he started to remove the hair from her arm-pits. Then a smile creased his grim visage. A large wart was revealed - a hidden teat!

Mary was lifted to her feet. "Look!" shouted Stearne, pointing to the offending blemish. "I have found it! This is the hidden teat with which she suckles her imps! It's the biggest I have ever seen - she *is* a witch!"

A roar went up from the superstitious Puritans. Hopkins drew a finger round his sweat-drained collar. "Thank Christ," he breathed.

Mary was to be taken away with the other condemned women, but the crowd still thwarted him. "Swim her!" they cried. "We want more proof of her witchcraft."

The men on the dais stared aghast at their audience. For all they were hard, cruel, avarious creatures, this day's work had left them shocked and exhausted; their eyes, red-rimmed, had a glazed, unreal look. Stearne suddenly flung away and would have ran off if Hopkins had not caught at his sleeve. "What are you doing man? We must see this thing through to the bitter end. They are out for blood today." And he laughed - the travesty of a laugh.

The Witchfinder General had long since dispensed with the swimming method of examination, but there was not much he could do at the moment to change the situation. His pallid features glistened with moisture as he called to the mob. "Away then, to the Mill Pool!" They turned and poured out of the building leaving Hopkins and his company to follow them.

Two of the assistants were delegated to take the other women to gaol, but Mary was carried, naked, in a different direction. She protested violently, cursing and mouthing oaths, but she was their last defence against ruin and none of them paid her the slightest attention.

The air smelt sweet as they emerged from the Assembly Hall - blinking in the strong sun-light. Their journey was a comparatively short one, the Mill being a mere quarter of a mile away. Surrounded on three sides by thick trees and vegetation, the pool lay deep and still. Even in mid-summer, the sun's warmth barely touched its surface.

Mary was dumped on the bank while she was tied; the right thumb to the left big toe; the left thumb to the right big toe - thus forming a cross. The church bells were ringing for evensong as Mary was prepared for the ordeal by water - the Judgement of God!

The formula was a simple one. If the suspect sank and remained at the bottom of the water, he or she was proclaimed innocent, and, when there seemed no likelihood of anything happening to the contrary, was duly hauled from the depths. Often, the victim had drowned meantime, or even died later from shock. Regrettable but unavoidable. If the water rejected the suspect, however, and he or she, floated, this was undeniable evidence of the person's guilt and resulted in the death penalty.

A rope was secured around Mary's waist, then two of the men threw her roughly into the centre of the pool, to the accompaniment of spiteful whoops from the crowd.

Mary gasped as she hit the green-dark water; her breath knocked out of her body by the force of the impact and the coldness of the pool. As she disappeared beneath the scummed surface, Mary hoped that she would sink and be proved innocent, little caring if she drowned. Stearne, however, was determined to make an end of the matter and whispered to his men to hold the rope in the manner they had been taught, so that it would be impossible for her to stay below the surface of the water.

Mary tried to prevent herself from floating, by relaxing her body, completely, but it was no use.

"Look!" roared the mob. "The water has rejected this daughter of Satan. She's guilty!"

Hopkins was forced to agree with the crowd, but he would

have given much for Mary to have drowned - for the water to have closed her mouth for good. She was still a danger to him while she yet lived.

Wet and slimed, her teeth chattering in a white, drawn face, she was hauled onto the bank where she collapsed on the flattened grass and vomited. Now, she would be thrown into a dungeon, tortured, and finish on the gallows. Hopkins, finally left the grim scene and crawled back to his lodgings, at the end of the longest day in his life.

CHAPTER 5

The noise of a key being turned in a rusty lock, awoke the inhabitants of the cell from their uneasy slumbers. The air was fetid with the smell of unwashed bodies and primitive sanitary conditions.

The four women peered through the gloom at the intruder, as the door closed behind Mary Summerset.

"Yon's that woman who pricked us," a fat, grey-haired female raised herself in the straw and blinked.

"Aye, that it is. If she 'ad pricked us wi' a proper bodkin, we would na' be 'ere," muttered another.

A young, slim girl, cried, "It must be a trick! What is she doing in here?" Her drowned eyes were huge, in a face, swollen from weeping.

What appeared to be a bundle of old rags in a corner, moved, and an old beldame staggered onto skinny legs. "Look at 'er now," she cackled, mirthlessly, "she trembles as much as we do . . . let's do for 'er, like she's done for us."

Mary retreated a step - her back to the door, her shocked eyes flickering over the haggard faces.

"Look! She's afeared of death as much as we are." The old one's mouth gaped in the mockery of a smile.

The fat woman said, "No, don't kill her yet, that would be too good for the likes of her. Let the torturers rip her innards out."

"I say, kill 'er now!" the crone snarled. "I'll do fer 'er wi' me own 'ands." She suddenly sprang at Mary, clawing at her face and kicking her with bony feet. The witchpricker fought back, and grabbing the old woman round the waist, flung her

73

onto the straw.

"She's too strong for me," gasped the crone, from where she had fallen. "She's got the strength of a man - move yersels and get 'er."

Her companions, not to be outdone, struggled to their feet and lunged at the new-comer, hitting, pulling and scratching. They grunted with pleasure at this opportunity to vent their fear and terror upon the enemy.

Mary gave as good as she got; her stout fists hitting jaw-bones and stomachs; her muscular legs shooting out and being greeted with howls of pain. Yet the women did not relent. They were beyond the point where pain could be considered - lost in an oasis of rage and despair. Their victim knew it was only a question of time before she was overcome, but she was willing to fight to the end.

The old beldame tottered over to the mêlée and managed to strike Mary across the cheek with a rusty nail. "That'll teach ye, ye she-wolf," she hissed. Mary's face altered with the sharp pain, as the blood oozed from the long gash and moved slowly down her cheek. Her mouth trembled - she was very close to tears, now.

The door of the cell opened and pushed her forward, as two gaolers edged their way in. "What's the bloody noise in here? Have you all gone mad?" But the desperate fight continued - the contestants totally oblivious of the men.

One of the gaolers disappeared and returned with a whip. He proceeded to belabour the frantic women with it and eventually they cowered back onto the straw.

"By the Book, we'd better put this one in a cell on her own before these hags tear her to pieces."

His companion grunted his agreement. "Yes, they'd only

blame us for it - we'd get the chop, too.''

Mary cried as they led her away and thanked God for her escape. They put her into an empty cell and she sank gratefully onto a heap of straw-filled sacks.

In the quietness of her new quarters, she had time to recollect her recent ordeal. She tried to pray but was unable to find any words. She smiled grimly to herself. It was a long time since she had performed such a task. Anyway, God must have long since deserted her. Not only God, but all those who had professed to be her comrades. Even these had turned against her. But, why? Mary wrestled with the problem.

She knew that she had incriminated many innocent women and sent them to their deaths, but surely, this was her job? This was what was expected of her. After all, the authorities approved of her master's business. She sighed, yet even so, in her heart of hearts, she had always known it to be evil.

Mary stroked her aching body and turned on the straw. She wondered how many of the victims had been real witches. Probably, not many at all! The genuine ones would be far too clever to allow themselves to be caught.

She took a sip of water from an iron mug which was chained to the wall, then spat it out in disgust. It tasted bitter and tainted. ''They even keep mugs in chains,'' she murmured, smiling at her little joke.

''I wonder what the real witches are like?'' she asked, addressing the mug. Mary remembered how a few of the victims had borne their sufferings with an air of dignity and gone to their deaths like martyrs. They believed that their god, whom the Puritans called the Devil, was the true god and would help them in their anguish. There was no denying that in many cases, he had! Some of the women had endured unspeakable torture in silence! "You know, mug, perhaps there *is* something in this witchcraft, after all."

She thought of the time she had joined up with Hopkins and his band. It was true she had made money, but Hopkins, too, had made money - a great deal of money - much more than she would ever have. So why had he turned against her, now?

Mary beat a tattoo with the iron vessel on the damp stone wall. Was it because of her preference for women? She knew that she was considered to be abnormal, but Matthew had had no time for her, sexually - "Thank God for small mercies!" Mary grimaced at the thought.

She had always performed her work well, so *that* could not be her crime. Anyway, there were others like her. Several of them had been historically famous and others came from good or noble families. No one condemned *them* for being different, moreover, it was not looked upon as a crime, in law! Well, she couldn't help the way she was made. Mary stretched herself on the sacks and stared up at the small grating in the wall. She knew many folk detested her. God, how that mob had revelled in her downfall, but surely they were ignorant as to her nature?

Just then, an unwary fly became caught in a large web on the grating. Its frantic buzzing seemed akin to her own plight and suddenly the answer hit her. Why had she not thought of it, before? If Hopkins had not used her as a scapegoat, the crowd would have turned on him! She had been sacrificed to save *his* skin!

Mary sat up and hugged her knees. It was true that there was no loyalty among thieves, and the Witchfinder General was as big a rogue as one could meet. It was he who had taught Mary how to turn the pin round so that the victim would feel no pain - and thus be convicted! She saw it all, now. He was only interested in condemning women of witchcraft to fill his own coffers. God's death, the man had no soul! Why, he would 'swim' his own mother for gain!

It dawned on Mary that Hopkins could be collecting his reward for her own conviction at that very moment! Her eyes darkened with hatred. 'If only I could escape,' she thought, 'I would join the other side! I might even become a witch, myself!'

She realised it would be difficult. Finding a coven in these times would be well nigh impossible. And as for becoming a member of it . . . still, nothing venture . . . and all that. "Yes," she spoke to the grey, forbidding surroundings, "that's what I'll do! Join the witches and fight their persecutors!" Mary started, at the sound of her own voice, echoing round the cell. She held her breath in case she had been overheard. But all seemed quiet and she breathed, again.

Then, another thought came to her. What if the witches hated her, too? They must do - knowing how she had harmed them. What a fool, even to consider such a course of action. Though, perhaps now that there was nothing to lose, there *could* be something to gain!

Mary knelt in the straw:

"God forgive me for the way I tortured those women," she whispered. "You have made me suffer to show me how much I made *them* suffer. Please, oh please, do not let them hang me. I swear I will make amends. I will do all I can to help the witches, but please help me to escape from this prison - Amen."

She felt a little more at ease after her prayer and fell into a light sleep. When she awoke, the cell had grown darker and she glimpsed an evening star through the opening in the grating. The sight cheered her and she resolved to try and think up a way of escape.

Mary had no money with which to bribe a gaoler. If such had been the case, freedom would be a fairly easy matter, considering the way the turnkeys lied about the women in their charge. Tales of them being spirited away by Satan, or changed into cats, or other animals, were quite common. Of course, these were the women who paid well for their release. Yes, the gaolers would do anything for gold and their fantastic stories were believed by those in authority.

Hunger, broke in on her thoughts and she held her complaining stomach in an attempt to ease the pangs. Mary had always been a good eater and enjoyed food. Her buxom figure indicated this in no uncertain terms!

A key turned in the lock and a gaoler entered bearing a bowl of greasy soup and a hunk of black bread. He was a much younger person than his colleagues. 'Quite a simple man,' thought Mary, with relief. She noted that he eyed her with the same lustful look that all the gaolers had, and she fully expected him to make a bawdy remark, but his glance belied his actions. He placed the bowl and the bread on the floor and left the cell. Mary tucked into the spartan meal, "I'll certainly not put on any more weight in here," she muttered, ruefully.

There was little she did not know about the way the turnkeys treated the women in their charge, and although she was no beauty, she was faintly surprised that the man had not attempted to molest her. Perhaps Jonathan's mysterious death had cooled their ardour for the time being.

Even so, it could not last; give it another few weeks and they would be up to their old tricks again. Mary wiped out the bowl with the bread and settled down on the straw. Then, an idea struck her. Maybe she *did* have something to barter with - her body! The very thought of sexual relations with a man, filled her with horror and she shuddered at the mere idea. Mary had never liked men - even as a child. She would sooner lie with one of the hags in the other cell than make love with the male of the species. Still, she would have to make *some* sacrifices if she was to escape. Could she endure such a thing for the sake of freedom? Mary fell asleep with the problem unresolved.

Next morning, the sounds of the gaolers waking the other prisoners for their frugal breakfast, aroused her. Mary performed her toilet as best she could, and made use of a piece of wooden comb, discovered in the straw, to arrange her dishevelled hair. She had come to a decision and was now determined to try anything in order to break out. Then, too, there was Meg. She badly wanted to see her again and this gave Mary added incentive.

Summerset realised that she had fallen in love with the girl. She could easily recall the perfume of Meg's hair. But who was the lovely, delicate creature and where did she live? Mary had to take drastic steps at once; get away and search for her. There were footsteps outside, and swiftly, she removed her dress and dropped down onto the sacks, feigning sleep.

She heard the door creak as it opened, and saw, through slitted eyes, the figure of the gaoler holding some more black bread and a bowl of - she knew not what! He halted when he saw her - naked, on the straw, and Mary sensed his surprise and made sleepy clucking noises so as not to alarm him. Slowly, he ambled across and placed the food beside her. For several minutes, which to Mary seemed like hours, he stood above her, his eyes moving over every inch of her body. Presently, he knelt down and began stroking her limbs. Mary cringed, inwardly, but made a pretence of slowly awakening from a deep sleep. Then, opening her eyes, she gasped, snatching her gown from the straw.

"It's alright, it's only me. I won't hurt you," his voice was nervous and uncertain.

"What's your name?" asked Mary, forcing herself to be agreeable.

"Oliver," he grinned, shyly.

"It's a nice name," she smiled up at him.

"Yes, I like it," his eyes continued their exploration of her.

"What's the matter, Oliver?" she asked, stroking her hair with a careless hand.

The man reddened, "Oh, nothing."

"Then why do you keep looking at me? Have you not seen a naked woman, before?"

His tongue moistened suddenly dry lips. "Yes, but not like you. They say you are different from other women."

"In what way?"

"It's only what I've heard, mind."

"Well, go on, what have you heard?" Mary nudged him, playfully.

Oliver did not reply. He contented himself by pulling at his red beard - now thoroughly embarrassed.

"Tell me. What have you heard?" She raised her body on one arm, displaying heavy breasts, provocatively.

The gaoler avoided her eyes. "They do say as how you never

go with a man . . . that you gets your pleasure with women.''

"Well, what if I do?" Mary's hazel eyes, widened.

"Oh . . . oh," stammered Oliver, "is it true, then?"

"What of it?"

"Nothing. It's just that I've never had a woman of such a nature."

Mary smiled, wryly. "That's not to be wondered at. You've had some wenches, then?"

He fiddled with his belt. "Aye, some, but not half as many as the other gaolers. They take any they've a mind to."

"Why don't you?"

"I don't like 'em all. I'm particular, see."

"Do you like me?"

"Oh, aye, I like you," he grinned, squinting in the poor light. "I've never had one of *your* kind."

Mary had met men like him. Oliver had a fetish for homosexual women and he would obviously enjoy bragging of such a conquest to his friends. If she played up to him, she might be in luck. At any rate, she had discovered his weakness - his Achilles' heel! She looked straight into his eyes, "Would you like to possess a woman like me?"

Oliver stared at his boots. "Yes, I would."

'He is certainly unlike others of his profession,' thought Mary, 'well, here goes,' and she turned her body and moved restlessly so that he could obtain a better view of her.

The gaoler began to perspire. "You're very nice; your bones are so well covered," he murmured, his hand laying like a dead thing on her thigh.

Mary knew she had won the first round, but she would have to go very carefully; he might not be so willing to help her to escape. She could sense a certain obstinacy in him.

"Better wait 'till dark," Mary winked and carefully removed his hand from her leg.

All that morning, Oliver kept peering through the grill in her door, and Mary remained unclothed to keep the ground she had gained over him. He imagined possessing Mary, but he dared not enter her cell until the time arrived for her supper.

At last, he was carrying a bowl of soup through her door. She was still reclining on the sacks, but had donned her dress, arranging it nicely to expose her thighs, while the bodice revealed her cleavage, enticingly. He placed the food near her and said he would soon be going off duty. His voice had a breathless quality and Mary knew that this was the time to act.

"If I give you my body willingly, will you help me to escape?" Her face was a mask.

He dithered. "Oh, I don't know about that."

"But, you know I'm not really a witch?"

"So they say."

"Well, don't you see that I am only here under false pretences? It was all done for spite."

Oliver was in a quandary. He desired the woman, but he was mightily afraid of what would happen if it became known that he had aided a prisoner to escape. He bit his lip in annoyance.

"But, how could I help you to escape? They would make me take your place if they found out."

Mary sat up, displaying her ample bosom. "You could tell them that the Devil came and took me away."

The gaoler was torn between fear and lust - he stood looking at her like a sullen hound, his brow, shiny with sweat.

She reached up and pulled at his sleeve. "Come now, why don't you?"

Oliver, however, was a crafty man. Her eagerness made him realise that she was only trying to use him for her own ends. He turned away - jingling the bunch of keys - busy with his thoughts. It sounded too easy. This kind of female would not give herself willingly to a man. She wanted something in return and he was not going to put his head in a noose for the sake of gratifying his lust - strong as it was. No, he would take her and promise to aid her, afterwards. There was no urgency. He could tell her he would plan it for the next day, or the day after that! He grinned to himself. She did not know he was due for a week off work. Then, when he returned, she would be gone. Yes, that was it!

Now, his lust rose, unimpeded by self-doubt. She might be a virgin! "Alright," he said. "I'll help you to escape . . . *after.*" Mary flashed him a smile and posed, seductively. "Come! Take me then." He stood there, breathing heavily, his glazed eyes contemplating her body.

She flung at him. "Don't you want me? Can't you manage it?"

"Yes," he growled, seemingly unable to move.

"Then, don't waste any more time - come on! You don't want me to change my mind, now, do you?" Mary held out her arms.

Without warning, Oliver flung himself down on the sacks and Mary bit her lip to control her involuntary cry. His body was hard against hers and she felt his rough hands caressing her breasts. The gaoler was fiddling with his belt, now, and Mary closed her eyes and awaited the final horror. But, before he could cover her mouth with his own, she had turned

83

her head away.

It was then that she saw it! The iron bowl filled with soup! She stretched out her arm, but it lay just beyond the reach of her fingers. Mary teased the man, laughingly, and pretended to push him away; at the same time, moving her body beneath him.

She reached out again, and this time her hand closed on the cold metal of the bowl. Mary tipped it over, spilling the greasy liquid over the stones, then lifting her arm and employing her considerable strength, she brought the bowl down with a resounding 'crack' onto the gaoler's head. He merely grunted, as the blackness received him.

She managed to struggle from under Oliver's body, then, undressing him, she climbed into his clothes. They were a reasonable fit, on the whole, and stopping only to turn up the bottoms of the trousers, she carefully opened the door and peered out. It seemed quiet enough outside, so she stepped into the dimly lit passage and locked the door behind her. Mary had taken the precaution of draping her dress and petticoat over Oliver, and as there was but poor illumination, it was possible he would lie undiscovered until the next day. He would have a terrible headache when he awoke, but that would be the least of his worries.

Mary walked along the passage and succeeded in passing a sleepy gaoler. In a few minutes, she stood in the prison yard, breathing the fresh night air. How good it felt! But she was not out of trouble yet. She had to go through the main gate!

Turning up the collar of her jacket, Mary walked jauntily across the yard. Approaching the gate, she kept within the shadows cast by the high wall, her head sunk in her chest. As she passed, the gate-keeper bade her 'Goodnight', and Mary grunted a reply, walking into the street - a free woman!

She continued walking until she was well away from the prison and the town houses rose around her. Then she ducked into the shelter of a doorway to gather her wits and recover for a moment. But Mary's legs suddenly gave way beneath her and she sat where she had fallen. Her recent experiences had left their mark. She would have given a lot for some liquor at that point. Still, she had succeeded in escaping from that dreadful place - not altogether a mean feat - and her prayer had been answered. Maybe a way would be shown to her, even now!

The important thing was to find a hiding-place - and quickly! The town was no good. She would make her way to the forest for the time being. At least she could hide there, and with luck, she might find a stream, too.

Walking slowly through Belford, she dodged from one doorway to another, keeping on the look-out for the night watchman. Mary was nearly seen, when a door she was leaning on, suddenly opened, and an old woman let her cat out. Luckily, the door did not open too widely and she was able to dart away into the darkness. But the incident shook her and she resolved to be more wary where she sheltered.

It had started to rain and was soon pelting down. 'It's a blessing in disguise,' she thought, a little out of breath now and quite soaked. The streets and alleys were deserted, except for the occasional vehicle which lumbered past, its wheels splattering her with muddy water. A few link boys with bobbing lanterns, hurried on their errands and strumpets, who braved all weathers, lurked in dark passage-ways and called out to Mary, describing their wares. One, the worse for drink, tried to grab her, but was flung aside, her oaths resounding in the cavernous archway. A lean dog followed her for a while, whining at her heels, and once, she nearly fell over a shadowy, recumbent figure which growled obscenities at her.

Mary knew, roughly, where the forest lay, and plodding along, she eventually reached a lane which led out of the town and appeared to go in the right direction. Here, although she felt safer, there were no lights at all; merely the faint outline of the track, uneven and full of stones.

The downpour was rapidly churning it into slimy clay and the going was difficult. Mary stumbled along, dragging her feet in the slush. A young woman, she was not, and her plump, overweight body, clothed in Oliver's now rain-sodden suit, was nearly exhausted.

She panted and swore, hoping to find cover before the field labourers started out for work. They were always early - a little before the dawn. Mary knew it would not be long before her disappearance was discovered, then, the hue and cry would be up!

She tried to quicken her pace a little, but what strength she had left was quickly evaporating. Mary hung onto the fact that she would be easily recognised in the gaoler's uniform - but how and where to find other clothing? She had no money now, so could not hope to buy any. Then, too, there would be plenty of folk to track her down! Not only the lawmen, but the young bloods of the town. They would greatly enjoy a witch-hunt. Hopkins, too, would do everything possible to see that she was recaptured, and she knew that the public loved hangings, it was almost a national sport!

In her mind's eye, Mary could visualise an execution day with hundreds of people jostling for a good position; many of them travelling miles to attend. Tradesmen putting up their shutters and taking their wives and children to see the gallows - the grim sentinel of death. Special booths were always set up to dispense food and drink and other goodies, with pedlars plying their wares. Oh yes, the familiar scene was indelibly stamped into Mary's brain and went round and round like a dreadful nightmare, as she imagined herself in the position of the star performer!

The very thought of capture made her feel sick and ill. She would rather kill herself! She grimaced at her macabre joke. Now, she was feeling desperately hungry. God - would this lane never end? The path twisted on its way like a wet serpent, then suddenly, she heard something behind her. It sounded like an animal of some kind; panting and whining in the blackness. 'Not that cur from the town,' she thought, and looked back, just as the creature loped past. Black, it was, and quite large - a dog for sure. A little way ahead, it turned and faced her and Mary thought it was going to attack. Her hand flew to her throat. 'God's death!' She halted, staring in horror at the great beast. Its huge eyes were green and shining like lamps. It flung back its head and howled, once, before leaping over the hedge and vanishing as abruptly as it had appeared.

Mary remained rooted to the spot, shaking with fear. If only she could sit and rest a while, but she knew she must press on. With slow, faltering steps, she began to move again. Eventually, round one of the bends, she saw the dark shape of a building in the distance. Well, it was no use going there and putting herself at the mercy of its owners, that would be suicide. It was a chance she was not prepared to take, even at this late hour.

As she drew nearer, Mary could see that the building was a

small house, with a barn at the rear, and she could just make out the beginnings of the woods a little way beyond. Soon, very soon now, she might curl up and sleep.

Trudging past the house, she noticed something white, swaying above the garden. "I'm seeing things now," she muttered, "I must be ill." Stopping to recover a little, she could see that the pale object was a gown, hanging on a clothes line. She chuckled weakly, leaning drunkenly over the gate, unable to believe her luck. It seemed like a gift from heaven, and would at least give her a change of dress until something better came along. Of course, the gown would be as wet as her own clothes, but she could dry it when the sun rose.

Quietly, Mary opened the gate and picked her way towards the clothes line, but she stumbled and fell over a stone, which formed part of the edge of a flower bed. She gasped as she hit the ground, and when she tried to rise, found that she had sprained her ankle.

Mary was filled with terror. It was not possible to remain where she had fallen. She must try and walk, somehow! The pain was bad but she finally managed it; gritting her teeth to prevent crying out.

Slowly, she dragged herself towards the tantalising gown, which appeared to wave, mockingly, at her inability to reach it. Mary was almost there, when her other foot found a ridge, hidden in the grass, and down she went again, but this time, her head hit the stump of an old lilac tree. She experienced a blinding flash of pain before losing consciousness.

Early, the following morning, Bess sallied forth into the rain-drenched garden to gather some flowers for her mother. They were lifting their sleepy, wet heads to the bright touch of the sun, as he covered the earth with his radiance.

After the night's downpour, the plants and herbs exuded exotic aromas and it seemed to Bess as though all the growing things were glad that she and Robert were soon to be united. As she made her way, snipping here and there, she noticed that the gate was swinging on its hinges. 'That's strange,' she thought, 'I'm sure it was fastened last night.' She strolled across, then her eyes widened in alarm as she saw the marks of muddy feet on the lawn. Bess followed their tracks, anxiously, and then she saw it - a body lying half-concealed near the rosemary bushes. The shock sent her speeding back to the house - red hair flying, the flowers, forgotten.

Mistress Nokes was busy baking bread when Bess ran into the kitchen. "Come quickly, Mother, there's a dead man in the garden!"

"Lord-a-lovee, whatever do you mean?"

Bess dragged Agnes outside. "Look! Over there by the bushes."

Her mother walked over to the still figure and bending down, lifted Mary's head. "He's not dead, child. He must have had too much to drink."

"But, Mother, don't you see? He looks like one of the gaolers from the prison." Bess was now thoroughly alarmed, "What is he doing in *our* garden?"

Her mother straightened up, holding her back with one hand, a look of pain passing across her face. The stiffness in her bones seemed to be getting worse these days. She sighed, "Maybe someone robbed him and left him here - who knows?"

Her daughter frowned, "I don't like it at all. He might have been sent to spy upon us." She looked round apprehensively, half expecting to see a face peering at them over the wall.

"Now stop this nonsense," Mistress Nokes returned sharply. "We don't know how he came to be here, but we can't leave him here to die. A dead body would certainly be a dangerous thing to have around - especially if he *is* a gaoler. They might think we had killed him and that would never do. Quick, Bess, give me a hand to lift him. It's a pity Meg went off delivering eggs so early."

Slowly, they lifted Mary and between them, managed to carry her indoors and heave her upstairs into one of the bedrooms.

"Phew! What a job!" gasped Bess. "Have a rest, Mother, and then we'll get him onto the bed. I'll fetch an old coverlet, we don't want him to soil the counterpane." She dashed away and returned with a patched sheet. "This will do. Now, one more heave, Mother dear."

The sunlight streamed through the casement window, illuminating the pale face on the pillow.

"Mother!" cried Bess. "It's Mary Summerset, the witchpricker. I've seen her in Belford. It was she who tortured Meg!"

Mistress Nokes was well nigh exhausted from her labours and her temper, as well as her breath, was short. "No matter who she is, or what she's done, we cannot allow her to die. Fetch some hot broth at once, while I undress her. She's soaked to the skin."

Bess stared disbelievingly at Agnes. "I'm really sure now that you want to see us all on the gallows," she panted. "First, it was that wretched cat and now it's this wicked woman. I'll not help her." She flung away and gazed out of the window - her nostrils flaring.

"Be quiet!" snapped Mistress Nokes. "You seem to have

forgotten that she no longer works for Hopkins. In fact, she, herself, has been convicted. Yes, that's it. She must have escaped. It takes a brave woman to overcome a gaoler."

Bess turned, a look of absolute amazement on her features. "How do you know what happened?"

"How else could she have obtained these clothes?" Agnes smiled, thinly. "She must have some courage."

"You'll be making out she's the Queen of the May, next," sneered Bess, glaring angrily at the form on the bed.

"Well, we'll see what she has to say when she comes round. She's in our power now, so there's nothing to fear. If it comes to it, we can surrender her to the authorities."

Bess, her hand on the door, stared at her mother, her face, troubled, "No, not that. Whatever she's done, she does not deserve *that* fate."

Her mother smiled - an understanding smile. "I knew you would come to my way of thinking. Let the matter rest until we have heard her story."

After her daughter had gone, Mistress Nokes made Mary as comfortable as she could. Although she had not shown her concern to Bess, she was deeply troubled about the whole affair. However, she had learned to refrain from reacting to a situation before knowing all the facts. In the end, it saved one's time and energy.

Bess returned with a bowl of hot broth and between them they managed to force some of the liquid past Mary's lips. In a few moments, her eyelids fluttered open, but when she saw the two women, she shrank back into the pillow.

"Where am I? Don't let them take me away."

Mistress Nokes gently patted her hand. "Calm yourself. No one is going to take you anywhere. Now, finish this soup and we will talk when you feel stronger.''

Mary tried to raise herself, but fell back. There was nothing to do but obey. They fed her slowly, then left her to rest.

The invalid gazed round the pretty sun-filled bedroom. After her initial shock, it was difficult to reconcile the horrors of the previous days with the surroundings in which she now found herself. Perhaps she had died and gone to heaven? The bed was so comfortable with its clean white sheets and pillows smelling sweetly of lavender. How different it was from the terrible conditions in the prison. And these women appeared to be kind - she could only hope for the best. Certainly, she was not strong enough to move at the moment - nor did she wish to! God had answered her prayers, again!

The details of her ordeal the previous night, filtered slowly through her mind. She must have been discovered and brought into the house. The vague memory of the 'ghost' dress hanging in the garden, evoked the flicker of a smile across her countenance. But, what had they thought of her strange attire? Did they know who she was? Would they send her back? At length, Mary fell into a troubled sleep, yet a sleep which gave a long needed rest to her tortured body and brain.

It was late afternoon when Mistress Nokes re-entered the bedroom. The sun had passed over to the other side of the house and the room was pleasantly cool with a strong scent of roses wafting in through the open window.

Mary had already awakened and was enjoying the peace and luxury of the feather bed. She felt much better and smiled shyly at her hostess.

''Well, how do you feel now?'' asked the old lady, drawing up a chair and settling into it.

''Much better, thank you ma'am.'' Mary attempted to straighten her hair.

"Good! Now, we know who you are, and we know you are a fugitive from justice, but I would like to hear *your* story."

"I'm not really a witch."

"Of that, we are also aware," affirmed Agnes. "Why not tell me everything in your own words."

Mary acquiesced and related all that had happened to her, from the moment in the Assembly Hall when the crowd had turned on her. Mistress Nokes listened intently and at the end she said, "You must be very brave."

"I don't know about that," smiled Mary, ruefully. "I know now that I have led a wicked life and caused the deaths of many innocent women." She clutched at the bedclothes, fearfully. "What are you going to do with me? Are you going to turn me in?"

"No."

"But, how can I trust you? How can I trust anyone?" Tears welled up in her hazel eyes, which were large and lustrous and altogether one of her best features.

"I have every right to give you up, because of what you did to my daughter - apart from anything else. But, I do not bear malice and neither do I seek revenge," replied Agnes, calmly.

"What do you mean? I have never seen your daughter, if such was your companion, until this day."

Mistress Nokes looked at her keenly. "Bess is indeed my daughter - but not my *only* daughter." So saying, she rose and opened the door, beckoning to someone outside.

When Meg entered, dressed in a pale green gown, her fair tresses around her shoulders, Mary stared at her - unable to believe the evidence of her own eyes. Surely, she must be dreaming?

"Oh, please forgive me," she pleaded. "I *had* to do it. Believe me, I'm sorry for everything I did to harm you. Please don't give me up. I swear I'll never go back to witch-hunting. I'd sooner join the witches, myself!"

Meg and her mother exchanged glances.

"I have told you that I have no intention of doing that, despite your treatment of Meg," answered Mistress Nokes. "It was partly her own fault. She should not have poked her nose into what did not concern her. I know she was trying to save her friend, but she would not have seen Margaret Wall if she had been minding her own business. Nevertheless, this family lives by a code . . . 'An it harm none, do what ye will'."

At these words, Mary began to weep, "God bless you. Perhaps one day I will be able to do something for you. I hope I can become a good Christian like you."

The other two smiled at each other and Mistress Nokes passed Mary a handkerchief. "To show you that we trust you, I will tell you a secret. We are all followers of the Old Religion."

Mary gaped. "Y - you mean that you are witches?"

"If you like to call us witches - yes," replied Meg from the window seat. "Now, you see why we cannot give you away."

Mary wiped her eyes. "Then, it is best if we all stick together. You have been so honest with me . . . may I kiss you, ma'am?"

Agnes bent over the bed, "Why, bless you, my child. Now, we must find somewhere for you to hide until such time any danger is past. You must not be seen by any visitors. Not all our friends are witches." She smoothed her apron - as always, concerned about her appearance.

Meg was eager to help, "Would the loft be any good, Mother?"

"Yes, of course, that's the place," nodded Mistress Nokes. "It's small, but comfortable. We have always kept it a secret, in case we would one day have a need for it." She smiled, "It appears *that* day has come. There is a hidden door into it, which we discovered by accident many years ago. I will have a bed put up there for you."

"In actual fact it lies next to the loft - on the same level," Meg chipped in, "but no one would guess it was there," she smiled at Mary.

"How can I thank you?" asked their visitor, wonderingly. "I have never known such kindness."

Then, she was alone, finding what had passed in the last few hours, very difficult to believe.

In a few days, Mary was a familiar figure in the Nokes household. She was almost accepted as a member of it and returned their benevolence with a most willing heart.

After a thorough search of the forest and the surrounding countryside, the hunt for the witchpricker was finally abandoned. The story was spread around that she had been taken away by the Devil and there were those who swore they had seen her riding through the air on a goat, accompanied by an army of imps!

Mary helped with all the chores of the house and made herself generally useful. Despite what she had undergone, she had not changed in her outlook towards women. To her, they were a recompense for the lack of femininity in her own personality.

Mary Summerset really loved Meg, and often thought that she sensed a certain attraction in Meg, for herself. She wondered if the girl thought about the time they had spent together in the Assembly Hall - she never alluded to it.

One thing struck her as being unusual. She had not heard Meg speak of any boy-friends, and had not seen her with any young men, which, for such an attractive young woman, was strange. Mary shook herself, mentally, she really must not think such thoughts in her present situation.

One day, when Mary was in the secret room, Meg entered, carrying a bunch of wild flowers, picked from the hedgerows. She shyly presented the bouquet, then said, "I'm going to ask Mother if she will make you a witch - I mean, put forward your name for initiation into the Craft. Our last coven meeting was abandoned when I got into trouble and Mother thought she had been followed at the previous one." Her smile flashed in dimpled excitement. "But, there *is* a meeting in the near future and if all agree, you can be initiated, then."

Mary smiled back, "There is nothing I would like better than to be one of you."

"I am so glad!" cried Meg, and threw her arms round Mary.

Their love for one another was consummated that day, in the secret room under the eaves, without any thought of shame or regret.

CHAPTER 6

Hopkins swished the ale round and round the pewter tankard and stared into its golden depths. "I'd give a great deal to know where Mary went, especially as she was wearing the gaoler's clothes," he stroked his beard, thoughtfully. "She could not be seen in the day-time dressed like that, so where in God's name is she?"

"Perhaps she was *really* taken by the Devil," suggested Stearne.

"I'd like to think she's now burning in Hell - the bitch!"

"Keep your voice down," Hopkins looked furtively round at the other customers in the Black Swan - it was busier than usual, today. Then, his cold eyes returned to his companion. "I know you disliked her, but I was not aware you loathed the woman as much as that."

Stearne, grimaced, "Words cannot express my feelings towards that she-wolf. I'm glad we're rid of her. Aye! Well rid!" he blustered.

Hopkins shrugged, "Well, she did her work thoroughly. I doubt if I'll ever find a better pricker."

"Think you she's left town?"

"What else can I think? She can't be in the forest - they combed that two or three times."

"Perhaps some carrier gave her a lift on one of his packponies. Even gypsies could have helped her get away."

Hopkins took a long pull at his ale before answering. "That's more than likely. But if such *is* the case, I'll catch up with her one day, mark me well! Summerset's not going to get the better of the Witchfinder General."

One or two heads turned in their direction and Stearne growled,

"*Now*, who's attracting attention?"

Such was Hopkins' arrogance, however, that he merely nodded towards the men and proceeded to light his pipe.

"Then you don't believe that the Devil took her?" asked Stearne.

His master snorted into the blue smoke. "Of course not. Who but an idiot would swallow such stories?"

Stearne leered at him. "Then according to you, all the townsfolk are idiots!"

The other allowed himself a thin smile. "I wouldn't deny that. They'll believe anything about these witches."

"Yes, but Mary wasn't a witch."

"Nor are many women we convict as such." Hopkins examined his finger-nails - he was fastidious to the point of eccentricity.

"Are there no real witches, then?" Stearne's face creased in dismay.

"Of course there are, but I don't expect we find many."

"Then, who are these women we convict?"

"Mostly old crones who have upset some neighbour in one way or another." He drew long on his pipe. "We supply a type of revenge, you might say, and also an easy way of getting rid of hags who are disliked." Hopkins leaned over the table. "Were you not pleased when the crowd accused Mary of being a witch?"

Stearne's ruddy features wore an expression of disbelief mingled with anger. "Do you mean to say that these women have no powers at all?"

"Only what folk bestow upon them. Did not Shakespeare say, 'Some are born great, some achieve greatness, and some have greatness thrust upon them'? These witches fall into the latter category.''

His servant prodded the table with a stubby finger. "Ah, but the women *confess* they work spells and have dealings with the Devil." Hopkins grunted then quietly delivered his *coup de grâce.* "And so would you if you were put to the question."

Stearne's jaw dropped, "Do you mean they are charlatans? Don't they work magic spells?"

His master chuckled behind his hand. "In that, they are probably as good as the anti-witch charms we sell to the people."

"But, you only do that to make money."

"Exactly! Mine is a two-edged weapon. If folk refuse to buy the charms, I can accuse them of being witches, themselves, or suggest that they have sympathy for the witches - either way, I have them!" He smirked into his ale. "Stearne, as long as there is money in witch-hunting, I intend to find as many of them as possible." He replaced his tankard; wiped his mouth delicately on a lawn handkerchief, and rose to his feet. The other man belched loudly and departed to find the inn's latrine. The room was fast emptying now, as the customers left to resume their afternoon's work.

Hopkins strolled over to the window and was joined by Stearne, who complained about the condition of the latrine.

"It must be bad if *you* complain," sneered the witchfinder, gazing through the thick, bottle glass. Then something caught his eye.

"See that boy, yonder?" he pointed with a thin forefinger. "He informed me that Mistress Nokes is a witch, and I gave him a crown to keep an eye on her and to let me know where she goes - especially at night. I have to be very careful how I act in that direction. She is much respected. I dare not convict her on hearsay. There must be evidence - and strong evidence, since John Gaule intervened on her daughter's behalf and proved she was not a witch. A pox on that meddling old fool."

"May!, the boy brings you news of her," said Stearne. Then his eyes narrowed as an idea suddenly dawned. "Do you think that Mary could be hiding with the Nokes family?"

Hopkins snorted. "Hiding with *them*? You must be mad! What woman would aid someone who had ill-treated her own daughter? She would be the first one to surrender Mary to justice. She may appear a kind woman, but she would fight like a hell-cat if anyone touched a member of her family."

He waved the matter away. "Mary would be safer with the torturers."

Stearne coloured angrily, wishing he had kept his mouth shut. He was always putting his foot in it.

Hopkins took a pinch of snuff from a silver box and patted his nose delicately with two fingers. "Personally, I believe that Mary is living in some other town, disguised as a man. She always had a mannish look about her."

"Those paps would give her away though, two beauties, they were." Stearne licked his lips, appreciatively.

The lawyer eyed him with distaste, "You don't miss much do you? I'd forgotten you were so lecherous."

"I only said they *might* give her away." Stearne's face wore an injured expression. Despite his coarseness and cruelty, he could not overlook any criticism of his character, and Hopkins despised him for this.

"Not if she bound herself tightly and wore a coat - numbskull!" replied his master, scathingly.

100

At that moment, Joseph passed the inn. "Quick! Go and bring that boy to me," he commanded.

Red-faced and scowling, Stearne did as he was bid and returned holding the struggling youngster by the scruff of the neck.

Hopkins, his hands behind his back, asked sternly, "Now, young man, what have you to say for yourself?"

"N . n . nothing," stammered Joseph.

The witchfinder towered over him. "Well, it's about time you had! Did I not give you a crown to bring me information about Mistress Nokes? Have you forgotten that?"

"No . . . I tried," the lad shuffled, uncomfortably.

"But you have not been successful, eh?"

Joseph gazed at the floor. "No . n . no sir."

Hopkins began to lose his temper. "I don't believe you have done anything about it, at all."

Joseph's eyes, owlish, shot up to the man's face. "Indeed I have, sir."

"Well? Where does Mistress Nokes go?"

"She don't go anywhere, except to the market. I followed her whenever I could."

The lawyer glanced down at him and spoke through clenched teeth.

"I'm not interested in what she does in the daytime. Where does she go at night?"

"She stays in," the lad said flatly, his mouth, trembling.

Hopkins subsided into a chair. "So, she stays in, does she? I thought you told me that she went into the forest and danced with demons - eh? eh?"

Joseph's cockiness had apparently deserted him - never to return. He clutched feverishly at the edge of his jacket. "I've watched her house every night - I have! Except for the night of the storm. She never leaves it - I swear!''

"But, does she not go to meetings with the Devil - as you said?''

His questioner drummed the table with impatient fingers.

"She used to.''

"And she does not do it now. Have you converted her?''

"No, sir.''

Hopkins' face whitened with anger and Joseph took a step backwards and looked round for a way of escape, but Stearne barred any retreat.

"You are either a liar, or the woman is no witch. I believe you made it all up to obtain money from me.''

The boy hopped from one foot to the other in his anxiety. "I swear to you, I did not. You *must* believe me.''

"Then what about the cat that turns into Satan and those pins you vomited?'' Hopkins brought his face close to Joseph's, his eyes, cold as stones. "Do you know what happens to liars?'' he gritted.

"I swear that Mistress Nokes *is* a witch,'' the boy croaked.

The flat of Hopkins' hand met Joseph's cheek with a loud 'crack'.

"Now get out and bring me no more lies,'' he panted.

Joseph staggered back, whimpering, then turned and fled.

Stearne watched him go, a grin on his usually surly features.

"Do you really think the woman is a witch?''

"I have never thought such to be the case, and I don't think her daughter is, either.'' The lawyer stroked his beard, thoughtfully. "The boy's a confounded liar.''

"But, are none of these young girls we prick, guilty of witch-

102

craft?"

Hopkins shrugged his shoulders, "Not as far as I know.

"Then why do folk bring them to us?" Stearne scratched his thatch of blonde hair.

"Don't you realise, man, that this country of ours is sex-starved? The Puritans have condemned all pleasures - so the people delight in seeing a naked wench. *You* know that. You're as bad as any of them."

Hopkins stood up and donned his hat and gloves. "I've watched your face when one is pricked." He gave his associate a knowing wink; picked up his cane and left the room.

Stearne kicked at a convenient stool - he was furious. He hated the way Hopkins poked fun at him and would have left him long ago, had it not been for the comparatively easy and well-paid work. He waited a few minutes, then followed Hopkins out of the inn, cursing him quietly with a few well chosen oaths.

Meg asked her mother if Mary could join the Craft.

"Would you like her to be one of us?" asked Mistress Nokes.

"Oh, I'm sure we *all* would," replied her daughter, smiling softly.

The older woman gazed at Meg, steadily. "Yes, I think it would be better for us if she belonged to the Brotherhood. Especially now that we have accepted her as one of the family. I will have a talk to her and see if I consider her worthy of initiation."

"By the way, Mother, Mary told me about something that happened to her on the night she arrived here."

Meg proceeded to relate the incident concerning the black dog and Mistress Nokes listened intently, her brows, furrowed.

103

At the end, she said, "Well, you know what she saw, don't you?"

Meg shook her head. "No, not really, but I thought of the ghost dog that some folk talk on."

"Exactly! I believe she saw 'Black Shuck' - and that is not a good thing to see. Whoever sees this demon dog sometimes does not live long enough to tell on it."

Her daughter shivered. "Oh, I do hope it is not an evil omen for her."

"So do I, but remember, here in Essex, it is supposed to be a more kindly hound, and is known to protect travellers. We will hope his appearance was a blessing rather than a curse. Anyway, I think we should keep the information to ourselves - Mary has had too much to worry her, lately."

That afternoon, Mistress Nokes took Mary into her bedroom.

"I want to have a talk with you," she said, "sit over there."

Mary obeyed and settled herself in a chair, while her companion sat by the window.

"Meg wants you to become a member of the Craft," the old lady began.

"I know. She told me she would ask you about it."

"What have *you* to say on the matter?" Agnes inclined her head, questioningly.

'She looks like a wise old owl,' thought Mary, and quickly reassured her. "There is nothing I would like better."

Meg's mother turned to gaze into the garden. "That may be, but you must realise that you are seeking to join the Priesthood of a very ancient religion which has been in existence for a very long time. And, for the sake of this faith,

104

hundreds, nay thousands of people, all over Europe, have suffered torture and death."

"I fully realise that," nodded Mary, but Agnes continued as though there had been no interruption. "The witches worship the Mother Goddess - the Queen of Heaven, and the Horned God of Death and Regeneration. The twin forces behind nature - male and female. The Horned God, or Old Hornie, as he is affectionately called, is the deity that the Church turned into the Devil. We do not believe in the Devil. How could we? Our religion existed long before that of Christianity."

"What is your god's name?" queried Mary.

Mistress Nokes smiled, faintly. "That, I cannot tell you, neither can I speak the name of the Goddess. These things will be revealed to you if you enter the Craft. And when you *do* know their names, you will be sworn to secrecy."

Mary's large eyes never left the old lady's face. "I will swear to keep them secret," she said, solemnly.

"As it should be," agreed Agnes. "Even those who are tortured never reveal the names."

In spite of herself, Mary quaked, inwardly. Would she be strong enough to uphold such a faith - one which inspired such loyalty and courage in its followers? And then again, surely there must be some truth in the dreadful stories of black magic that she had heard.

Mistress Nokes had a far-away look in her eyes. "I know what you are thinking. You are wondering about the tales of witches who fly to the Sabbats and copulate with the Devil."

Mary gasped and gripped the arms of her chair. "How did you know what I was thinking?"

Agnes Nokes smiled, a slow smile. "Think you I have been a

105

witch some forty years for nought?'' She adjusted her white cap with deft fingers. "Such stories have been put into the mouths of the victims by those who torture them, in order to justify the persecutions - if such a thing were possible! They will say and do anything they are told to, hoping to avoid further torture. Those who *are* of the blood, keep to the story in order to hide the truth.''

Mary expelled her breath in a sigh of relief. "What else must I do?''

"You are bound by oath to keep the secrets of the Brotherhood and also to help all your brothers and sisters of the Craft - when *that* help is needed.''

You must realise that the coven is the kernel of the Old Religion and you must know that the initiation is part of a mystery tradition which will place your feet on the first rung of the ladder, leading to perfection of soul.

Unlike the many, who observe the Old Gods through customs and folk festivals, such as the May Day revelries and the lighting of boon-fires on hilltops; the Craft admits only the few who are capable and intelligent enough to be entrusted with the Mysteries.

As you may know, the number of witches in any one coven must not exceed thirteen - twelve, and a leader. Because, Lady Moon shows her full face but thirteen times in a year, and *that* orb is a symbol of the Goddess in her three phases - Virgin, Mother and Crone.''

Mary clasped her hands. "Oh, it's all so interesting, I hope I will be acceptable in your eyes. But, one thing puzzles me - do men belong to the Craft?'' The question seemed to irritate Agnes but she answered readily enough. "Nowadays, yes, but originally, the Craft was part of the Feminine Mysteries.

106

When men became priests in the new religion, they took the power away from the priestesses and also infiltrated the older faith. Today, they are usually the husbands of the women who are initiated, yet the female still remains the one who holds the highest rank. There is a deep mystery here and it takes a *very* special man to understand why this is so."

"Does it make any difference that I . . ." Mary stopped in mid-sentence and colour suffused her features.

"Go on," prompted Mistress Nokes, relentlessly.

"I don't know how to tell you." Mary's eyes were fixed on her shoes.

"Let me help you. You are different from other women." Mary looked up - amazed. "You know?"

"Yes, I know. But who am I to condemn anyone for what they are?" A veined hand was waved as if dismissing the subject.

Mary blinked away the sudden tears which rose, unbidden. Swiftly, she went over to her friend and kissed the deceptively fragile hands. "You are very tolerant and understanding," she whispered.

Agnes flashed Mary a knowing smile which momentarily transformed her into a younger woman. "Tush, tush, that will do, now." She patted the strong, dark hair. "We believe in reincarnation - that we are born again on this earth. So, if you are born in the wrong body, or if it is your fate to be as you are, who can blame you? It is something only the Gods understand."

"Then, you don't despise me for what I am?" asked Mary, anxiously.

"Despise you? Bless you, no, my dear. I will tell you something that must go no further than this room."

"I swear I will never breathe a word of what you tell me."

"So be it! This is my secret. I know that my younger daughter, Meg, has the same instincts as yourself. I have watched her grow from childhood, and I know! But I blame myself entirely for what she is. After Bess was born, I wanted a boy, and prayed continually for the Gods to grant my wishes. When Meg arrived, I mentally, refused to accept her. I know I was wrong, and have long since asked the Gods forgiveness. But then, I was so determined to have a son that I brought Meg up as a boy. I allowed her to play boy's games and dressed her, for a while, in boy's clothes! In the course of time, I realised my foolishness, but it was too late.

My husband did not approve, but there was no stopping me in my younger days. Yes, I have failed as a mother. She will never marry now and may well have to go through life, unloved."

Agnes sank back in her chair - exhausted. Baring her soul to her listener had cost her more than she cared to admit.

After hearing such a story, Mary dared not tell Mistress Nokes of her feelings for Meg. She wished fervently that she could, but it was quite out of the question. "I do understand - I do," was all she said as she gently stroked the old lady's hands.

"Well, now you know my secret, let us talk no more of it. Our next coven meeting is but a few days off. It will be a full moon and if the Gods and the omens agree, you shall be initiated. Now, I must go and prepare the supper." Agnes patted Mary on the head and walked slowly from the room, leaving her guest alone with her thoughts.

That night, when the house was still, Meg crept up to the loft and slipped between the sheets of Mary's bed. Its occupant, a light sleeper, instantly awoke.

"You shouldn't be here," she whispered. "The others might hear you."

Meg giggled. "It's safe, silly goose, Bess sleeps like a log .. . even an earthquake would not disturb her."

"I was not thinking so much of Bess - it's your mother," came the reply.

"That's no problem. She knows."

"What?" The sheet rose in the gloom as Mary pulled it from her head.

Meg heaved with silent laughter. "Who's waking them up, now?" Then, "Listen, I told Mother about us this evening."

"You *told* her?"

"Yes." The newcomer thumped the pillow into shape. "Is it not time *I* had a lover? Bess has Robert Maxwell."

Mary snorted. "That's different."

"Why is it? What's wrong with two women loving each other?"

"Nothing - I suppose. It's just what people say, Meg."

"I don't care what they say. They are always poking their noses into things which do not concern them." Her finger prodded Mary. "Poke, poke, poke! Besides, apart from the family, no one knows you are here."

Mary caught and held the offending finger. "What about your mother?"

"I've already told you - *she knows.*" Meg's free hand added emphasis to her words with a playful pinch.

"Ouch! Whatever did she say?"

"Nothing - would you believe? I think she was quite pleased, really. If I'm happy, I think it makes Mother happy."

Almost absentmindedly, Mary stroked her friend's shoulder.

"But, I trust your mother and I know she trusts me. I cannot deceive her."

Meg kicked at the sheets, impatiently. "How can you deceive her when she knows about us? I said I have *told* her - mugwump!"

"What will she say to me, tomorrow?"

"Not a word, my dear, and she certainly will not inform Bess. Our love does not hurt anyone - does it?"

Mary thought for a while. "Not if you are sure your mother does not mind."

"Cross my heart! She will keep our secret locked in her heart. Isn't it exciting?" Meg threw her arms round her friend and hugged her.

"She's the strangest woman I have ever met," mused Mary. "She never says an unkind word about anyone."

Meg chuckled. "Except the witchfinders, of course. Mother cannot abide Matthew Hopkins and his cruelty."

Mary winced at that remark, but had to agree. 'How glad I am to be away from all that,' she thought. 'And all my prayers have been answered. How extraordinary!' Mary whispered into Meg's ear. "If everyone was like your mother, the world would be a far better place to live in."

"That is because she worships the Old Gods - the Ancient Providence - and believes that folk should be allowed to live their own lives, as they will. Providing they do no terrible harm."

Meg began to respond to her lover's caresses and the room receded. Her newly awakened passion drew her beyond the mundane, as she discovered the secrets of her body for the first time. Wave after wave of exquisite, sensual pleasure rolled inexorably over her - and her mind dissolved in that darkly, purple cavern of voluptuousness.

CHAPTER 7

Mary woke early to find Meg still asleep, her fair head laid trustingly on Mary's shoulder. She lay still and listened to the sleepy twittering of the birds in the eaves - aroused by the call of the sun - new born.

Her mind drifted and she thought of the past and all that she had been through. It was because of her nature that she had first joined the witch-hunters. It had given her the opportunity to be close to women, and, to be honest with herself, she had enjoyed the excitement of the contact with their naked bodies.

Mary shuddered with repulsion when she thought how perverted she had been, and how her ordeal, and sudden love for Meg, had at least saved her from sinking further into the pit of loathsomeness. She could not help her feelings, or what she was, but she could at last make up for a part of her wicked life, by aiding those who had come to her rescue.

Mary had not long worked for Hopkins. Her previous employer could be considered a kind man, compared to the Witchfinder General. He would often free the women who had been brought to him, because of pity - especially young girls. But this had never happened with Hopkins. He thought only of silver and was determined to become a rich man. His avarice and cruelty prevented any woman escaping the gallows.

The witchpricker had been loaned to Hopkins' party because her namesake, Mary Phillips, had been taken ill, or had been in an advanced state of drunkenness, as to be incapable of carrying out her duties.

Goodie Phillips, as she was called, was a fat, greasy slut, who could down a quart of ale at one go, and in this doubtful accomplishment she was equal to any man. It was no feat for her to drink a couple of gallons at a night's sitting, and while in her cups, she would lay with any man who was drunk enough to fancy her.

It was rumoured that both Hopkins and Stearne had possessed her, although Mary doubted this, as Hopkins was extremely fastidious in his personal habits. It was a mystery how even Stearne could lay with such a vile, repulsive creature, especially, as he, like the gaolers, had the choice of all the convicted women. Mary, however, had refused Stearne's advances, which resulted in his hatred of her.

Hopkins had encouraged her homosexuality and had given her every opportunity to be left alone with young girls, so that he could spy on her. Once, she had caught him in the act, and his voyeurism was the source of their initial dislike of each other.

She now realised that it must have been a regular thing - to satisfy his own perversions. She yearned to lay hands on him - to strangle him would be a pleasure. Mary clenched her fists beneath the sheets, nails digging into flesh. Then, the moment passed, and with it, her anger. At least she had found contentment with this family, and when Hopkins and his followers moved on, she would be free! Provided there *was* such a thing as complete freedom, which she doubted.

In every country there were always people ready to persecute those who held philosophies or faiths, dissimilar from their own - who did not know the meaning of tolerance.

Would there ever be such a thing as the Brotherhood of Man? Astrologers had foretold that it would come to pass in what they called, the Aquarian Age, but that was in the far distant future. The Age of Pisces, in which she was now living, had a long way to go, they said, four hundred years, or more!

Mary was confused. She had listened to the Puritans quoting the words of the Master Jesus - 'Love thy neighbour as thyself', yet there were more wars and persecutions carried on in the name of Christianity, than in any other faith. She had heard the Calvinists ranting abut damnation and the agonies of the fiery pit, yet she could not believe that a god of love would allow his children to burn forever - no matter how wicked they had been.

She remembered the commandment - 'Thou shalt not kill', but she, herself, had aided in the killing of witches! The commandment did not say - 'Thou shalt not kill certain people', it merely stated, 'Thou shalt not kill', and she believed it meant *every living soul.*

Mary was aware that many folk refused to accept the fact of witches being human, and imagined, therefore, that they were excluded from this commandment. But she knew they were as human as the next person, and indeed, had the same feelings. Had she not seen them suffer the most inhuman torture and witnessed how they reacted to pain as much as anyone else?

Despite the sanctimonious teachings of the Puritans, they were just as eager as other sects to destroy their rivals and this did not only apply to witchcraft. Even priests of the Roman Church were hung, drawn and quartered without the least compunction.

Many of the older churchmen were against the persecutions. Had not Cannon Lees claimed that the war waged in

115

the name of idealism was controlled by material interests? Had he not called the witch-trials, a newly invented alchemy by which human blood was transmuted into silver and gold?

The apologists of the persecutions excused their actions by quoting from the Bible, Exodus XXII, 18 - 'Thou shalt not suffer a witch to live', but she had once been told, by an old monk, that the Hebrew word 'chasaph', which had been translated to mean 'witch', occurred *twelve* times in the old testament with *various meanings*. As Reginald Scott had pointed out in 1584, in this instance, it meant *'poisoner'*, and certainly had nothing to do with the highly sophisticated Christian concept of a witch.

Mistress Nokes' immense tolerance had changed Mary's outlook on life. She was now free from the dogmatic attitudes of the Church and the ideas they instilled into their followers. She could view the present situation as an individual! Reincarnation was something she had known very little about until her benefactress had discussed it with her. It explained many things that were omitted from the teachings of the Puritans. It made clear why some children were born as infant prodigies. A soul might carry learning with it through many lives!

Her thoughts were interrupted by her friend, awakening. Meg yawned sleepily and kissed her, but eluded Mary's embrace and slipped quickly out of bed, her smile flashing into dimpled wickedness. "No, darling, it's too late, I must hurry. I promised the others I would see to the animals this morning."

She donned a blue cotton gown; blew Mary a kiss, and left the room on small, bare feet.

One evening, at table, Mistress Nokes suddenly froze - a
bowl of vegetables in one hand and a spoon in the other.
"They want me at the Hall," she said, a far-away look in her
eyes.

"Whatever is the matter?" asked Mary. She seemed utterly
mystified and quite unable to take her startled gaze from
Mistress Nokes' face.

"It is well," Bess reassured her, "it's only Mother's far-
sight. She has received one of her messages."

Meg nodded. "Yes. Obviously, the quickest way to deliver a message is to send it direct - from one mind to another.
It's very common amongst the Brotherhood. Surely, you
have heard of it? There are various names for it - clairvoy-
ance, second-sight, but we always call it, 'the gift'."

"We are taught how to develop it in the Mysteries," Bess
chipped in. "It can be extremely useful at times."

"When will you go, Mother?" enquired Meg, helping herself
to a piece of apple pie.

"I think it best to make the journey tomorrow, after mid-
day," replied Agnes. "You see, Mary," she smiled at her
guest's puzzled countenance, "there is something I must know
from other members of the coven. I gave them the task a few
days ago and they are now ready with an answer."

Next day, Agnes Nokes set off for Monkton Hall. It lay
two miles east of Elm-tree farm, if one knew the short cuts.

It was hot, even for the month of August, and heavy, with a
hint of thunder in the air. Agnes was wearing her best gown
of cream cotton, embroidered with clusters of lavender-col-
oured flowers. She had folded her purple cloak and put it in
the bottom of her basket - in case it rained, later.

117

Leaving the farm by way of the orchard and the wicket gate, she was soon walking through a meadow and knee-high glorious marguerites. Her errand led through a series of lanes which weaved their way between the countryside of the Tendring Hundred. Wild flowers ran riot in the hedgerows. Pink heads of the willow herb and ragged robin, mingled with the yellow, spiked yarrow; the white stars of the dead nettle and the deep-blue flower heads of the wild borage. Mistress Nokes' sharp eyes noted them all and greeted them as old friends, recalling their medicinal qualities and testing her memory.

Presently, she struck a lane which led to the nearby village of Monkton. It ran alongside a high, red-brick wall, which bounded a large estate. A little way along, she came to a studded oak door, set in the wall, and after making sure there was no one in sight, she turned the heavy iron ring, and pushed. The old wood protested loudly as it creaked inwards on rusty hinges. 'It's a good thing they remembered to leave this entrance open for me,' she thought, as she passed through and replaced the bolt.

Agnes followed a narrow path which hugged the inside of the wall. On her right lay a beautiful copper-beech hedge, which sheltered a herb garden. Her nostrils twitched appreciatively as the pungent aromas assailed them and she stopped for a moment. "I must be getting old," she smiled to herself, "a short walk like this never used to tire me."

She continued along the path before striking off to the right through some undergrowth. This part of the estate had been left to run wild, but despite the lack of anything to guide her, she seemed to know exactly where she was going.

At the top of a rise, Agnes looked back and saw the grey roofs and chimneys of Monkton Hall. Memories came flooding in of the ball she had once attended there - "it must be forty years ago now, give or take a year," she mused.

It was there she had met her late husband for the first time. Richard Nokes had danced with her all that evening; entranced by the slim, pretty, auburn-haired girl and her scintillating conversation. He, too, had cut a handsome figure with his doublet and breeches of dark, wine-coloured velvet - a perfect foil for her gown of ice-blue satin.

They had married a few months later, in the tiny church at Monkton. Of course, she was already an initiate of the Craft - a fully fledged witch - by her mother's hand. But who was to know that?

Agnes told Richard of her secret on one of his leaves. And when he left the ageing Queen's service, and his role of a royal bodyguard, he expressed a desire to join her in the Mysteries.

He proved an excellent pupil and duly became the High Priest of her coven. Richard's father left him a legacy with which they bought Elm-tree farm, and their life together had been a happy and interesting one. They both preferred a simple existence, close to nature, and Richard was not sorry to turn his back on the intrigues of a life at court.

It was not generally known that Agnes Nokes came from good stock. Her mother, Elizabeth Bowes, had been a cousin of the then, Lady Anne Ashley of Monkton Hall, and when Elizabeth became a widow, after only three years of marriage, she had been lucky enough to secure the position of housekeeper at the Hall. Agnes, then only one year old, had had the best possible upbringing with Lady Anne's children. She had learned her lessons with ease and spoke French, fluently.

Mistress Nokes shook herself, mentally, she must attend to

the matter on hand and not lose valuable time in dreaming of the past - however pleasant.

She hurried on, down an incline; across a stream by way of stepping-stones, and came at last to a small cottage near the main, griffin-guarded entrance to the grounds. Walking quietly up to the door, she glanced swiftly at the window, in which stood a small carving of a human hand. It was turned, so that the back of the hand faced outside, and this told her it was safe to enter. The palm, displayed, would have warned her off. A simple, yet effective device.

Agnes tapped on the door and entered. The two women who awaited her, greeted her with obvious affection.

"Merry meet, Agnes - you received the message, then?"
Betty, a cheerful body of some fifty years, settled Mistress Nokes into a comfortable chair. "My, my, but you look tired. I'll bring you a drink and a bite to eat."

Agnes had grown up with Betty, whose mother had held the post of head cook at the hall. Betty had married David, the woodcutter's son, who was now the head gardener. The slim, raven-haired Joan, had come down from Scotland to work as a lady's maid. Her family back home were all affiliated to the Craft.

They had both heard about the Nokes' family's unhappy experiences with Hopkins, but insisted upon Agnes relating all the details. They were lucky, living on the estate; it was the kind of place the witchfinders left well alone.

When Agnes had answered all their questions and refreshed herself from a laden tray, Betty locked the door and drew the curtains.

"Now, dear, I performed the divination as you requested in your letter. I gather your friend would like to be one of us?"

120

"That is so. We have come to know Mary very well. What did the divination say?" Agnes twisted her hands, anxiously.

"Well, it was not too good a reading. It seems your friend has led a bad life, although she has now mended her ways. However, there is much Karma to be repaid - mainly of retribution - she will certainly come to a violent end."

"Oh dear, I had hoped for a better future for her," Agnes said, sadly.

"Look you here." Betty took her hands. "It seems to me that if she was to be made a witch, it would help her spirit and give her some solace and peace, in the meantime. Surely the Old Ones would give a blessing?"

Agnes sighed. "Aye, to be sure, but I thought she had passed through all her troubles. I would have performed a reading myself, but I'm too involved with the situation."

"Now, don't you fret, you cannot control or alter another's fate, you know." Betty paused, then, "There is someone in the cards who loves her dearly and whom Mary loves in return. That cannot be bad! Now, our Joan is going to cast the runes for you. She has the sight as you know." Betty patted Joan's dark, silky tresses and the three women clasped hands, smiled knowingly at one another, and were still.

Presently, Joan stood up and opened a velvet pouch which hung from her waist. She produced some stones of assorted shapes and breathed over them. "She brought them with her from North Berwick," whispered Betty, "what a clever thing it is," she teased, winking at Agnes.

Joan grinned and began to weave a pattern with her bare feet; shaking the stones in her hands and flinging her black hair from side to side, a silent spell on her lips.

The others watched her with rapt attention, remembering

121

their own youth, yet totally without envy. Rather, admiring the girl's lithe figure, writhing in the green, homespun gown; young breasts straining against the white, gathered bodice.

Joan stopped suddenly in front of Mistress Nokes, her face, a mask; holding the runes high above the grey head. Then, down to the floor - casting them away from her.

The stones scattered and rolled and came to rest in their appointed places. Betty gripped her friend's arm - expectant, while the seer drummed lean fingers on the floor, her dark eyes running through the pattern of the stones, then, "It seems likely that your Mary will be made a sacrifice. And her fate is closely linked with that of another woman. I think it is either you, Agnes, or one of your family."

The enquirer nodded, thinking of Meg.

"She will die violently, in the near future - again - this will be a sacrifice, albeit her own." There was sorrow in the girl's eyes.

Agnes stirred uneasily. "Would it not be better to deny her initiation?"

"No. The runes show that she will become a member of the Craft, but, as I say, her fate is linked very strangely with yours."

Joan sighed, her hands stroking her hair. "One thing is certain," she continued, "the Nokes family will be remembered with honour and love for a very long time to come."

"Well, that's good, dearie," Betty beamed at her friend.

"Yes, but I am worried about Mary's future," said Agnes. "Still, the question *has* been answered, and for that I am thankful."

Joan rose gracefully to her feet, a slight frown spoiling her features. "There is one more thing I have to tell you." She paused, weighing her words with care. "You will have the power of the Goddess with you in your darkest hour."

At these words, the room seemed to fill, suddenly, with a strange energy which encircled the three women. They felt it as a cold breeze passing round each of them. "It's the Goddess," breathed Betty, as their faces crawled and tingled. They were suspended - out of time - while the power continued to flow between them and through them . . .

The sound of footsteps outside, scattered the atmosphere and brought the witches back to their surroundings with a jolt. Joan jumped up. "Wait, I'll see who it is." She darted to the window. "Oh, it's only David, back from work," she said, unlocking the door.

Agnes rose to her feet. "Yes, and I must get home. It's past the hour of five." She gathered up her basket. "Thank you for the readings, dears, and I'll see you at the meeting."

"You'll be safe getting back?" Betty asked, kissing her.

The old lady nodded, as David walked in.

"Well, well, it's good to see you, Agnes. Can I give you a lift in the cart?"

She shook her head, but Betty intervened. "Oh do let him take you part of the way, Agnes, you must be tired. And listen, it's started to thunder; if you walk you'll get soaking wet."

Their visitor found herself accepting the proffered lift, thankfully, and in no time at all, they were trundling out of the gates, while the first drops of rain fell from a darkening sky.

David put her down half a mile from home and she was soon hurrying through the field of marguerites which lifted their parched heads to welcome the moisture. 'It's a good thing I brought my cloak - although it does smell so lovely with the rain,' she thought. All the same, Agnes was relieved when she had gained the entrance to her orchard.

During the next few days, everyone's interest was centred on the forthcoming Esbat.

"They will all be there, except the old and the infirm," remarked Agnes, as she busily swept out the kitchen.

Mary smiled to herself as she cleaned the oil lamps. Her friend never thought of herself as old, and indeed, she had a lot more energy than some younger women.

"I do hope we will not be seen. It all seems very risky to me." Mary's face was troubled as she shook a stray lock of hair out of her eyes.

"Aye! Hopkins will be more watchful now. He hasn't convicted anyone since your escape, so he will, no doubt, do his best to capture someone. Your disappearance must have riled him."

"Knowing Matthew as I do, he'll be seething with rage to think I've outwitted him - he's so conceited." Mary grimaced at her reflection in the now shining lamp. "I'm glad I'm not with him, he'll be pouring out his venom on his assistants. Look how he used *me* as a scapegoat when Gaule snatched Meg from his clutches."

Agnes wiped her hands on her apron. "That is why we must be extremely careful this time. He knows the dates of the main festivals and he might have had his spies out on the eve of Lammas, but that meeting was postponed and this one is not taking place on an important date. Even so, we cannot take any chances."

Mary put the cleaning rags down. "How do you keep the locals away?"

124

"Well, most of them are too scared to leave their homes when they think a Sabbat is taking place. A Sabbat is one of the eight major festivals of the year, when all the covens in the neighbourhood attend. But, you never know, even at a small meeting, who might be around. That is where Robert's clever idea has come in handy."

Agnes smiled mischievously at her friend.

"Oh do tell me what it is."

"Well, sit you down."

The two women faced each other across the scrubbed and spotless kitchen table.

"You know the stories they tell about witches dancing with demons?"

Mary nodded.

"Robert suggested we should all dress up as devils and demons and wear masks, so that a stranger seeing us in the forest would be frightened away," she beamed. "So far it has been most successful and has kept outsiders from spying on our rituals."

Mary helped herself, absentmindedly, from a bowl of currants.

"Where do you obtain these masks?"

"Every witch makes their own. It matters little *how* they are made as long as they look terrifying. Some members have shown great ingenuity and carved marvellous wooden masks, real works of art. While others just used old flour bags with eye-holes and faces painted on them. They are hidden in various places, usually in hollow trees. Each person knows where their own mask is hidden. They put them on when they enter the woods, and so disguised, proceed to the sacred grove."

Mary laughed at the thought of some lonely traveller being confronted by such a sight. "Will I be made a witch at this meeting?"

Mistress Nokes smiled at her enthusiasm. "Yes. It will be a long night. There is your initiation and also the Handfasting to join together Bess and Robert."

"Shall I have a mask?"

"Most certainly!" Agnes nodded. "I have some spare bits of material. You must see what you can do with a needle and thread."

She went to an old chest and handed Mary a linen bag. "Now, off you go and see what you can make."

In her secret room, Mary set to work and when she had finished she showed her creation to Agnes, who laughed until the tears ran down her cheeks. "You'll be shot with a silver bullet if they see you in that! People will think you are a werewolf," she gasped.

"It is really very good, and in the darkness, you would swear it was a real wolf's head. It is to be hoped that you don't scare the witches away, too!"

Mary collapsed, and the house rang with the sound of their uncontrollable laughter.

CHAPTER 8

The full moon shone down from a clear sky. Her bright orb shed its light over the countryside, covering everything with a silvery radiance. Her light, however, failed to penetrate the dense forest, which, by contrast, seemed darker than usual.

The trees whispered to each other and the contours of their branches cast alarming shadows. An owl hooted mournfully, and in the distance, a dog fox barked to its mate. It was an eerie place which local folk avoided at night, especially as it was reputed to be a meeting-place for witches!

Robert Maxwell stood in a small glade talking to an elderly man. "Have you brought the horned helmet, Arthur?" he asked. "I shall need it tonight."

"Aye, it's safely hidden, come over and I'll show you."

Arthur was a sprightly sixty-nine and an Elder of the coven. He was a farrier by trade and the owner of a dozen horses which he hired out from time to time.

As the two men walked towards the trees, they encountered a hideous-looking monster. Large, glaring eyes protruded from their sockets and long, yellow tusks drooped from its mouth. The face was a vivid green!

Robert chuckled and turned to his friend. "Would you believe that this creature is to be my future wife?"

"I suppose beauty is in the eyes of the beholder," grinned Arthur, as Bess removed her mask, shook her fiery tresses free, and greeted Robert with a kiss.

"Wel-come, my love," he said.

"I understand that you two have to be congratulated,"

commented Arthur. "I have been told that you are to be joined as man and wife."

"That is true," replied Robert, giving Bess a bear hug.

"I do love you, Robert," she murmured.

"That is what I like to hear," smiled Arthur. "Perfect love is hard to find. May you continue to love one another through many lives," and his fingers formed the gesture of the Craft Blessing.

Robert scanned the surrounding darkness. "Are the others with you?"

"They will be here, darling," Bess assured him. "But we deemed it best not to travel together. I left first, then Mother. Meg and Mary will be following her."

"Very wise," Arthur nodded his white head. "We dare not take any risks now, after what happened to poor little Jane. Incidentally, my dear, you were extremely brave in what you did for her."

When Bess heard the name of her friend, tears gathered in her grey eyes. So much had happened to them since her death.

"Poor, dear Jane. I wonder if she will be with us in spirit, tonight?"

"Very likely," muttered Robert, wiping her tears away. "But, come dearest, monsters don't cry," he cajoled. "Here, put your mask on."

Arthur cleared his throat. "I believe we also have an initiation tonight. I know the 'Pentacle' has approved the woman."

"Yes, we have a lot to do," replied Robert. "I hope the rest of the coven come soon."

"Look! Here is Mother, now," cried Bess.

They all turned as another fantastic creature came into the

clearing. Arthur said, laughing, "That mask idea of yours was splendid. They even scare *me* and *I* know who they are!"

"It has at least kept our meetings free from interlopers," agreed Robert. "Some of the locals have seen one or two of our masked witches, and you should hear the stories that are being circulated. Even a sceptic like Hopkins is beginning to believe the tales that his victims confess, and Stearne is too scared to come anywhere near these woods. If Hopkins had less power over him, I believe he would quit witch-finding altogether."

"How *does* Hopkins manage to control a man like Stearne?" asked Bess, her eyes on her mother who had stopped and was looking behind her into the trees.

"Well, they both know so much about each other's filthy dealings, they keep together for safety."

"Oh dear," sighed Bess. "Fancy having to go through life like that. Still, they *do* deserve their fate."

Mistress Nokes joined them, but as she removed her mask, Bess was quick to notice the worried look on her mother's face. "What's the matter?" she asked, anxiously.

"I may be wrong, but I still have the feeling that I am being followed."

"Think no more of it, Agnes," Arthur volunteered with a wave of his hand. "One is always prey to strange imaginings when walking in the forest at night."

His remark appeared to reassure her. "I hope you are right, Arthur. We've had nothing but trouble, lately."

He took her hand between his own. "Let's hear no more about it. We don't want the night spoiled by silly fancies, do we? Now, what of your new candidate?"

"It's Mary Summerset. She was originally one of Hopkins' prickers, until he turned against her. We have taken the normal precautions of course, and the omens favour her joining us."

"Do you think she will make a good witch?"

"I'll stake my life that there will be none better, and you know I'm a pretty good judge of character."

Arthur, smiled. "That's true enough." He turned to Robert, "We'd better go now and collect that helmet."

The two men walked across the glade to a hollow tree, where Arthur, removing a heap of leaves and moss, lifted a bronze helmet from its hiding-place. It was a handsome piece of work, studded with polished amber and crowned with a pair of stag's antlers. Robert placed it carefully upon his head.

Hidden in the undergrowth, scarcely daring to breathe, the boy, Joseph, watched the two men disappear behind the old oak. He had followed Mistress Nokes all the way from her cottage; keeping well within the shadows and leaving a good distance between them. When they entered the forest, however, the crackle of twigs under his feet, had very nearly revealed his presence.

Joseph was not really the kind of child of which heroes are made. It was only his frantic fear of Hopkins that had decided him on making a final attempt to find out something that would convict Mistress Nokes of witchcraft.

Now he was here, he began to feel frightened. What if she *did* join the demons in these woods? He looked around and his mind started to play strange tricks. The branches of the nearby trees resembled claws trying to reach him. They seemed to be alive! He believed, too, that he had seen the old woman change into a monster! This metamorphosis had taken place in a few seconds, as she passed behind a large tree. Had she really changed, or was it only his imagination?

He peeped out from his cover just as Robert stepped from behind a tree on the far side of the glade. And Robert was wearing the horned helmet! Joseph cowered in terror. Not only did the apparition prove to him that Mistress Nokes had changed her form; but she was meeting the Devil, himself!

Paralysed with fear, Joseph very nearly screamed out, but managed to check himself in time. There was no one here to help him, even if he did! He would be captured by the demons and most probably eaten alive!

He wobbled unsteadily to his feet and parting the leaves, looked into the clearing. What he saw loosened his insides and made his flesh crawl. The clearing, bathed in moonlight, was full of hideous, evil-looking monsters, the sight of which he had never before imagined. They must have come straight from Hell!

"God help me," he muttered, and slowly backed away. Lucky for him, Robert was intent in conversation, and Joseph crept off without being detected.

Once he started to move, it was easier. His trembling legs began, albeit reluctantly, to obey him, and stumbling onto a path, he fled, believing all the fiends of Hell were on his heels.

"What was that?" asked Robert. "I thought I heard something in those bushes over there."

"Maybe a fox," Arthur shrugged, "there's plenty of them in the woods at this time of the year."

Robert continued to scan the trees, and thought that Arthur was a bit too easy going for his own good. But, he said, shortly, "I suppose you are right. Let's go."

The group moved on towards the sacred site - the incident, forgotten.

Joseph did not pause in his headlong flight. He tore through the forest, leaping over logs; falling over protruding roots and scratching his hands and face badly on the overhanging branches. He feared to stop - even to draw breath! He imagined hands coming from all sides, dragging him back to the clearing, and what might happen to him there, he dared not think. He wished he had never seen Matthew Hopkins, and would have willingly given him his money back, if he had not already spent it!

Joseph soon had difficulty in breathing and was forced to slow down. Was he going to die? He steadied himself for a moment against a sturdy tree. It was then that he heard the sound of approaching footsteps. Ducking back into the bushes, he was just in time to prevent himself from being seen.

Joseph tried to whisper the Lord's Prayer, but could not remember the correct words. Two vague shapes came into view and his hair, quite literally, stood on end, the perspiration oozing from his body.

Rooted to the spot, he crouched, jaw agape, as the figures passed by. One was a hideous imp and the other had the head of a wolf! The latter, Joseph recognized at once. He had heard many tales of werewolves, but never really believed that he would actually *see* one. His brain reeling, the boy's senses departed and he collapsed in a pathetic heap.

The 'wolf' halted abruptly and Mary Summerset's voice came muffled through her mask. "What was that? I thought I heard something."

Meg squeezed her arm. "Could be a branch. Elm trees often shed them when hot weather follows a lot of rain. We had better hurry or we'll hold up the ceremony."

They set off again, quickening their steps.

Entering the clearing, the two women passed through it and a little way further on, turned left onto a small path which was marked by a large stone. A few minutes later they emerged into a large glade. It was a perfect, natural amphitheatre with a carpet of moss and short turf surrounded by the overhanging foliage of the forest.

Five witches had been delegated to prepare the site. Arriving much earlier than the others, they had already been joined by Mistress Nokes and her companions.

As Meg and Mary appeared, they were greeted with the familiar, "Merry meet" and "Wel-come". And while the others commiserated with Meg on her ordeal at the Assembly Hall, Agnes took Mary aside.

"Come with me," she said, leading her to the edge of the trees. "We will wait here while they erect the Circle and prepare for your initiation."

Mary, transfixed with awe, gazed at the centre of the glade, where a great circle of white rope had been laid down, surrounding a huge, flat rock - the Altar. Upon the Altar rested the symbols and tools of the Craft. She could not make them all out from where she stood, but recognised a sword, with the hilt shaped into twin, crescent moons; some bowls, a short knife, a round piece of metal which gleamed in the moonlight, and a container of incense, which spiralled its blue-grey smoke to greet the night sky. She sniffed, appreciatively, 'what a lovely aroma'. It assuaged her fears slightly. Her whole body had become tense and her heart beat so loudly she was sure it could be heard by all present. Mistress Nokes pressed her hand, hard. "It will be well, dear, you'll see. Everyone feels nervous before their initiation."

She guided Mary to a fallen tree trunk and sat her down. "There, we'll wait now, and watch."

The witches slowly disrobed and began rubbing their bodies with something from a large pot, which they passed round the group.

"That's the special unguent," whispered Agnes. "It has many uses, but it *does* keep the body from becoming too cold - especially in *our* climate."

The people formed a long chain and moved slowly towards the Circle. They passed round its circumference then broke into a quick trot, while Robert strode into the ring, and with the aid of a tinder-box, made fire upon the sacred stone.

He lit a great beeswax candle and took his place in front of the Altar with his arms crossed on his breast. Immediately, the tempo of the dancers increased, and the silence of the night was suddenly filled with life as they began to chant: "*Ah-ha, Aha! Evoh! Ah-ha . . .*" They moved as one, to the rhythm of the call; with the exception of a slim, dark-haired young woman, who left the circling witches and entered the ring.

She filled a large, drinking-horn with dark, red wine, poured from a stone jug. Then turning, she raised the vessel to the stars: "*Powers of Death in Life, and Life in Death, I call upon Ye and invoke Ye!*"

Joan's voice (for she it was), rose clear and resolute above the chanting. With the grace of a goddess, she stepped to the perimeter of the Circle, and slowly poured the liquid around its outer edge before replacing the horn upon the Altar. Then, she knelt before the High Priest; her dark hair falling like a cloak around her.

The movement acted as a signal. Coming to a particular point of the Circle, the witches leaped, one after the other, over the silver ring; the barrier between the quick and the dead. Slapping their bodies in the old gestures and signs and uttering strange, half-human, half-animal cries.

Their momentum carried them onwards, and joining hands, they circled, deosil - treading the Mill - making Magic between the Worlds - "*I - O - Evoh - Ee . . .!*"
Joan, the Maiden of the Coven, raised her arms in adoration, as the tops of the trees, the moon and the stars, whirled around them - joining in - the Dance of Life!

Mary shivered and pointed to a tall, forked staff, standing in the ground, just outside the barrier. "What's that?"
"Oh, that's the Stang. It represents the Horned God and also the South point of the Circle. See, there is another at the North, but with three prongs. That one is called the 'Goosefoot' - it's a symbol of the Goddess."

In spite of all that she had been told, Mary could not quite believe her eyes. Was it a dream? Would she presently awake in her bed, in the secret room? But, no, her companion seemed real enough. She was thankful for her friend's company in that eerie place.

The dancing and chanting suddenly ceased and all was silent. The witches standing round the Circle; the High Priest, crowned with horns - as a statue, before the Altar. Then, as they waited, seemingly suspended in time, they heard it in the distance . . . the faint, silvery notes of a pipe. A plaintive, yet compelling melody, coming ever nearer. The notes hanging in the still air and filling the glade with their magic.

As Mary watched, she saw part of the darkness, at the edge of the trees, move, as a tall, dark figure emerged and walked majestically into the Circle. The long black robe was fastened at the neck with a silver clasp, and the figure wore a mask in the shape of a goat's head, complete with horns. It approached the Altar, and the coven bowed in homage.

This was their leader, whom the Christians called 'the Devil', or the 'Man in Black'. Mary knew that although many covens had been caught and convicted, the 'Man in Black' had never been taken, and no one knew who he really was. Some said, he was the Devil, himself! She began to tremble in earnest, now. What had she got herself into? Mistress Nokes did not notice her fear, she was completely engrossed in the drama taking place before her.

The goat-headed being slowly mounted the Altar and proceeded to remove its mask. Robert turned to receive the mask and lay it reverently aside. The figure unfastened the silver clasp and the robe fell away to disclose the naked body of a beautiful, fair-haired woman. Her swan-like neck was graced with a necklace of moonstones, which reflected the pearly hue of her skin, and around her left thigh was a garter of deep-blue velvet, fastened with a silver buckle inlaid with sapphires.

She stood perfectly still, her body emitting a faint, bluish, glowing light. The witches gazed up at her, entranced, and Mary's jaw dropped. A woman? The 'Man in Black', a woman?

Mistress Nokes smiled - a secret smile. "Yes, it is a woman - not in every coven, mind, but in most," she said, answering the unspoken question.

"But, this could be the reason why the 'Man in Black' is never caught! They would naturally be looking for a *man*!"

"Exactly!" nodded Agnes, and she nudged Mary, playfully. "But, we live and learn - do we not?"

"Who is she?" asked Mary, her eyes never leaving the Circle.

"That, is the High Priestess and Queen of the Sabbat," replied Mistress Nokes, with pride. "She is chosen for her beauty, knowledge and wisdom, to represent the Goddess on Earth."

Mary noticed that Agnes had evaded her question by describing the woman's rank in the Craft, but this was not the time to debate the issue. The High Priestess was descending from the Altar, and Mary's friend whispered, "She is now going to erect and consecrate the Circle."

Robert, kneeling, presented her with the great, magical sword. She took it from him and approaching the Gate of the East, held it high in a salute. Then, slowly, she traced another, unseen, astral circle, deosil or sun-wise, with the point of the sword:

"May the power of the God dwell in it;
May the love of the Goddess protect it;
May the Lords of the Gates watch and ward it,
That no evil spirits pervade it."

The witches moved inwards to allow her passage, until she once more gained the East and had sealed the Circle. The High Priestess kissed the blade and raised the sword above the Altar:

"Circle of Space, Circle of Light,
Be thou raised, in the Old Gods sight!"

Mary blinked. Was it her imagination, or did a faint, blue light, glow, where the sword had passed?

Now, the beautiful lady was lifting a bowl from the Altar: *"I exorcise thee, O creature of water; by the Moon that rules thee, that all impurities and uncleanness of the World of Phantasm, be cast out from thee. In the names of the Old Ones."* Her voice had a vibrant, musical quality, and at the same time, a peculiar metallic ring to it.

Robert took the bowl from her and held it, while she lifted another: *"Be blessed, O' thou creature of salt; by the Earth that moves thee. Let all malignity and hindrance depart, and all good enter, therein."* So saying, she poured the salt into the water; exchanged bowls with the High Priest, and circumscribed the Ring, sprinkling the water as she went. The sky-clad witches cried in unison: "So mote it be! For the One in Three!"

Joan, the Maiden, received the bowl; replaced it upon the Altar, and presented the dish of burning incense. The High Priestess carried it round the Circle, raising it in salutation at the Four Gates of the compass. Finally, she gave it back to the Maiden who returned it to the Altar. Then, Joan knelt, kissing the feet of the Lady, who raised her and embraced her, giving Joan the sign of the Triple Goddess.

Once more, Robert presented the sword and took his own athame or magical knife, from the Altar. Joan did likewise, while the High Priestess stepped to the East; pointed the sword above the Circle and held it thus until she felt the power of the Gods within it. Robert and Joan stood behind her - one on either side, and after a short pause, their leader declaimed: *"I do summon, stir, and call ye up, ye Mighty Ones of the East; to be witness to these rites and to guard the Circle."* The sword's blade flashed in the moonlight, describing the sign of the five-pointed star - the Pentagram. The invocation was repeated at the South, West and North, with the members of the coven grouped in the form of a crescent moon, behind the 'Triangle'. Then, the sword was returned to its place on the Altar and the witches greeted the High Priestess. Each person was welcomed with a kiss and a special word.

Once more, the Priestess mounted the rough, stone steps onto the Altar and raised her hands for silence:

"We of the Craft are facing extreme cruelty at this time, and we must meet that cruelty with courage and strength. Not for us, the renunciation of all we believe in. We must endure, so that those who come after us will be able to carry on the Craft and teach it to their children.

Many will escape the persecutions, and those souls will become as beacons to our descendants. Already, an initiate of this coven has passed to the Summerlands. An it be for the courage of our Bess, Jane would have had to face the torturers. Let such a witch be a guide and example to all and let us thank the Old Ones for such a companion. We must also give thanks for the excellent harvest we can expect this Lammastide. Bring your wills and hearts to bear - now - in giving love and power to our beloved God and Goddess."

One witch, produced a small drum, and another, a pipe, and they struck up a fast reel. The High Priestess ran down the steps and led the band until all were dancing furiously, hand in hand, around the Circle. Their feet kept the rhythm and their exultant cries made Mary's blood leap in her veins.

The leader danced off, weaving a snake-like pattern - the others, following, and the music changed to a slower, more hypnotic beat.

Robert was at the rear, holding a scourge, and he whacked it across the buttocks of any witch whom he considered to be lagging, or not keeping to the tempo of the dance. A blow, coming unexpectedly from behind, caused much screaming and yelling and was answered by the laughter of the more fortunate!

Then, the music ceased abruptly and the company dropped to the mossy turf, but Robert raised the great sword to the stars, mentally thrusting the evoked power into the unmanifest, as a gift to the Gods. Now, all were concentrating - willing - with every ounce of energy at their disposal; visualising the sword, and its precious burden.

Presently, one of the group began to moan - it was the Maiden. The others rose to their feet and stood at a respectful distance, while the leaders attended her.

"Is she ill?" breathed Mary.

"No, child, she is in trance and will be giving the coven a message from the other side - you know - from the spiritual planes."

"There must be some spirits around. I have felt we are being watched for some time." Mary glanced over her shoulder.

"Oh, that's alright," replied Mistress Nokes. "You always feel that you are being watched at an out-door meeting. It's the power gathering, it gives one that sensation."

"But, how . . .?"

"Sh . . . it's not the time to talk of such things . . . later."

Joan was speaking now, in a clear, articulate voice which penetrated the air like a silver arrow:

"Beware! Beware! Ye Children of the Goddess! There is danger all around and the worst is yet to come! The old one will be sacrificed for the rest of the coven, and another will find death among the enemy. There is much spilt blood, and

140

the courageous one will lie in it. But, fear not! Your leaders will bring life to the dead and help to keep the coven together.

When the leaves fall from the trees, the cruel tyrant will leave Belford and you will know peace - of a kind. His 'reign' will end soon after, as sure as the Royalists were defeated at Naseby. I go!''

The Priestess asked for some wine and poured a little into Joan's mouth. In a few minutes she was back on her feet again and the coven huddled together, discussing the message in subdued tones. Diccon, the scribe, had carefully noted it down, and now the Priestess took up her position in front of the Altar:

''We thank Thee - Andred and Alderon, for the prophesy and we must remember the terrible times in which we are living. We cannot expect aught else just now, but at least we can look forward to a more peaceful time in the Autumn. Let us thank the Gods for that!''

''Aye! Aye! Thanks be to the Ancient Providence!'' came from all sides.

The Priestess asked if the neophyte was fully prepared, and if so, that she be brought to the edge of the Circle. Mistress Nokes told Mary to undress, then led her forward to the Eastern Gate. With a scarlet cord, she bound Mary's trembling hands behind her back and fastened it around her neck, leaving the knotted ends hanging loose.

The High Priestess declaimed:

''An it be our will that Mary Summerset be made a witch?''

''Yea!'' cried the coven in unison.

David (the head gardener from Monkton Hall), approached Mary. He was wearing a cloth hood upon which was painted a skull and in his hands he carried a scythe. Without any warning, he raised the implement and swept it over Mary, so closely that it brushed her hair. Seven times the scythe skimmed above her, and seven times, Mary flinched and shut her eyes.

"Only the imperfect are frightened by Death. If thou art afraid, what art thou doing here?"

"I *will* to *know!*" answered Mary, suddenly finding her voice.

"So be it!" replied Death.

Now, Agnes blindfolded her and Robert took his place opposite David:

"Thou art standing on the threshold betwixt the quick and the dead - the place where two worlds meet. Hast thou the courage to take the step which leads to knowledge and wisdom?"

"I have."

"It were better to have thy head sliced from thy body by Death's scythe, than to step across the barrier in fear and dread."

Mary uttered the passwords as she had been instructed, and Robert said:

"Raise the Gate of Horn and allow the neophyte, entrance to the Circle."

Mary was pushed into the Ring by Mistress Nokes, while 'Death' held the scythe above her head.

"You are now within the Womb of the Mysterious Goddess. And the Doorway of the Mysterious Goddess is the base from which Heaven and Earth sprang. It is there within us all the while . . ."

Mary was led round the Circle by Robert, who spoke to her in hushed tones . . . "Magic is composed of knowledge and strength, and describes the purpose of the Mysteries . . ." The High Priest was preparing her for the oath she was soon to take . . .

Suddenly, Mary was surrounded by the whole coven, their bodies pressing on her, then, with a witch pulling her by the end of the cord, and another pushing her from behind, they ran her round the Circle until her senses reeled and she gasped and cried out at the strange sensations. Unable to see anything, she was now completely disorientated; the strange chant in a foreign tongue, beating into her brain:

"Chaire Soter Kosmou
Io Panphage Pangenetor,
Agios Agios Agios
Io Pan! Io Pan! Io Pan!"

Brought to a sudden halt, her feet were tied together and she was gently lowered to the ground - curled up in a foetal position. She heard the High Priestess speaking - as if from a great distance:

"Now, you are in the centre of the Circle which represents the sacred womb of the Great Mother. There, you will lay and contemplate your birth into the Craft."

Silence filled the glade and time seemed to stand still. The only thing, moving, was a light zephyr which wafted the incense to Mary's nostrils. Her heart thudded heavily in her breast, both from the exhaustion of the dance, and from fear. Her mind floated in a dark void where flashes of light strobed the blackness . . . The fear deepened, but she was completely helpless - she could not escape, even if she tried!

The silence continued, and Mary began to feel more relaxed - her heart, steadying its beat. How long had she been lying on the ground? It seemed an age!

She was, at that time, being spiritually reborn, while curled on the Mother's green breast. Then, she heard the voice of the High Priestess. 'How good it is to hear a voice, again,'

143

she thought.

"You will now enter the tunnel of rebirth and be born again through the Triangle - the sign of the Goddess, and the First Degree of our ancient Craft."

Someone moved the blindfold so that Mary could see with one eye, and lifting her head, she saw an avenue of limbs above her. It was made by the female witches, as they stood, legs apart, forming a triangle and symbolising the vagina of the Earth Mother, through which, she, as the new initiate, would have to pass.

Bound hand and foot, as she was, Mary started her journey through the human tunnel. It was a difficult task, as she had to pull herself along by her elbows and wriggle her body - rather like the progress of a snake!

Mary stopped occasionally, to rest, while the witches moaned and cried, as if in the pangs of childbirth, which was, in itself, disconcerting.

When she at last reached her goal, a firm foot was placed upon her neck and the High Priest spoke to her:

"Art thou always ready to protect, help and defend thy brothers and sisters of the Art?"

"I am."

"Then repeat after me, saying:

I, Mary, in the presence of the Queen of Heaven, Her Consort, and the Mighty Ones - do of my own free will and accord - most solemnly swear that I will ever keep secret and never reveal the secrets of the Art - except it be to a proper person, properly prepared - within a Circle such as I am now in. - All this I swear by my hopes of a future life - and may my weapons turn against me if I break this - MY SOLEMN OATH. There is no hiding-place for a traitor to the Craft!"

To all outward appearances it sounded quite a simple warning. There were no awful invocations or threats of doom about what would happen to Mary if she did indeed betray the oath. Yet, the very fact of requesting her weapons, or tools, to turn against her, would appear to be equally as powerful a deterrent from oath-breaking, considering that the said weapons symbolised fire, air, water and earth! Upon abjuration, Mary was invoking the vengeance of the elements!

She was gently raised; the blindfold was whisked away and the cords which bound her were severed. Tears coursed down her cheeks. Whether from the pain of her grazed body or the wonderment of the ceremony, she knew not, but suspected that everything had contributed to her present inner turbulence. Then, too, there was the strange gut reaction to a situation where she had indeed been as helpless as a new-born babe.

Robert, the High Priest, appeared before her holding two silver goblets.

"One of these goblets contains wine, the other, a virulent poison. I command thee to seize, without reflection, one of them, and empty it at a single draught." His face was mask-like, the sapphire eyes seeming to pierce Mary's very soul.

The neophyte looked around for help or reassurance, but there was none, and although some of the witches were facing her, their faces told her nothing. A spark of anger ignited within her. Did they think she had no courage? Mary's lip curled derisively and she took one of the goblets and drained the contents.

The High Priest inclined his head:

"Thou hast bravely passed the test. Fear not! Both the cups contained wine. The only difference between them is that a

little myrrh has been added to one of them.'' He held up the full goblet and smiled, *"This one."*

The High Priestess approached Mary and assumed the Goddess position of holding her breasts, cupped, in her hands. Mary was told to kiss them. Then, the other women offered her their breasts, one after the other, and the Priestess handed Mary the cord with which she had been bound.

"This, represents the umbilical cord which is cut to free the new-born babe from its mother. The child thereby becoming an individual in its own right. In return, you must give the coven a part of yourself."

Robert, using a small pair of scissors, proceeded to cut off a lock of Mary's hair. He placed it carefully in a tiny skin bag, whereupon two other tokens were taken from her. Then, the bag was sealed and taken away.

The High Priestess smiled warmly at Mary and said, "We have offered you our breasts to symbolise that we all accept you as a Child of the Goddess. We will feed and help you in times of need, as a mother does, her child. You have displayed courage which is a necessary attribute for a member of the Craft, and now, as your birth sign is that of Scorpio, I present to you a topaz necklace set in gold. As you may know, the topaz is the jewel of that sign. You may not enter a Magic Circle without such an item of jewellery, because the Goddess, Herself, is portrayed wearing a necklace. It represents the Circle of Rebirth and the assurance of reincarnation.''

Mary gasped, her face lighting up with pleasure as the golden gems flashed and winked in the candlelight. 'It must have cost a fortune,' she thought, turning round while the Priestess placed it on her neck. Then, the Lady took her

146

hands, kissed her warmly and led her to Robert. The High Priest showed her the tools of the Craft and explained their meanings with a promise of instruction, later. Finally, he saluted her:

"We now accept you as a member of the coven. Mary - newly-born witch!"

The initiate, dazed and happy, smiled shyly at Robert, then the High Priestess took her by the hand and leading her to the edge of the Circle, spoke to the great forces of Nature:

"Hear and attend, Lords of the East! I present to thee, Mary - Child of the Goddess!"

The other three Gates were also acknowledged, then all the witches gathered round Mary and she was introduced to each person in turn. She had never been kissed so much in all her life!

Agnes congratulated her and Mary whispered her thanks for Mistress Nokes' care and friendship at a time when she had most needed it. Meg, a circle of amethysts at her throat, hugged Mary and generally made much of her new witch friend - highly delighted with the proceedings.

Their leader clapped her hands for attention:

"Now! We have another pleasant task to perform. Robert, our High Priest, and Bess, are to be joined together by our ancient rite of Handfasting."

The witches giggled and whispered together as they returned to their places round the Circle. Mary was now looked after by Meg who stood close beside her. Robert and Bess were left standing alone in front of the Altar and looking a little abashed by all the attention. They held hands and smiled at each other. The High Priestess smiled too:

"This night of the full moon, Robert and Bess are to be

147

joined together in the sacred names of our beloved God and Goddess. Is there anyone present who can give a reason why this ceremony should not take place?"

Her wide, blue eyes skimmed over the upturned faces; the fine line of her brows, up-tilted - questioning. No one stirred, but suddenly, Bess burst into tears! Robert, quite taken aback, put his arms round her and tried to comfort her, without success. The Priestess looked askance at the young woman as Bess lifted a tear-stained face. "Yes!" she cried. "*I* have a reason why this ceremony should not take place!"

"What?" exclaimed Robert. "Do you no longer love me?"

Bess clutched at him. "Of course I love you, Robert, and will do so to my dying day."

He frowned and held her from him. "Then, in the Lady's name, what is it?"

Bess continued to sob, then burst out, "I am not worthy of him. I am with child!"

Robert stared at her aghast, but the Priestess smiled kindly, "Fear not my dear, many women marry in that condition."

Bess hid her face in her hands. "But, Robert is not the father."

The High Priestess began to look as bewildered as Robert. "Then, who is?"

At this question, Bess burst out crying again and Mistress Nokes hurried over to her.

"Now Bess, are you certain?" she asked.

"Nothing is more certain," sobbed the young woman.

"There now, don't you take on so," Agnes put her arm round her daughter's shaking body and turned to face the High Priestess - her face twitching with emotion. "The truth is this, my Lady. Bess delivered the poison to the prison to save Jane from further torture, and she was raped by one of the gaolers.''

''Shame!'' came from all sides.

Mistress Nokes nodded. ''Aye, he brought shame on Bess right enough. She has certainly paid for her good deed,'' she smiled grimly, ''but he too has paid in full - as you well know.''

Robert intervened. ''That will not prevent the rites from being enacted, and when the child is born, I will love and cherish it, as my own.'' He gazed tenderly upon Bess and embraced her as the coven voiced its approval.

Then, ''She could have an abortion,'' called a witch. ''Mother Collins is an expert at it.''

''Never!'' shouted Robert, throwing the speaker an angry glance. ''Are we not taught that it is wrong to take life?''

''Aye! Aye!'' agreed the coven.

Robert knelt on one knee and addressed the High Priestess. ''Carry on with the rite. I accept Bess and her unborn child.''

Silence fell as their leader held her athame aloft:

''*Before all present and in the eyes of the God and Goddess, I join these two people as man and wife.*''

Then, exchanging the athame for a smaller knife which she unwrapped from a piece of white muslin, the High Priestess made a small cut in the wrists of both participants and held them together.

''*As their blood mingles - so will they be joined likewise, in perfect love and perfect trust.*'' She bound their hands together with a piece of scarlet cord and led them at a trot around the Circle. A broomstick was placed in front of the Altar and the couple leaped over it on their way round the Ring, to the accompaniment of much laughter and quite a few

149

bawdy remarks.

"He'll be clouting her cauldron before the night is out!"

"It's the last we'll see of them for a week or two!"

By the time their 'ordeal' was over, both Bess and Robert's faces were as red as the cord which bound them!

Everyone rushed over to congratulate them and Bess, throwing her arms round her husband's neck, whispered, "You have made me the happiest of women."

At last, the High Priestess held up her hand:

"We will now close the Circle. May you all dwell in safety until the next, Merry Meet!"

She picked up the sword and stepping to the East, drew the sign of dismissal:

"Ye Guardians of the East, we do thank ye for attending, and ere ye depart, we salute thee. Hail and fare-well!" She raised the sword and then attended the other Gates.

When the Circle had been closed, the witches relaxed and there was the usual flurry of activity. Some, packed away all the ritual implements, while others prepared the feast. There was much animated talk and gaiety as they donned their clothing. All, felt that inner glow of joy and wonder which the rituals always bestows upon the participants.

As Mary dressed, she caught snatches of conversation.

"I miss the old calls."

"What are they?"

"They used to be intoned by one of the Elders, to summon the Lords of the Gates. It filled one with terror just to hear them - and yet they were wonderful - quite awesome withal. They don't use them now for fear of discovery."

"I wonder what there is to eat, tonight? I brought freshly

made griddle scones, thick with butter. Let's go and see.''

The rope circle had been taken away and the feast was spread out upon the Altar so that each person could take what they wanted. Although there was plenty of food, it was nothing like the feasts of earlier times, when whole sheep and oxen were roasted on the huge fires. Nowadays, everything was partaken cold, as it was forbidden to light fires of any description. Still, it was a goodly spread, with chicken, duck and whole sides of beef. Not to mention, honey cakes, ginger bread and all kinds of fruit. Liquid refreshment took the form of ale, cider and a sweet-spiced herb wine, made by Mistress Nokes from a secret recipe.

Everyone let their hair down; sitting or standing in little groups. Two or three of them started to dance, and David produced a fiddle. The lively strains of a reel, soon had the witches on their feet; twisting and turning in time to the music.

Mary and Meg sat together, discussing the meeting.

"Who is the High Priestess?" asked Mary.

"Only the Elders - and that includes Mother, know who she really is. We call her by her witch name, Lucina. She received her rank through her mother, who was also a High Priestess. In time, she, too, will be replaced. Or rather, she will hand over her position to another," replied Meg, biting into a large piece of ginger bread and offering her friend an apple.

"Thanks. But what if she has no offspring?"

"It matters not. She can choose whom she thinks is fitting for the position, providing she is also willing to teach them. There is a rumour that Lucina is to be married and become the lady of a manor in Cornwall, but she will not leave us until a new High Priestess is found."

Mary bit hard into the red fruit. "Why did I have to be naked?"

"One must enter the Circle as one comes from the womb - naked or 'sky-clad', as we call it - without any material possessions. You are then reborn through the Triangle, which is a symbol of the Goddess. The cord that binds you is the umbilical cord, which is severed once you are 'reborn'."

"Will I be able to work magic?"

Meg squeezed her friend's arm. "In time. It takes a lot of practice." She grinned. "It might be difficult for you . . ."

This remark prompted a mild rebuff from Mary which took the form of a playful slap and Meg ran off, laughing, her golden hair flying behind her. But, as she was not pursued, she returned, making a face at Mary, who asked another question. "Listen, I know what you said, but do not the Gods help in this magic?"

Meg straightened her bodice. "Of course. But we do not believe that *our* Gods are all powerful. They need our help as we need theirs. Most people do not realise this. They think that miracles can occur, solely, through prayer. But that is not enough, as the Wise Ones found out a long time ago. Anyway, magic *does* work, and the proof of the pudding is in the eating, as they say. So, we keep to the old ways and produce the energy. Then, it is directed to whatever is desired. Dancing, is only one of the ways of doing this. You will learn of others in time. You know, Mary, we are much closer to our Gods than the Christians are to theirs."

Mary held up her hand. "Only one more question, I promise. Does the High Priestess always perform the rites?"

"Yes. A woman must always take the leading role in the

Craft. In ancient times, witchcraft was a feminine religion, and when the God was paramount in the Winter months, she would gird on a sword and represent the God. Nowadays, however, unless it is an all female coven, the High Priest portrays the male deity.''

"And this beautiful necklace," Mary took it off and gazed in wonder at the gleaming gemstones. "Why did Lucina give me such a lovely thing?"

Meg laughed. "We are lucky she is so wealthy - and generous, too! Shall I keep it in this little bag for you, until we get home?"

"Oh yes, do. I should hate to lose it. I will keep it, always."

Robert leaped onto the now bare Altar and called for attention. "Brothers and sisters, we must disperse as the hour is late. Take all possible care and make your separate ways home. Merry part and merry meet again!"

"Merry part and merry meet again!" chorused the witches.

"Betty and I have been asked to remove the remains of the feast," said Meg. "See you in a minute."

Mary watched, as the people made ready to depart. They took leave of one another with the familiar, "Blessed be!" It sounded rather like a bee-hive! She, herself, was soon caught up in the farewells and added her own voice to the rest. How good it was to be part of such a family.

Then, she and Meg were alone in the glade. Meg was busily throwing bits of food into the bushes for the birds and animals. Finally, the last of the liquid was poured into the ground.

"This is called a libation," she explained. "We give it back to Mother Earth as an offering for her generosity."

"It's rather cold," Mary glanced round the deserted clearing.

"It seems quite altered now everyone has gone."

"Yes, let us go, too, but we must put on our masks before leaving, like the others."

They walked off together through the forest and presently, Meg said, "I must hide my mask here."

"Shall I leave mine, too?" asked Mary.

"No, I think you should keep it on until you reach home. I don't want anyone to recognise you as the witch-pricker. I could not bear to lose my best friend. We must part company here, dear. You go first and I will follow in a little while."

"But, what if someone sees me in this mask?"

"Oh, just howl a bit and they will run like the wind," Meg teased. She gave Mary a little push. "Off you go now, and take care. I'll see you back at home."

She stood watching as Mary strode off and finally disappeared from view, then sat down on a large stone and suddenly felt unaccountably miserable. "Silly goose," Meg mentally shook herself. "Always thinking the worst will happen."

At that moment, she heard the whirring of wings, and an owl skimmed past, missing her by inches. "Get away, you bird of ill-omen," she cried angrily, scrambling to her feet. The owl hooted, as if in reply, as it continued its search for food.

A faint grey light was beginning to penetrate the thick foliage - it would soon be dawn. Meg, quite badly shaken and with her heart thudding in her breast, wearily began to follow the path which led out of the forest.

154

CHAPTER 9

Mistress Nokes arrived safely back at Elm-tree Farm. This time, she was sure she had not been followed and decided that she must have imagined her fears on the previous occasions. The first rays of the sun were showing behind the distant hills and a bird piped the Lord of Life's arrival from a nearby bush.

Agnes felt very tired after her long walk and the excitement of the meeting - it had been quite an event. Heaving a sigh of relief, she opened her gate and walked quietly up the path, hoping that the others would also reach home, safely.

She was just about to open the front door, when a figure stepped out from the shadows of the lilac tree. The sudden shock robbed Agnes of her breath and she clutched at her throat.

"Who's there?" she gasped, unable to move or think.

"Greetings Mistress Nokes," said Matthew Hopkins, doffing his hat. Her mind raced madly. Hopkins here - at her home - at this hour? Had he been in the forest and seen them? She recovered her wits and drew herself up, proudly, a frown creasing her brow. "Master Hopkins! What on earth brings *you* out at such an hour?"

His face was partly hidden by the shadows and his broad-brimmed puritan's hat, but she sensed his insolent smile.

"I was about to ask you the same question, Madam. Is it not unusual for a gentlewoman to be out of her bed at this time of night - or should I say, morning? Perhaps you are returning from some midnight merrymaking?"

Mistress Nokes' eyes were flint but she managed a thin

smile. "I'm afraid I'm somewhat past the age for merrymaking, sir. I leave that to the younger folk."

She heard steps on the path and turned . . . Joseph! . . . She stared at him blankly as he pointed a grubby finger at her. "She lies!" he cried. "She's been to the Witches Sabbath. I followed her there."

"You hear this boy?" Hopkins' voice was soft and menacing. "What have you to say to the accusation?"

Mistress Nokes drew her cloak more closely around her and laughed harshly. "The poor boy imagines things. He's afflicted by the Moon."

"It's true," insisted Joseph. "She was dancing with demons. The Devil, himself, was there! I saw him! He had horns sticking out of his head and he came out of a tree! I had to fly for my life or he would have had my soul - but he's gained hers! She's signed a pact with him. I know!" He gesticulated wildly. "He comes and lies on her bed in the form of a black cat. I've seen the way she strokes and kisses him."

Agnes shook her head. "Dear me, he *is* mentally afflicted. Such lies in one so young."

"If what the lad says is untrue, what *have* you been doing, abroad all night?" asked the witchfinder. His narrowed eyes seemed to pierce her very soul, but she returned his gaze calmly.

"I have been visiting a sick friend and I'm very tired. I must go to bed, now." She turned to the door, but he quickly put his arm across it, barring her way.

"That is very unlikely," he sneered. "There are no dwellings in the direction from which you came just now."

Agnes realised she was trapped and could have bitten off

her tongue for saying such a thing. "I swear I'm not a witch." Her bones ached with tiredness. She was very close to tears and that would never do. Her proud spirit struggled to assert itself, but her body was screaming for rest. She listened to Hopkins' words as from a great distance - they were unreal - the whole scene was unreal. What was he saying?

"We shall soon find out whether you are a witch or not. I have my own methods which are very successful." He grinned, evilly, "Perhaps a ducking or a few sleepless nights will loosen that tongue of yours. I feel sure we will find some devil's mark on that old body. My prickers don't miss very much."

She would have fallen had not one of Hopkins' assistants, who had strolled up the path, stepped forward and caught her. "I am but a feeble old woman," she cried, now utterly at their mercy.

"Then you are more likely to be a witch," he laughed, arrogantly, waving his cane in the air.

Just at that moment, the black cat darted from the bushes and ran forward to rub itself affectionately round Mistress Nokes' skirts. Hopkins feigned surprise. "So, the boy *does* speak the truth," he said. "Her familiar comes to her aid. What have you to say to this?"

"It is but a stray cat." She felt physically sick, now.

"Aye! It has the form of a cat at this moment, but does it not change into a handsome young stripling and copulate with you?"

"You speak evil and disgust me with your foul talk." Rallying again, she kept her dignity.

He pulled at his neat beard with gloved fingers. "Is it

filthier to talk of such things, than it is to sell your body to Satan?"

"I have not had intercourse with Satan," her voice trembled with indignation.

His eyes caught and held hers. "Perhaps I should say an incubus, or is it a succubus? I can never remember the difference."

Agnes dragged her gaze from the face of her tormentor. "I know of no such words. Let me go!" She struggled, but to no avail.

"Come, come, is it not a succubus that appears in the form of a woman, and draws the semen from men in order to inject it into women, while in the shape of a man?" Hopkins was enjoying himself.

"If you know, why ask me?" Her wits sharpened again on his words.

"I thought that one who had been so injected would know more than I, who have only heard of such abominations."

"You have a foul mouth." Her gall rose. She suddenly felt very ill.

"Aye! But not as foul as the things you do at your meetings." His voice was hard, as a frozen pond in winter.

Mistress Nokes' mind teetered between horror and hysteria. She could think of no reply. She knew that nothing she could say would convince Hopkins she was not a witch. He barked a command for his men to take her away and they dragged her down the path and out of the gate.

Joseph watched the proceedings - a smug expression on his face. He was about to follow when he heard a rustling in the grass behind him. Turning, he saw the black cat glaring at him, its back arched - fur bristling, as it snarled and spat. It must be the Devil seeking revenge! He screamed in terror and rushed after the others.

Mary, still glowing with a tired happiness from her exciting experience, hummed softly inside her mask as she reached the lane leading to her new home. The sky was bright and clear - 'it is going to be a lovely hot day,' she thought, as she neared the farm.

But the scene which met her eyes when it came into view, stopped her in her tracks. Mistress Nokes was being taken away by two men! She suddenly recognised Hopkins. His wide-brimmed Puritan's hat, short cloak and cane, were unmistakeable. Mary started to run towards them, completely forgetting that she still wore her mask! They were trying to harm her dear friend who had been so good to her.

Hopkins looked back when he heard the sound of running feet behind him, but before he could do anything, Mary had felled him with a blow to the stomach. She threw herself down upon him, scratching and clawing at his face. The lawyer felt the blood trickling into his beard. He had had all the breath knocked out of his body, but he struck out to defend himself.

He might have been attacking the wind for all the good it did him. With strength borne of fury, Mary heaved him upright and dealt him a hefty punch to the chin which sent him sprawling again in the dusty lane.

The suddenness of the whole incident and the macabre appearance of Mary, had robbed the rest of Hopkins' party of their wits, and they stood as if rooted to the spot - their mouths, dark, gaping holes.

Young Joseph broke the spell. "Look!" he screeched.

"It's a werewolf!" And one of the men drew a pistol from his belt. "Don't shoot!" screamed Mistress Nokes, but her appeal came a second too late. The man fired and Mary fell to the ground, gasping.

The old lady struggled to break free from her guards. "Quick! See to her! She may not be dead - we may yet safe her life."

Matthew Hopkins was very badly shaken. He staggered drunkenly to his feet, wiping the blood from his ashen features, and threw himself at Agnes, shaking her like a rat. "She?" he screamed. "How do you know that monster is female?"

Too late, she recognised her second mistake. Hopkins flung her aside and bending down, ripped the mask from Mary's face.

For a moment, he stared, transfixed, at the still, white countenance, then, "Christ's Blood! It's Mary Summerset!" He put a hand under her cloak. "She's dead right enough." He lifted his head and stared at the distant woods. This was something even *he* could barely comprehend.

Deep down he had admired the witchpricker, though he would never have admitted it - even to himself. The fact that Mary had attacked him - he, her erstwhile master, made his throat contract in the most unaccountable way.

Hopkins had not, at any time, been on the receiving end of cruelty or violence. It was a new experience for him. His mind turned from the uncomfortable sensation; sought, and found, its usual outlet. "So! She was hiding with you!" he snarled. "Not only do you attend the Devil's Sabbath, but you harbour escaped prisoners, too."

Tears streamed down Mistress Nokes' face. She was stunned with shock and horror and could only stare at Mary's body, lying in its pool of blood. She felt somehow to blame for her terrible end. And the mask, instead of being a protection, had proved to be her downfall! Oh, why had not Mary kept out of sight and saved herself? If only she had remained hidden until they had gone. Agnes had no thought for her own situation. Now this had happened, she was past caring.

"It looks as though Mary *was* a witch, after all," muttered Hopkins, his eyes, downcast, following a bright red rivulet of blood, as it slowly made its way through the uneven surface of the lane. "Or have you made her one?" He rounded on Mistress Nokes, savagely. "Not content with selling your own soul to Satan, you must force others to join your filthy band."

Agnes made no reply, she was lost in her own private world of misery.

But now, Meg came - running, to that still group, her hair flying behind her. And the sight of her daughter brought Agnes a tinge of comfort.

"Mother!" she cried, her face white with anxiety. "What's the matter? What are they doing to you?"

Mistress Nokes shook her grey head; she could find no words, and Meg stared at the still form on the ground.

"Why, Mary!" she exclaimed, bending over her. "Are you hurt?"

And her blue eyes widened with horror as she saw the blood. "Ah, no, no," she breathed, and looked up piteously at the empty faces for reassurance.

"Aye, dead." One of the men answered her silent question, clearing his throat. "Dead as a doornail."

His words smote her like a spear. She shrieked in anguish and clasped Mary's head to her breast, cradling the body in her arms, and her cries were such that even Hopkins looked uncomfortable. Agnes, half-fainting, was lost in her daughter's grief. Finally, Hopkins went over and pulled Meg to her feet. "She's dead," he said, "let her be." And he dragged her, screaming and struggling, from the corpse.

Just then, Joseph appeared, carrying a long branch, pointed at one end, where he had whittled it.

"What's that for?" demanded the witchfinder, holding Meg, firmly.

"It's a werewolf!" yelled the lad. "It can only be destroyed by plunging a wooden stake through its heart." He gibbered and capered like a thing possessed.

"Nonsense! I know this person! Anyway, it's a vampire one kills in that way - not a werewolf."

Hopkins knew he had lost control of a situation which was fast becoming a nightmare. The only thing he wanted now, was to retire as gracefully as possible. And this boy was rapidly developing into a damned nuisance.

But, 'this boy' took no notice, or did not hear the words. He was completely lost in his own crazy thoughts, and running over to Mary's body, he plunged the stake into it with all the strength at his disposal.

The blood gushed profusely from this second wound; some of it splashing on his face and clothing. The sight sobered him immediately and he gazed at the results of his action, unable to move.

Meg shrieked anew and swooned in Hopkins' arms; her golden hair spilling over his tunic, her face as white as his broad collar.

"Christ Jesu!" One of the men crossed himself, and for a time, the participants of that awful drama, appeared as statues, bathed in the sun's brightness.

Hopkins, for the second time that morning, knew not what to do and fingered his beard, nervously. His assistants shuffled their feet and avoided each other's eyes. The only sound was the cawing of the rooks, as they floated lazily, like pieces of black tissue paper, high up over the elm trees at the edge of the forest.

Agnes sobbed bitterly. "Have mercy, sire, let me aid my daughter."

Hopkins, glad of the interruption, growled, "Quiet woman! Look to thy own peril."

He laid Meg down and turned to his men. "It's no use trying to arrest this girl again, she's already been free'd from the accusation of witchcraft. The old woman will be enough for the time being. You can come back later for Mary Summerset's body."

He pulled at his beard, his eyes bright with malice. "Maybe I'll have it hung in chains as a warning to others." Then, he caught sight of Joseph, skulking in the background. "Be off until I send for you. Be off I say!" He advanced, threateningly, and Joseph needed no second warning. He departed as fast as his short legs would carry him.

In spite of his hatred for Mary, Hopkins seemed unable to leave her. He stood surveying her mutilated body. "I said we would meet again," he muttered, then flung the edge of her cloak over her face. "It's a pity you escaped the gallows." At last, he turned on his heel and strode off down the lane, followed by his assistants, dragging between them the unfortunate Mistress Nokes.

When Meg regained consciousness, she found herself alone.

163

Rising unsteadily to her feet, she peered around through blurred vision - her head swimming, until her swollen eyes rested upon Mary's body. The flies were already engaged, thereon, attracted by the smell of fresh blood.

Meg's memory swiftly returned and recoiled in horror from the events of that fateful morning. Had she been ridden by the Nightmare? Could such a terrible thing have actually happened? Yet, the still form, remained, a silent witness to the tragedy. She knelt down beside it. "Oh Mary, my dearest friend, why did they have to kill you?" Tears made tiny grooves on her dust-smeared cheeks. "I loved you so much." She buried her face in her dark-green gown, then suddenly looked up, her thin hands clawing at the material. "I'll not allow your body to leave my care. You'll have a proper Craft funeral, I'll see to that, never fear."

With a strength borne of despair, Meg attempted to drag the corpse to the farmhouse, but the task was well nigh impossible. She had only just managed to reach the gate, when Bess and Robert came hurrying down the lane, and with an anguished cry, Meg collapsed into Robert's arms.

The couple were stunned and not immediately able to grasp the horrific details, but they had the presence of mind to pull the stake from the body and bundle Meg and her terrible burden, up the path and into the house as quickly as possible.

Once inside, Bess rushed to make a posset of honey, beer and herbs, for all of them, while Robert tried to calm the hysterical girl. He eventually heard most of the story and Meg was quick to question him as to why they had not come home earlier. Where had they been? Robert's red face answered her.

"Huh, making love in the woods! You should have come

164

straight back here. It would have saved Mary - I know it would."

"Dearest," Bess entered with a tray. "We cannot be blamed for such a thing. If that was Mary's fate, it would have happened sooner or later. You must not upset Robert, so."

Robert, did, in fact, feel responsible for the whole affair, although he knew that nothing could have kept the Nokes' family from the meeting. His mind raced, trying to think how on earth he could protect them. It was damnable luck, but it had happened and must be faced, and, if possible, overcome. He was not one for shirking a duty, and his oath, taken all those years ago in the sacred grove, to protect his brothers and sisters of the Craft, had not been taken in vain.

Between them, they managed to settle Meg in her mother's chair, by the fire. Mistress Nokes had left plenty of logs in readiness for their return. Her idiosyncrasy of having a fire burning at all times of the year, now proved to be a comfort to them and helped considerably in combatting the coldness which shock always brings to the body.

They sat, sipping the sweet-smelling drink and gazing at the new flames, greedily engulfing the logs. Meg, utterly exhausted, had fallen asleep; Mary's blood still on her gown, and Bess sobbed quietly on her new husband's broad shoulder. They were dazed by the awful fact of Mistress Nokes and Mary no longer being with them.

"Do you remember the messages at the meeting?" Bess blew her nose into a large, linen handkerchief. "It said, people were going to die - didn't it?"

Robert, his face, set and grim, nodded, but remained silent, staring in front of him; thinking out ways and means of outwitting the infamous witchfinder. Only the crowing of the cockerel in the yard disturbed the misery of their thoughts.

At length, Maxwell ran sturdy fingers through thick, brown hair; groaned with tiredness, and lifted his wife to her feet.

"Come now, Bess, we must be up and doing. No time to rest, yet. Hopkins might return at any time and there is a lot to do. We've got to outwit him, somehow. Wake Meg. You must both help me with poor Mary."

Bess gently roused her sister, but Meg broke into floods of tears. Bess embraced her, lovingly. "There, there, dear. Don't take on so, you'll make yourself ill."

"We're all heartbroken," said Robert, his arms round their shoulders, "but we cannot remain inactive at this time of danger. And I promise that Mary will have the last rites as a true witch should. Now, you must help me." He walked over to where the body lay, hastily covered with a patch-work quilt, and with the help of the two women, he was able to convey it upstairs, through the concealed door and so into the secret room under the eaves.

Once there, they laid it reverently on the bed. It would be quite safe now, even if Hopkins *did* decide to search the house.

"I will inform the rest of the coven of this outrage," panted Robert, "and speak with the Summoner to pass the message on. Tonight she will be cremated on the sacred hill."

"You can't do that," protested Bess. "They would see the fire from the town."

His lips twisted into the ghost of a smile. "So much the better. I hope the flames light up the whole sky. This new witch gave her life in an attempt to rescue your mother. She deserves the best funeral that we can give her - in true Craft tradition."

Bess looked up at Robert with an expression which was somewhere between love and admiration. "Dearest, I'm sure Mary would have wanted that."

His fighting spirit was infectious and flooded the sisters. They realised that their sorrows would have to be temporarily pushed into the background in order to concentrate upon these new responsibilities.

"But, what about the witchfinders?" asked Meg, her sad eyes never leaving the form on the bed.

"To Hell with the lot of them. By the time *they* reach the hill, it will all be over," replied Robert, moving to the door.

"But, how are we to convey Mary's body there?" enquired Bess. "This house will surely be watched when they find she has disappeared."

"Have no fear," answered her husband, darkly. "I have an idea. I think we can beat the filthy swine at their own game. Come now, Bess, there's work to be done. I must go and make arrangements for the cremation and the removal of the body from this house."

"Yes, but what about poor Mother?" cried Bess. "How can we help her? After all, Mary is past her troubles, but Mother is in the hands of those cruel men."

Meg began crying again and the sisters held on to each other in their grief and comforted one another as best they could.

Robert stood awkwardly in front of such anguish, his hand flicking away the moisture on his brow. "Listen, my poor sparrows, first, we must attend to the matter on hand. Then, when all is done, we will devise a plan to rescue your mother - never fear."

Bess held Meg from her and stroked her sister's swollen face. "Bob is right, dear, I'm sure they will keep Mother in

167

gaol for a day or two, until . . ." her voice trailed off and she gently turned her sister's glance to the bed. "I will help you . . ."

"Don't worry," there was sudden courage in Meg's voice. "I can manage to lay Mary out. I will dress her in her new nightgown. I *want* to do this for her, so please - go with Robert, dear."

Her brother-in-law nodded kindly to Meg, then putting an arm round his wife's trim waist, he led her wearily from the room.

"Ye Gods," he muttered, "what a way to start a honeymoon."

Hopkins' men returned for Mary's body and stood scratching their heads and staring stupidly at the blood-stained spot where it had lain. They searched both the house and the outbuildings, heedless of any damage they caused; the hens scattering from their huge boots - clucking and squawking their indignation at the disturbance. Finally, they left in disgust.

Hopkins was furious when they reported their failure to him. This was the second time Mary had eluded him. Once alive - and now, dead! "How in God's name can a dead woman vanish?" he fumed.

"Mayhap she wasn't dead?" suggested Stearne, wiping the froth from his moustache.

They were in their usual haunt - the Black Swan, or the 'Mucky Duck', as the locals called the inn.

"Are you completely mad? Of course she was dead. Could *you* live with a stake through your heart?"

John Stearne knew that whatever he said, he couldn't win. He yearned to thrust his fist into the man's visage and watch that sarcastic expression disappear, but decided that discretion was the better part of valour and attacked his opponent, verbally.

"If you had left someone to guard it, the body would be there, now," he growled.

Hopkins lashed back at him. "And if you had been there instead of hanging round the backside of some serving wench, *you* could have stayed with it."

The argument ended in the same way as previous ones. Stearne jumped up in disgust and flung out of the inn. The Witchfinder General smiled thinly to himself; it was always a great pleasure to better his assistant.

On this occasion, however, Stearne was determined not to be beaten. Why should he always be on the losing side? He walked along in the sunshine, his head lowered with hands thrust deep in his pockets - thinking the matter out.

If the body *had* been concealed in the farmhouse, someone would have to bring it out - it was not something which could remain there for long. He grinned at the thought. The stench of a corpse in this heat, would become unbearable in a few hours. Perhaps they would feed it to the pigs? The idea was very unlikely, but if it was there, he determined to find it, here and now. That would show the bastard!

He made his way out of the town and along the lane to Elm-tree farm. Once there, he concealed himself carefully in a clump of trees which were almost opposite the gate. From that vantage point he had an excellent view of the front door and could see anyone who either entered or left the house. Of course, there would be a back door too, but he could not be expected to be in two places at once!

Several hours passed while he waited, but the place re-

169

mained silent and brooding in the afternoon heat.

"I might as well be watching an empty house for all the good it's doing me," he grumbled, stretching cramped legs.

The gnats continued their remorseless attacks on his head - their high-pitched whining seemed to be inside his skull. He felt the bumps gingerly and swore to himself. His body was stiff and aching and he was feeling very much in need of a drink - and food, too, come to that.

He was just about to forget the whole exercise when he heard them . . . voices singing lustily in the distance. He could see them now - feet tramping noisily; stirring the dust in the hot, sun-baked air. Three drunken louts - probably farm hands, by the look of their rough, hemp-sewn smocks, leather gaiters and floppy-brimmed hats to protect them from the sun while they worked in the fields.

'They must have had some ale,' thought Stearne, his small eyes narrowing as he watched them making their way and giving tongue to the popular bawdy songs of the day.

"Drunken sots," he muttered; thinking of the old witchpricker, Mary Phillips, and the times he had had to take her back to her lodgings in a similar condition.

One of the men suddenly tripped and fell flat on his face. His companions jeered at him as they helped him to his feet, and between them, dragged him along. They had just reached the farmhouse when he stumbled and fell again. "Christ!" cried one, "You'd think he was still at his mother's paps to look at him."

The other man helped him to rise. "Here, look - blood! He's cut his hand badly. The blood's fair pumping out. Give me a rag to bind it up."

His friend searched his pockets. "Don't seem to 'ave any-

170

thing 'andy. I could tear a bit off me shirt, though,'' he added, helpfully. ''No, no, don't bother. Look after 'im while I go to this 'ouse and see if they can give me a bit of cloth. We don't want it turning skeptic.''

He left his companion holding the injured man and made a zig-zag track to the door. But he had to knock several times before it finally opened. Stearne could see Bess, framed in the doorway, but was too far away to hear what was said. However, she must have agreed to help because the man touched his hat to her and returned to the others.

Between them, they helped the injured man into the house and it was not long before they emerged, dragging their friend with them. Stearne could see the man's hand was now bandaged, but he must have lost a lot of blood because his friends had to almost carry him along.

He watched as they walked unsteadily up the lane and disappeared round a bend. 'That poor chap's for it when his wife sees the state he's in,' he thought, idly.

Stearne was now thoroughly disgruntled and bored with his uneventful watch, and at last he could endure it no longer. ''To hell with the body,'' he muttered. ''If only Matthew would believe that witches could be snatched away by the Devil, I need not have wasted my time.'' Pausing only to relieve himself on a tree, he departed thankfully for more hospitable climes; his thoughts full of large tankards of cool, frothy ale. John Stearne's personality was not one which could withstand its creature comforts for long.

From his hiding-place behind a window in the house, Robert observed Stearne walk off towards the town. He grabbed his wife and whirled her off her feet. ''We've fooled them again,'' he cried. "The plan worked perfectly! Mary's body is now on its way - out of that demon's grasp!"

Despite her sadness, Bess smiled at his enthusiasm. "Oh, Robert! If only Stearne had known that *you* were the 'injured' man, and that Mary left here in your place! What a fool he would think himself - and will do, if he ever finds out."

"Aye!" Robert winked at her. "He would never believe that a dead woman walked away under his very nose. Come, kiss me Bess."

His wife put her arms around him and for a little while, the tension of the previous hours, receded.

A huge bonfire lit the top of the sacred hill. Lying three miles from the forest, in a south-westerly direction, Maiden Tor had been a regular haunt of witches in times gone by, although the local covens had not frequented it since the reign of Elizabeth. This well-loved Queen is said to have danced, naked, with her ladies-in-waiting, on the palace lawns under the light of the full moon! However, her act regarding conjurations and witchcraft was replaced by a much more severe statute under her successor, James the First of England - 'the wisest fool in Christendom'.

This unfortunate son of Mary, Queen of Scots, was a tyrannical, pedantic monarch who thought himself threatened by plotters using the black arts, and presided over many examinations of witches. Small wonder that the hill, like others, had been abandoned!

A circle of stones - the Nine Maidens, marked its summit and the place always had an uncanny feel to it. Visitors to the site would remark on an unseen presence which lurked there, but the Wise Ones knew it for the Guardian of the Stones. The hill had been sacred to the Old Religion for a very long time. The stone circle was only one of thousands, similar, scattered throughout Britain and the continent. As the witches stood round the funeral pyre, the flames leapt into the dark, moonlit sky, as if trying to touch it, and illumined the solemn faces of those assembled with a false ruddiness. Dark-robed, the figures were - dark, as their unspoken thoughts. Was it only one short day since the Esbat? Had this new initiate *really* died and passed so soon to the Summerlands? Despite the heat from the fire, many shivered and wondered who would be next.

They watched silently as the High Priestess walked into the Circle. Lucina wore a black-velvet cloak and hood, lined with silver thread, over a gown of purple satin. She addressed the coven: "This night, we pay our last respects to our new sister, who gave her life in an unsuccessful attempt to free our trusted friend and Elder, Agnes Nokes. Agnes, who, at this very moment, languishes in prison on a charge of witchcraft."

Four men carried Mary's corpse into the circle. It was resting on a frame of branches, lashed together with rope. Lucina raised her arms to the first scattering of stars: "Hear us, dreaded God and gentle Goddess. We commend to Thy care the earthly remains of one of Thy brave Children. One, who willingly gave her life to save another. Please accept Mary Summerset into Thy Summerlands. Strengthen and purify her soul until the time comes for rebirth upon this Earth.

Mary leaves this world through the fires of purification so that her body may quickly return to the Elements from whence

173

it came. Her etheric and astral bodies will likewise dissolve swiftly and leave her soul free to enter the lovely realms of the Gods.''

Lucina sprinkled Mary's body with consecrated water: ''We commend ye to the Mighty Ones - the Kings of the Elements. Fare-well!''

The men lifted the corpse onto the pyre. The flames caressed it - making it, one, with them and the body was rapidly consumed.

Meg stood, watching with the others, her pretty face swollen from weeping at this last 'goodbye'. As she gazed at the fire, she thought she saw the astral body of her friend, rise from it. Mary hovered - her arms outstretched - welcoming, and Meg moved towards the vision, her face transformed with happiness. She would certainly have thrown herself onto the pyre, had not her sister and Betty intervened.

''Let me go!'' screamed Meg. ''Mary wants me.''

Bess and Betty held her fast as she struggled to free herself - she was quite determined to perish. ''I love Mary,'' she cried. ''I must go to her, *now*!''

Bess slapped her sister's face, hard, and it seemed to have the desired effect, as Meg slumped back into Betty's capable arms.

Lucina had observed Meg's distress and forthwith dismissed the coven, leaving the Nokes family with their private grief. ''She'll be right enough now, Betty,'' said Bess, softly. ''We'll see to her - thanks - Blessed Be!''

Betty, her eyes bright with tears, rejoined her husband and Joan and they returned to their horse and cart which had been hidden in an old barn at the foot of the hill.

Bess edged her sister away. ''What do you mean - you loved her - didn't we all?''

"Yes, but not as I did," whispered Meg, between sobs.

Bess looked puzzled. "I don't know what you are talking about, dear. You would have been burned to death had not Betty and I saved you."

"I did not want you to save me. I cannot live without Mary."

"You must be deranged. It's all the worry we are having."

"No, I'm not! I have nothing to live for now."

Something dawned in her sister's mind. No! It could not be true! She shook Meg, gently. "Tell me what you mean," she demanded.

"I have already told you. I love Mary." Meg's eyes burned with an inner fire - her face, quite altered.

"You mean . . ." Bess hesitated, then looked away. "Were you and Mary, lovers?"

"Yes!" The defiance in her sister's voice brooked no denial. But, Bess, due partly to everything she was suffering, fairly bristled with indignation. "You've brought shame on our family! I never thought my sister was a . . . was a . . ."

"Was a - what?" snapped Meg.

"Well . . . are you not ashamed?"

"No, I am not!" Meg glared at her. "I am ashamed to hear you talking like a Puritan! I always imagined the Brother-hood to be tolerant, in that they believe people should live their own lives." She flung away and sat down on one of the stones, wrapping her cloak tightly around her and gazing down into the valley.

Bess watched her helplessly. She could think of nothing to say. Presently, she joined Robert who was attending the now smouldering ashes.

"What troubles thee, dear one?" he asked, his eyes on her dismal countenance. "Have we not done all we could for

175

Mary?"

"It's not that," she replied, shortly.

"Then, tell me what ails thee?"

Bess proceeded to relate what she had learned. She encountered those amazing blue eyes, and waited. "Meg's right," he said, at length. "We must be tolerant because love *is* universal. It cannot be enchained within man's puny laws and dogmas. If two people, of the same sex, have a loving, responsible relationship with each other, they have an obligation to express that love in whatever way they deem appropriate." He smiled at his wife, fondly. "Not everyone is as lucky as we are, Bess." His wife wondered at his words and was left to digest them in her own way as Robert went off to collect Meg.

Matthew Hopkins and Stearne, stood in the street in Belford, watching the conflagration on the top of the distant hill. Hopkins was certain he was witnessing Mary's funeral pyre - she had most probably been given the last rites by those accursed witches. And this, in spite of his efforts to seize the body. His face, twitching, he turned to Stearne. "If only I had known this was going to happen. I could have captured the whole coven, red-handed."

"Well now, it's like closing the stable door after the horse has bolted," grinned his companion, picking his teeth with a sliver of wood as he strolled off.

But Hopkins could not take his eyes from that glowing signal. "Those witches have more courage than I thought," he muttered.

"Well, I shall have to make do with Mistress Nokes for the time being." He screwed his gloves, absentmindedly, be-

176

tween manicured fingers. "Aye, by the Rood . . . I'll have *thee . . . witch!*"

CHAPTER 10

It was the day after Mary's funeral, and Robert, Bess and Meg were seated round the table, discussing how they could rescue Mistress Nokes. It was difficult. Their minds were tired and fogged with fatigue, yet something had to be done - and done quickly! Ideas were exchanged and abandoned; there seemed to be snags in all of them. As they sat, gloomily staring into space, a knock was heard at the door.

"Go and see who it is, Robert," sighed Bess. "My heart misses a beat every time someone calls. I'm forever expecting Hopkins to come and arrest us."

Her husband went over to the window. "It's only Arthur, I'll let him in."

Their visitor's face was grave as he entered. Robert pulled up a chair for him and he sat down without speaking. Meg, glanced at him, anxiously. "What is it, Arthur? What's the matter?"

Arthur smoothed his white hair, nervously. "It's about your mother. I'm afraid the matter of releasing her is going to be the very devil of a business. I have made discreet enquiries and it appears that Agnes is incarcerated in one of the lower dungeons of the gaol. She is guarded at all times, by two gaolers. Hopkins has realised that an attempt may be made to rescue her and has taken precautions against such an event." Arthur lowered his head. "I cannot see any possibility of saving her."

There was silence when he had finished speaking. The two women comforted each other - their eyes, moist, with unshed tears. Then Bess clenched her hands and stood up. "In that

179

case, we must shorten her agony and distress, as we did for Jane," she said, resolutely.

"Oh, not that!" cried Meg. "Anything but that." And she laid her bright head on the table.

Bess stared down at her sister's grief, her throat, contracting. Oh, what she would give to see Meg happy once again. Was it only two short days since their terrible troubles began? It seemed an eternity since the meeting. She suddenly realised that the men were looking at her. Of course, *she* was the mother of their family, now. At least until her mother returned. Very well, she would attempt to fill the vacuum. She answered their troubled faces:

"There is nothing else to do. You know Mother would wish it. Do you want to see her shamed and degraded before the mob, and then done to death like a common criminal?"

Meg raised her head, the violet eyes, huge, in the tear-blotched features. What was her sister saying? Very slowly, she came to the realisation that Bess was right. Of course, her dear mother would sooner poison herself than face such an ordeal.

"Then it is agreed?" queried Bess.

There was no reply, for the others were deep in thought. Finally, Robert answered her - his voice, flat. "If there is nothing else - I must agree."

Arthur cleared his throat. "Your mother would wish it. I have known her for a great number of years and she is a brave woman, but she would prefer to take her own life rather than face such a death."

Robert paced restlessly round the room. "I don't like it, yet I know it would be for the best . . . who will attempt to deliver the poison?"

"I will!" said Bess.

Robert turned on her. "Impossible! You have suffered enough at the hands of those lecherous swine," he gesticulated wildly. "Besides, you would be recognised, and there is the babe to consider."

"Then, I'll do it," announced Arthur, quietly.

"A man would never slip past the guards. Your going would be a disaster and you would endanger your life for nothing." Robert kicked at the rug - breathing an oath.

Meg stood up and folded her arms. "I'll go, I have nothing to lose, now."

Arthur put his arm, protectively, round the girl's thin shoulders. "We all know you would go, dear, but you have already faced the witchfinders once, and they will not easily forget the face of one who escaped from their clutches. Did not Hopkins also see you, when . . .?" His voice trailed away. "You might not be so lucky a third time, you know." Arthur was a good man, but diplomacy was not his strongest attribute.

Meg grasped his hand, her eyes brightening. She did not appear to have heard him. "I know! I can wear boy's clothing, then I won't be recognised." She warmed to her theme. "I will say that Mother was my old nurse and that I want to bid her farewell, as she was so good to me. I am sure they would allow me to see her for a few minutes - especially if I paid them well!" Her pale face was suddenly alive with enthusiasm. "If I took a small phial, I could give it to her through the bars in the cell door. It would only take a minute."

Arthur's grey brows lowered as he watched his friend's reaction to Meg's words. "What do you think of that?"

"It *might* work," Robert stood on the sides of his feet and rubbed his chin thoughtfully, his eyes fixed on Meg's flushed countenance. "It's worth taking a chance. They can only refuse her permission to enter the prison."

"And if we dress her in fine clothes, they may believe her story," added Arthur, slowly. "That is . . . if we make the bribe big enough, I suppose. Those gaolers will sell their souls for gold."

"Then you agree?" asked Meg, a catch in her voice.

They nodded, reluctantly.

" You have a dangerous mission to perform, Meg," said Arthur. "We must take every possible precaution. To start with, you would have to alter your voice."

"Like this?" she asked, in a low, husky tone.

"Why, that's perfect, dear," exclaimed Bess. "That would certainly convince me."

Arthur grasped his walking-stick and prepared to leave - pleased to have something positive to do. "I must away, now, but I'll be back early tomorrow morning with a good suit for Meg. In the meantime, I should cut her hair short. It will help with the disguise."

When he had gone, Meg said, "I never thought! We could have dressed Arthur as a woman and *he* could have gone."

"Please don't joke," said Bess. "I'll fetch the scissors."

Meg regarded her flaxen tresses with an air of resignation. "Ah well, it's a small price to pay if it will help Mother."

"It will grow again, don't worry." Robert patted her head then went out to feed the pigs. He had no wish to see the operation performed.

Arthur arrived the next morning with a sack on his shoulder. It contained a smart suit of blue linen. The doublet had a velvet collar, with cuffs edged in creamy-coloured lace. A blue velvet cap, silver-buckled shoes and a pair of silk stockings, completed the outfit.

"Let's see what you look like in these," he chuckled.

"Lordy me!" gasped Meg. "Where on earth did you get such fine things?"

"Never you mind," smiled Arthur. "Let's hope they fit you."

Bess fetched him a mug of ale, while Meg ran up to her bedroom to change. When she returned there were cries of admiration.

"You make a fine lad, Meg," pronounced Bess, "and what a beautiful suit, it fits you perfectly."

Her sister strutted round the room, hands in pockets, and grinned at her reflection in the mirror.

Robert came in from the yard and gaped at the resplendent creature. "It's not our Meg, is it?"

Arthur laughed at his expression. "I think she should carry off the deception very well. Do you know what to say and do, Meg?"

"She should," smiled Bess. "She's been practising half the night."

Robert took a purse from his pocket and handed it to Meg. "Here's the money with which to bribe the gaolers, love. There's enough there to bribe Hopkins, himself."

Meg opened the purse. "It's an awful lot of money," she murmured.

"Aye, it's most of our savings. But if it prevents your mother from suffering, it will be well worth it."

Bess opened the secret cupboard and brought out a small

phial. "Now, this is the poison. I remember Mother saying that it was a very special one. Keep it in a safe place - and may the Gods watch over you, dear." She hugged Meg tightly. "We are all depending on you, but *do* take care."

"Have no fear. It may be a lot easier than I thought."

Robert was not convinced, but concealed his fears. "You better go now. Our thoughts and prayers will go with thee. Hurry back."

They made light of their farewells, and Meg sauntered off like one of the young bloods of the town.

"I hope she succeeds," sighed Bess, straightening the curtains.

"We can only hope," said Arthur, frowning with worry.

"And they can but refuse her permission to enter the gaol."

Bess and Robert thanked their friend for all his help. Then, he too, made his departure, promising to return later in the day. Arthur was nearly three score years and ten, but he was still fit enough to perform his trade - and there would be horses waiting to be shod at his forge. Now, there was nothing for Bess and Robert to do, but wait!

Meg invoked cat-calls and whistles from the townsfolk on her way through Belford, but she ignored them all - intent on her errand of mercy. When she reached the gates of the prison, the gate-keeper emerged and looked her up and down; his beady eyes missing nothing.

"And what would a fine lad like you be wanting, 'ere?"

Meg told him the story about her old nurse. He listened to her attentively, his head cocked on one side like an old raven, but he appeared to believe her story.

"So, yer old nurse was a witch?" he said, spitting on the

ground.

"I had no idea at the time, sir."

The man, a stranger to courtesy, was visibly affected at being so addressed. "You must be a very thoughtful lad - coming to a place like this to bid yer old nurse, farewell. Ye don't find many young folk who would take such an interest in the aged, these days."

Meg scuffed her shoes on the cobbles. "Well, she was very kind to me when I was young."

The gaoler grinned. "Yer only a sprog, now," he shook his head. "I don't know - when ye were young, eh?"

Meg grinned back at him - sharing his joke.

"Still, I daresay ye mean well." He stared into space. "Aye, it's a pity she's bin caught. We get so many old hags in 'ere who they calls witches, but between thee and me, I 'ave me doubts." He winked at her, slyly. "Still, who am I to argue with the Witchfinder General? It'd be more than me job was worth."

Meg said casually, "I'll pay you well if you let me see her." She took out the purse and held up a guinea. It sparkled in the sunlight - a small, golden world.

The man stared at it - hypnotised. "You mean . . .?"

"Yes, that's for you." She dropped it into his calloused hand and he gazed at it without speaking; then:

"Yer a right royal gent," he said, touching his forelock.

"Well, there will be another one for you when I come out."

Meg watched his reaction to the bribe.

"It's not really in me 'ands, lad, but I reckon them in charge will let ye see 'er. Especially if ye grease their palms with a coin like this un."

"I'll do that, sir."

185

Reaching a decision, he pocketed the guinea and took Meg to the gaoler.

"Now then! Let this young gent see Mistress Nokes." This with an assumed air of importance.

"On whose orders?" asked the gaoler, sarcastically.

"Mine!" barked the gate-keeper.

The other man brought his swarthy visage close to the guard's.

"And wat right 'ave *you* to give *me* orders?"

The guard was unable to think of a reply.

"Am I not in charge of these dungeons?" continued the gaoler. The gate-keeper nudged him and winked, extravagantly. "Aye, but wait till ye see wat this young sir has for ye."

"And what might ye 'ave, young sir?" asked the gaoler with a wicked grin.

Meg opened her purse again and held out another guinea. With the speed of a spider attacking its prey, the gaoler grabbed the coin; tested it between his teeth; spat on it, and finally pocketed it. "Well, maybe I can bend the rules for once," he announced, gruffly. "Especially for a rich, young gent like you." He indicated a doorway with a grimy thumb. "Follow me."

He led Meg along a dark passage, past several, even darker, cells. The prisoners yelled and jeered when they saw the finely dressed 'boy' pass by.

She followed her guide, apprehensively, down some winding stone stairs, to the lower dungeons; her hand, sliding, as it met the wet, slippery walls. The dark smell of mould was overpowering.

They gained the ill-lit guard-room, where another gaoler sat drinking rum. He was even more repulsive than her guide - if that were possible! His unwashed face gleamed with sweat from the light of a single lantern, and he had the bloated features of a perpetual drunkard. His shirt was open to the waist displaying a hirsute body which he scratched every few minutes. He blinked in surprise as they entered:

"Who have you got there, Luke?"

"A rich young popinjay," leered Meg's guide.

"Aye, I can see that by his clothes. Them must have cost a pretty penny."

"He's got money on 'im, too, Toby."

"As 'e now?" The gaoler leaned over the trestle table and fixed Meg with an avarious stare. "And has the little gent got some to spare for the likes of me?"

Once more, Meg opened her purse and casually tossed him a coin. It rang on the boards and lay - shining.

"Gold!" His eyes bulging, Toby gazed at it, then, "And what might you be wanting in exchange for this?"

"I want to see Mistress Nokes." Meg stood defiantly, hands in her breeches pockets; nostrils quivering in the fetid air.

Behind her back, Luke raised his shoulders and shook his head at Toby.

"And what might you be wanting with that old witch?" questioned the gaoler.

Meg sighed inwardly and repeated her story.

Toby took a swig of rum, wiped his mouth on the back of his hand and belched loudly. "I wish I'd had a nurse," he simpered, mockingly.

"Aye, and she'd 'ave bin well poked if I know you," grinned Luke.

"Now, that wasn't a nice thing to say before a young nob like what we 'ave 'ere," protested Toby.

Meg was beginning to feel frightened now. "Well, can I see

her?'' she asked.

"Go on, let 'im in, Toby," pleaded Luke. "He's promised us another piece of gold - after."

The other man rubbed his chin. Something grew in his mind, yet he could not consciously remember what it was. He stumbled to his feet. "Not so fast. Why should he pay so much to see an old crone - even if she was 'is nurse? He could get a dozen bucksome wenches with that kind of money - aye, and a better time, I'll wager."

Luke was losing patience. He wanted to get his hands on the money and be rid of the boy, before he was seen.

"Let's take 'im to see the witch and be done wi' it."

"I only want to see her for a minute," pleaded Meg.

Toby sucked his teeth. "Aye, it's easy money for us, but we can't be too careful. Remember what happened to Jonathan?"

The mention of Jonathan sent a cold shiver down Meg's spine as she thought of what he had done to Bess. But that could not happen to a *boy*, and her disguise had fooled them completely.

"To hell with yer yellow streak," snapped Luke. "I'm in no mood to turn down gold."

Toby, however, was determined that Luke should not get the better of him. After all, he, Toby, was over the other gaolers - Hopkins had said so! He hitched up his breeches. "How do I know he's got this gold?" he asked, taking another swig from his bottle.

Meg was becoming more agitated with every passing second. She held out the purse with a not too steady hand and waved it under Toby's nose. In a flash, he grabbed it and emptied the contents onto the table. The gaoler's eyes gleamed avidly.

188

"Seven gold guineas, eh? Me and Luke could 'ave a real good time with that. Eh, Luke?"

His partner decided to placate him. "You're right there," he chuckled. "There's a few wenches who'd show us their petticoats for that."

They then proceeded to exchange a stream of obscenities on the kind of females they preferred, while Meg fumed with frustration. Oh, for a chance to deliver the poison and be gone from here. She decided upon a final attempt. "Very well! Take *all* the money and let me see the witch."

But, Toby ignored her. "Perhaps the young gent would like to accompany us to the whore-house." He grinned and held out the bottle of rum. "Have a swig, it'll put 'airs on yer chest."

Meg fretted and folded her arms against the offer, which seemed to annoy the gaoler. "Now, come on lad. I'll not do business with one who won't drink with me. Sup up."

He waved the bottle in front of her face, and much against her will, Meg seized it and took a drink. The fiery liquer made her cough and splutter, much to the men's amusement.

"Ye'll 'ave to do better than that if ye go out wi' me and Luke. We can't 'ave a pewling bed-wetter wi' the likes of us." He grinned lecherously and winked at Luke. "It's to be hoped yer better wi' the wenches than wi' yer drink."

"He should be," Luke eyed her curiously. "Yon's a real pretty boy."

Meg groaned inwardly. When would they cease their chatter and allow her to see her mother?

Luke's foxy face was avid in the lantern's glow. "When did ye last ease the itch in a doxy's belly, eh?"

Meg turned away and studied the walls of the chamber, suddenly sickened by the remark.

"See, now, ye've made 'im 'ot under the collar," said Toby, affecting concern. But Luke was warming to his theme. "Come on, lad! Tell us about the lasses ye've bussed. I bet ye've slipped one across many a serving wench."

"Maybe 'e don't like doxies," quipped Toby. "Some lads 'ave other fancies."

The comment took time to sink into Luke's dull brain, then its implications ignited a small flame in his loins. He sidled over and pawed at Meg's shorn locks. "Aye, 'e do look a bit effeminate. Perhaps 'e's like them young pages to the fighting men. What say you, Toby?"

Toby was beginning to enjoy the situation. He leered at Meg, his eyes sliding over her slight figure. "Ye could be right. I 'alf fancy 'im, meself." His lust, never far from him, stirred. "I bet 'e's got a beauty. 'Ave ye a good yard, lad?"

Meg coloured and stared down at her shoes, her mind, empty.

"Come now, yer acting like a simple country wench. Ye should be proud if ye've got a good weapon. 'ere, let's 'ave a feel."

Without warning he grabbed Meg and slipped his hand between her thighs. She fought to free herself - now thoroughly alarmed.

Toby grunted with surprise. "I can't feel it, it must 'ave shrunk." He held her as easily as a doll and pushed his hand down the top of her breeches. Meg gasped with shock as the gaoler kneaded her flesh, then:

"I tell ye it's true. I can't feel a thing! See fer yerself."

Luke needed no encouragement, and while Toby held Meg, he pulled down her clothing and surveyed her eagerly, his face, flushed with lust.

"If me memory 'aint failed, it's a wench." He peeled the lawn shirt slowly above her head. "Aye, and a fine pair o' dugs she 'as, too." Luke's mouth was suddenly dry and he passed his tongue over thin lips.

But Toby emitted a curse and flung Meg against the wall. "God's blood! Wat the 'ell are ye about - dressed as a boy?" Meg cried out as her back hit the uneven stones, and she crumpled; flinching with pain. She had nothing to say - all was now lost.

Toby's sudden anger quickly evaporated as he saw Meg's white skin and he began to chuckle, evilly. "Let's show 'er wat we do wi' a lad-lass, eh?"

Luke nodded, unable to speak. He held the screaming girl while Toby stripped her, grunting with pleasure. At last, she stood naked, her beautiful eyes brimming with tears. She tried to plead with them, but they ignored her remonstrances.

"She's got a fine body. I'll toss ye for first go, Luke."

Toby took one of the gold coins and flicked it into the air. Luke called in a hoarse voice, but his luck was out and Toby ordered him to lift Meg onto the trestle table.

She shrieked and kicked to no avail. She was held down on the rough board while Toby hurriedly unfastened his belt; the sound of his breathing clearly audible in the small room.

Standing, he took her. The slim legs forced apart and hanging over the edge of the table, his hot, throbbing flesh violating her virginity. And while he was thus engaged, Luke pawed her breasts and forced his tongue into her mouth.

The pain of her 'awakening', mercifully robbed Meg of her senses, but the swoon was temporary and for the next hour she was submitted to all the horrors of perverted lust.

At the end, she lay on the floor, the blood trickling down her legs, her body full of pain. But, yet again, she begged to see Mistress Nokes.

"Not a chance," growled Toby, reaching for the rum.

"Why not?" Meg's eyes were huge in her drawn features. "You've both had what you wanted - I beg you, let me see her, now."

Luke straightened his jacket. "Better chuck 'er out."

"No!" Toby spat on the stones. "I 'aven't finished with 'er yet."

Meg moaned and covered her face.

"Now then, me fancy, I've done fer now, but later, maybe . . . ye know, ye'r not 'alf bad." Toby's lust-warped thoughts were manifest in his slurred speech.

She cried out in desperation and fury, "Let me go!"

The gaoler, irritated, shoved her with his foot and a red haze formed in front of Meg's eyes. With a bound, she leaped at Toby, digging her nails into his blotchy face. He yelped with pain and threw her off as if she had been a troublesome insect.

"Ye bloody bitch!" he snarled. "Ye'll pay for that." He cocked his head at Luke. "Tie 'er up."

Meg froze as she saw Toby indicate the wooden post in the centre of the room. She rushed for the door, but Luke nonchalantly thrust out a heavy boot and tripped her up. He held her while Toby seized a whip from its peg on the wall.

"No! No!" Her screams filled the confined space and rebounded off the stones, but Luke began to bind her.

"The other way round," barked Toby. "I like to see their pretty faces when the thongs bite into their flesh."

Meg was turned to face him and secured to the post.

192

Toby allowed the thongs to slip between his thick fingers; a glazed look in his eyes. A second later, Meg shrieked, then fainted. Thin lines of blood marking her pale skin.

Luke grabbed Toby's arm, delaying a second stroke. "Are ye mad? Do you want to kill 'er?" His eyes were moons in his thin features.

Toby's lip curled arrogantly. "Mayhap yer right. I'll keep 'er for later."

"But, she can't stay 'ere." Luke gesticulated wildly. "The gov'ner will be coming on 'is rounds."

"Well, throw 'er in with old Polly. 'er's never 'ad company for years, and 'e never goes down there." Toby laughed, harshly.

Much relieved, Luke untied the unconscious girl and carried her down another flight of steps to a solitary dungeon. Unlocking the door, he entered and threw Meg onto a heap of dirty straw.

As he closed the door behind him, a figure which crouched in a corner, opened its eyes. This was Polly. She had been convicted of witchcraft some years earlier. But the evidence against her had not been sufficient to warrant her death, so she had been virtually abandoned in the prison.

Her one-time friends had either forgotten her or believed her dead. Only the gaolers knew of her existence and it was a wonder, even to them, how she survived in those terrible conditions.

Polly, now, had the appearance of a ghoul. Her skin was the colour of old parchment and hung on her thin frame in wrinkled folds. A skull-like visage held rheumy eyes which blinked constantly in the puny gleam of a solitary lantern set high up in the wall.

A filthy tattered shift exposed shrivelled breasts and Polly's straggly white hair hung in matted rats-tails. Added to this, her body was covered with scabs and sores where the vermin had taken their sustenance.

The old woman gazed in wonder at the body lying on the straw. The girl's pearly-hued skin glowed faintly in the poor light and Polly hugged herself and crooned with pleasure at the sight of another human being.

Presently, she wobbled unsteadily to her feet and crept over to the still figure. Timidly, she put out a claw-like hand and stroked the soft skin; then taking courage, she nuzzled at the pale flesh; saliva dripping from cracked lips.

Meg slowly regained consciousness and opened her eyes. She could see nothing in the gloom, but quickly realised that she was not alone. A voice was mumbling close to her ear and there was something wet touching her body.

Gradually, her eyes became accustomed to the poor light and turning, she met Polly's awful countenance. Meg screamed in terror - scrambling away in the dirty straw.

"There, there, dearie, you've nothing to fear from old Polly," mouthed the hag. "I'll not let 'em hurt ye."

Meg felt desperately ill and could only lay panting, and staring at the crone.

"Thy young body's so nice and warm," continued Polly, "let me feel thee against me old bones."

She crawled up and pressed her skinny form to Meg's nakedness. The girl shuddered as she felt Polly's hands exploring her flesh.

"Ye've shapely breasts me cosset," whispered the hag as she cupped them in her hands. "Look at my old dugs. All dried up and useless, yet them suckled ten childer 'afore I was

194

thrown in 'ere to rot. Said I was a witch, they did, but they couldn't prove it." She gazed into space and cackled, shortly. "I envy them women who get turned off - a quick drop and it's finished."

Meg began to sob, convulsively. Her poor mother! After all, the plan had failed . . . she wanted to die. It wouldn't be too difficult, the way she was feeling. Why had she been put into this awful place? Her thoughts buzzed round and round in her head like angry bees, but Polly was wiping her eyes with a filthy rag. "There, sweet duck. I'll look after ye like me own. Mayhap you'll learn to love me like a mother. I've forgot 'ow long I've bin 'ere. Sick as a lepered sow, I've bin."

There were ashes in Meg's mouth. She lay like a trapped animal - tense and unmoving - her body, chilled and hurting. The other woman crooned over her bestowing sloppy kisses. "It won't be so bad, now thee's 'ere. We can clam together and keep warm at night." But Meg merely groaned and turned her face to the wall.

Presently, there was the sound of heavy footsteps outside and the door creaked open. Toby's huge bulk appeared, silhouetted against the spasmodic flame illuminating the stairs. He swayed slightly, then advanced, the phial of poison in his fist.

"What the devil's this?" he bellowed, thrusting it into Meg's face.

She flinched, visibly. "It's a physic for my chest," she stammered.

"Liar!" he snarled. "You brought it for the old witch. It's poison!"

"It's *not* poison!" screamed Meg, kneeling up in the straw.

"Then, drink it." The gaoler's bulk towered above her. "Drink it, I say!"

"Why should I?" Fingers of terror seized her bowels.

"Because you *know* it's poison and you're lying!" Toby was revelling in her discomforture and fear. His eyes were slits as he pulled her upright. But Polly hung on to Meg's legs; her mouth, a vacillating cavern.

"Leave 'er alone - piss-pot!" she screeched, clawing ineffectually at the intruder.

"Shut yer mouth ye old sow!" The gaoler kicked her in the stomach and she fell back, gasping and clutching at her scrawny body.

"You've killed her," cried Meg, struggling to break from Toby's iron hold.

"So much the better," he growled. "We've 'ad 'er long enough."

He turned and grasped Meg's face in a huge hand; pushing her back to the wall. "Now, are ye a-going to drink this, or must I force it down yer pretty throat?"

In vain, Meg tossed her head, while the gaoler pulled the cork from the phial with his teeth and spat it out. Then, despite her frantic efforts to keep her mouth closed, he forced the bottle brutally between her lips and pulling back her head, made sure that the liquid trickled into her mouth.

Meg held it there and even managed to spit some of it out, but Toby dropped the now empty phial and held her nose, and eventually she was compelled to swallow.

As she slid to the floor, he stood, as if rooted to the spot, "By the Rood . . . it *was* poison."

Not knowing what else to do, Toby threw Meg's limp body over his shoulder and carried it upstairs to Mistress Nokes'

196

cell.

"There's someone to see ye," he announced, sarcastically, as he tossed her inside.

Agnes, screamed, once, at what she saw, then gathered her daughter's body in her arms. "My poor, dear child," she cried. "My poor baby . . . not dead . . . no, not you . . ."

CHAPTER 11

The churchbells were giving throat for Evensong when Matthew Hopkins and John Stearne marched into the prison to see the convicted witches. Luke met them in the doorway, and immediately, Hopkins noticed the worried look on the gaoler's face. "What' amiss, Luke?" he asked with a smirk. "You're not your usual cheerful self."

"There's nothing wrong," Luke shuffled, uneasily.

"Well, we'll soon see." The witchfinder strode along the passage and down the rough steps followed by Stearne and the gaoler.

In the guard-room, Toby lay with his head on the trestle, snoring contentedly, empty bottles strewn at his feet.

"Wake that drunken cur up!" roared the witchfinder, slapping his cane on the table.

Luke shook the man's shoulder until he was answered with a string of oaths. "Get the hell out of it and let me alone." Toby belched loudly.

"It's the General," insisted Luke.

"G - G - General?" The gaoler peered through bleary eyes. It took him a while to realise that Hopkins did indeed stand before him. The shock partly sobered him and he tried to stand up, but failed miserably.

"Get on your feet, sot!" hissed Hopkins, ominously.

The lawyer's words acted as a douche of cold water and Toby sprang to attention, and stood, swaying.

"What's the meaning of being intoxicated while on duty?"

"I'm not int - int -, I'm not drunk," blustered the gaoler.

The General's gimlet eyes swept round the dismal room and alighted on the whip. He ordered Stearne to bring it to him. Traces of dried blood still adhered to the thongs. "Well, well, been flogging someone have we?" A muscle twitched in the witchfinder's cheek.

"N - no!" squeaked Toby, gnawing at a begrimed thumb and unable to take his eyes from his master's grim features.

"Liar!" Hopkins held out an immaculate gloved hand. "Give me the dungeon keys."

But Toby still stared - transfixed - as a rabbit, before yielding its breath to a stoat.

Luke cleared his throat then responded to the command and placed the keys in the outstretched palm. Hopkins wheeled round and flung out of the room, his cloak flying behind him. Stearne followed, pulling nervously at his blonde beard.

The witchfinder's nose twitched with repugnance as he inhaled the unwholesome air of the dungeon and he drew from his pocket a nosegay of rue and hyssop.

Mistress Nokes still sat on the straw, rocking her daughter's body in her arms. She seemed not to notice their presence.

"God's death! What's this?" Hopkins held the herbs to his nostrils and glared at his assistant. "See who that is."

Stearne lifted Meg's head and his face creased in disbelief.

"It's that wench the minister free'd - the one who was screaming her innocence in the Assembly Hall, that day."

"Her *daughter*?" cried Hopkins. "How in God's name does she come to be here?"

"She's dead, too, Matthew."

"Dead?" croaked the witchfinder. "What do you mean - *dead*?"

Stearne left the question unanswered and stood back. Hopkins reluctantly approached Mistress Nokes and between them, they managed to release Meg from that desperate embrace. The old woman merely moaned and cried softly - her pain-wracked eyes fixed on something beyond the walls of the cell.

Hopkins examined the body with an expert eye, then: "Not only is she dead, but she's been flogged and, methinks, most likely raped, too." His mouth tightened and he drew himself up. "Bring that gaoler, Luke, in here . . . *now!*"

"Right." Stearne hurried out.

Hopkins realised, only too well, that unless things could be explained satisfactorily to the Belford magistrates, an innocent person, being found dead, while his own men were on guard, could bring about his downfall.

His critics would rub their hands with glee at the thought of bringing him to his knees, and, no doubt, inform Westminster, too! The would-be reformers could even call a halt to witch-finding and arraigning - at least, as he, Matthew Hopkins, conducted it!

By the time Stearne returned with a whey-faced Luke, Hopkins was ready for him. Drawing his cloak tightly around him and looking not unlike a sleeping bat the wrong way up, he barked at the unfortunate man. "Well? What is the meaning of this?"

"By our Lady, I don't know, sir," stammered Luke, wishing he were miles away.

"You don't *know*, varlet?" Hopkins face flushed and his cane suddenly cracked across the man's legs. "Do you think I am mad? Who killed her?" he bellowed.

The gaoler gazed down at the stained floor and said nothing.

Hopkins' eyes were stones. "Tell me who did this, or I

will have your unwilling tongue torn out by its root."

The threat died on apparently deaf ears. The gaoler either could not or would not answer.

"Christ Jesu!" Hopkins found it extremely difficult to refrain from leaping at the gaoler's throat and throttling the information out of him. But Stearne intervened and jerked Luke's arm up behind his back; grinning at the howl of pain which greeted his effort. "I'll make him talk, Matthew."

The witchfinder renewed his interrogation through clenched teeth. "I am the one who says a victim has to die - not vermin like you, or that other. This girl has already been proved innocent and now I find her dead in this cell. Do you want to see me banished from England? Have you not one whit of respect for your superiors?"

Luke's bowels turned to water and beads of perspiration ran down his thin cheeks. He trembled for his own worthless skin, knowing the power that Hopkins could wield. Finally: "It wasn't me . . . Toby done it."

Hopkins scanned the man's features, his mind, racing. He would have to obtain the truth of the matter - and fast! The people of Belford accepted him as the Witchfinder General, and as such, feared him. But if they even suspected him of being linked with the death of a proven innocent . . ., his thoughts recoiled from the ghastly prospect.

Then he remembered the Rev. John Gaule! The priest would take great pleasure from seeing the townsfolk turn against him. Hopkins shivered suddenly as he realised how easily the mob had turned on Mary. Striding out of the cell, he barked, "Bring him back to the guard-room."

When they entered, Toby was drumming thick fingers, apprehensively, on the board. Hopkins pointed at him, "String

202

him up!" he ordered. Toby's mouth dropped and his eyes bulged. In no time at all he found himself tied to his own whipping-post.

Hopkins seized the whip and walked towards him. Grabbing the neck of the gaoler's threadbare shirt, he ripped it down to the waist. The gold coins, concealed in a pocket, fell out in a gleaming shower. "So, you have been accepting bribes, too," roared Hopkins. His knuckles showed white as he clenched the weapon, raised it, then brought it down across Toby's hirsute back.

The victim emitted an unearthly shriek but the lawyer did not relent. His mind was filled with the frightening possibilities caused by this man's indiscretions, and in Hopkins, fear begat a pitiless cruelty.

He became drunk with malevolence and sweated profusely as he brought the whip down again and again, until the gaoler's flesh was covered with rivulets of blood.

Luke shuddered as Toby's screams and moans filled the air. He had no especial liking for the man, but Luke was the more humane of the two, and in the depths of his soul, he disliked any form of violence. Weary, sick and frightened though he was, his manhood finally won.

"Stop it!" he yelled. "Have mercy! In the name of Christ - have done!"

His words had as much impact as a falling leaf on the earth. Their master was in a world of his own, where the fear which tore at his belly could only be assuaged by vindictive, ruthless savagery.

"Did *he* show mercy to that girl?" Hopkins arm ached with the effort of his punishment.

The gaoler fingered his beard, his face, pale and strained.

"He did no more than you have done." Luke heard his own voice in amazement.

The witchfinder's movements were suddenly arrested; the whip suspended in mid-air. Tiny droplets of blood spattered onto his hand, spoiling the cuff of white lace. He turned to the speaker. "I'll not take that from scum such as you," he snarled, and brought the thongs across the gaoler's face.

Luke threw up his hands to protect his eyes and hindered the second stroke from blinding him.

"Now - get back to your work - *dog!*"

The man reeled out of the room, and Stearne, who had watched the proceedings with a callous indifference, hawked and spat, after him.

Hopkins suddenly felt dizzy. His head throbbed and his breath rasped and rattled in his thin chest. Bile filled his mouth and he looked round for a convenient receptacle. The pail in which the gaolers urinated, was just recognizable in the darkest corner of the room and Hopkins walked over and emptied the contents of his mouth.

Stearne, grinned at the idea which spawned in his mind. He followed Hopkins to the pail, relieved himself, then picked it up and threw its contents over Toby's back. "That'll heal his wounds," he guffawed.

The man shrieked anew as the liquid trickled into the open flesh, but he was ignored.

Stearne tossed the pail aside. "What about the girl's body?" Hopkins, partially recovered, frowned. "Aye, we must be rid of it before it's discovered here." He wiped his brow with a cambric handkerchief. "Tonight, we will take it down to the river. They will think she drowned herself because her mother was taken."

Stearne leaned on the wall and folded his arms, arrogantly. "What, with no clothes on?"

Hopkins' head shot up. "Where *are* her clothes? She couldn't have come here naked."

Stearne strolled across to a solitary cupboard which hung on loose hinges, and brought out Meg's suit. "It looks like men's clobber," he said, giving the bundle to Hopkins.

"I see it all, now," mused the witchfinder. "She came here in disguise to deliver something."

Stearne cocked his head. "Poison?"

Hopkins threw him an angry glance. He hated Stearne to be even *one* step ahead of him, but he knew the man was right.

"Of course," he nodded. "Poison for her mother. Someone tried that trick once before and succeeded, but this time I'm not going to lose my fee. Which reminds me." He bent and picked up the fallen coins. "Not bad for a day's work, eh?" Hopkins smiled grimly, jingling them in his hand.

"Take the clothes and dress the girl. And while you are there, see if you can find the poison. Mayhap it will help in convicting the old woman."

When Stearne had departed, Hopkins sighed with weariness and sat down to await his return. Toby had lapsed into unconsciousness, but he moaned and muttered from time to time as the pain brought his mind to a passing awareness.

The witchfinder, cooling, was sick of the whole episode and desired nothing better than to be out of the dismal place. One of the cheap tallow dips suddenly flickered and went out, leaving the room darker than before. He was relieved when Stearne returned, carrying Meg's body, now fully clothed. He dumped it unceremoniously on the flagstones.

205

"There's nothing in the cell," he reported. "The old 'un's still alive, but only just."

"I'm not worried about the witch. I'll deal with her when the time comes." Hopkins pursed his lips. "At the moment, I want to find what the girl brought here. Are there any more cells?"

Stearne, bellowed into the passage for Luke, who shuffled in avoiding their eyes. He glanced uneasily at the figure hanging on the post. He would have to wait until they had gone before releasing him.

Hopkins read the man's thoughts and smiled grimly. "That will be *your* fate unless you answer all my questions correctly. Now, are there any more cells?"

Luke nodded, dumbly.

"Who occupies them?"

"Only old Polly. She's bin 'ere for years," muttered the gaoler. Then he remembered Toby telling him that he thought she had kicked the bucket! "She may be dead, now," he added, hastily. "She weren't too well, yesterday."

"*You* are paid to look after the prisoners in your care."

"I've bin a bit busy, lately, like," replied Luke, looking the picture of misery.

"I should say you have - busy with that girl!" Hopkins motioned him away. "Take me to the dungeon, at once!"

Luke led the way into the bowels of the prison, but as they approached Polly's cell, they found the door open and the cell empty!

"Well? Where's the prisoner? Is it customary to leave doors unlocked?"

Luke stiffened with fear. "She's . . ."

Hopkins silenced him with a raised hand. "I want no tales

about the Devil taking her. I know those fables. Now -
where is she?''

He stepped back and something crunched under his foot.
The witchfinder picked up the broken glass phial. ''You
were right, Stearne. It *was* poison. But what in the name of
Jesu is it doing here?'' He looked at Luke, but the gaoler
remained silent, biting his lip.

''Speak up, man!'' roared Hopkins, and Luke realised the
game was up.

''Toby locked the girl in 'ere.''

''Why?''

''To keep 'er fer later.''

''Then, why poison her? And where is the prisoner?'' The
lawyer coughed on his words and put the nosegay to his face.
The stale air of the dungeon, combined with the stench of
human faeces, was overpowering. ''Well?''

''I don't know,'' mumbled Luke.

''Well, stay here until we find out!''

Hopkins swept out while Stearne grabbed Luke by the jacket
and threw him, sprawling, onto the rotting straw. He locked
the door and grinned evilly through the grill. ''That should
cool your blood down a bit.'' He whistled as he returned to
the guard-room. Once there, he said, ''I've been thinking,
Matthew.''

''Is that possible?''

Stearne made to leave, a look of disgust on his round face.

But Hopkins caught his sleeve and indicated the chair. He
had to mollify the man - he was in a quandary - and he
needed him.

''What have you been thinking?'' The witchfinder's dispas-
sionate eyes met the anger in Stearne's.

207

"Do you really want to know?"

"Yes."

"Then shut up while I tell you."

Hopkins smirked behind his hand. "Carry on, John."

The unexpected mention of his christian name came as a shock to Stearne. Such familiarity was unlike Hopkins. He suddenly felt embarrassed and settled his large frame on the rickety chair - head lowered - hands clasped over his knees.

"Well, it's like this. I've been thinking that if this girl's sister took possession of the body, and if they really *are* witches, she would probably have it cremated on that hill and we could capture the rest of the coven, there." Stearne thrust his head forward - eyes gleaming, now.

Hopkins pulled at his beard, careful not to appear too interested in the idea, then, "You've got something there, but we don't know if they *are* all witches, yet. Do you see?"

Stearne splayed his hands. "If they be Christians, she'll be buried in the church-yard - and so much for that!"

Hopkins inclined his head. "Well, it's worth trying. We'll deliver the body to the farm, tonight, but we'll stick to the story that she drowned herself, because of her mother. See to it that she's sopping wet before we take her round."

Inwardly, Stearne glowed with pride - and at the door:

"Shall I free this turd?" he asked, indicating Toby with his thumb.

"Aye, but it will be a long time before he receives a gaoler's wage, again," replied Hopkins, peevishly.

Dusk was now fast approaching, and Bess, Robert and Arthur were still anxiously waiting for Meg to return. Robert sat with an arm round his wife, trying, without success, to comfort her.

"If only we knew what has happened to her," she cried. "She must have been caught. What think you on it, Arthur?" The old man's face, wrinkled with worry. "Aye, I'm afraid you are right, Bess."

"Let's not give up, yet," said Robert, clenching a great fist. "While there's life, there's hope, and bad news travels fast. She might be in hiding - waiting until it's dark."

A sudden tap on the window made them all jump. "Oh Lord, what was that?" Bess stared at the closed curtains. "A bird or a bat, perhaps?" suggested her husband.

The tap was repeated - this time, much louder, and Arthur rose to his feet.

"No, let me go," cried Bess, running over to the window. She peered out, then gasped and stepped back; her usually rosy cheeks, blanched with shock.

"What is it?" Robert sprang to her side. "I don't know, but it was horrible." She shuddered and went into his arms.

Arthur drew back the curtain. "I think it's an old woman. I wonder what she wants?"

"Tell her to go round to the back door," instructed Robert, "it's safer."

Arthur motioned to the figure and went into the kitchen where he opened the door. He gaped at the creature which stood in the pool of light, then quickly pulled her inside.

The others stared in disbelief at the hideous old hag who muttered and crooned incoherently; plucking at her tattered rags with filthy, claw-like fingers and blinking in the light of the oil lamp.

"In the God's name, what do you want?" cried Bess, clinging to her husband.

The old woman tried to speak and her eyes filled with tears.

"She looks spent," said Robert, "I'll fetch her a drink of ale."

When he returned, the crone grasped the tankard, greedily, and swallowed its contents in one gulp. Then she drew a skinny hand across her mouth, and spoke. "I'm Polly Weston," she croaked. "Arthur, 'ere, used to know me."

Arthur stared at her in astonishment. "Why, yes, it's true! But I thought you were dead, Polly."

She grinned, toothlessly. "Aye, they all thought that. Old Polly died in prison, eh? I might as well 'ave died for all the use I've been these last years. God knows, 'ow many."

Arthur, explained. "This is Polly Weston. She used to be the High Priestess of a coven near here. But when she was arrested, there was not sufficient evidence against her, so they could not execute her. Agnes knew her, but we all thought she had died in prison. It was long before Hopkins arrived in the county."

Polly said, "I cum 'ere, cos I knew Agnes Nokes. Is she 'ere?"

The others exchanged glances and Robert volunteered a reply. "No . . . we'll tell you about her, later, Polly."

The mother in Bess, manifested. She clucked sympathetically and drew the old woman to a chair by the fire. "Sit there, you poor thing and I'll fetch you some hot beef broth, eggs and porridge. There's honey cakes, too, in the larder. Then, when you've eaten, I'll wash you and attend to those horrid sores."

She bustled off while Polly stretched her poor limbs and soaked up the heat.

210

"I 'aint seen a fire for years. I must be a hardy old besum to outlive yon hell hole."

Robert brought a blanket and wrapped it round the thin shoulders.

"Bless you. I've not known human kindness since I was took."

"We'll have you in some decent clothes when you have eaten," said Robert, "but, can you tell us how you escaped?"

Just then, Bess entered with a laden tray. Polly's eyes boggled at the feast, and when Arthur had drawn up a small table in front of her, she attacked the food with appreciative grunts. The others looked on - smiling at one another.

Finally, she sat back - sated, and when prompted, related her story of how she had escaped from prison, when Toby took Meg out of her cell.

"So, my sister is dead," cried Bess, bowing her head in her apron.

"Yer sister - eh?" Polly stared into the flames.

The two men were unable to believe their ears, and the shock temporarily silenced them.

"Well," continued Polly, "the gaoler made the sweet duck drink the poison, right enough, but don't cry, lass. There may be hope, yet."

Bess raised a tear-stained face. "Please don't say such things. What hopes are there when she's dead?"

The crone wagged a bony finger at her. "I'm not in the mood to raise false hopes, lass. Just tell me what poison you used."

"I have no idea! It came from Mother's poison cupboard, but we used the last of the hemlock for Jane - so it could not have been *that*. I only know that it was in a bottle marked with a Pentagram and I remember Mother saying it was a very special poison.''

"Have you any of it left?" asked Polly.

"Oh yes, I think so. I only sent a small phial of it."

"Then, let me see it, at once."

Something suddenly revived in Polly, and they sensed the ghost of the woman she had been in the past. One who expected an order to be obeyed without argument.

Bess went to the dresser and opened the secret panel. From a number of bottles, she selected a small, blue one. Polly snatched it from her and held it under her nose. Then, putting a spot of the liquid onto her finger, she carefully tasted it.

"As I thought. Your mother is a very learned witch."

"What is it?" asked Robert.

"This is a very special bane, known only to the Elders of the Craft," mused Polly. "It paralyses the whole body very quickly, putting the victim into a trance-like state which gives every appearance of death. But, mayhap they can be revived by the use of a special antidote."

Robert drew up a chair and sat opposite to Polly - completely engrossed. "How long can a body remain in this trance, without harm?" he questioned.

There was a brief pause, then, "The antidote mun be administered within three days - otherwise, the victim will die, for sure."

"Do you know what the antidote is?" enquired Arthur.

Polly smiled, grimly. "Aye, but see, it would take far too long to gather the necessary herbs and plants to concoct it, as each ingredient mun be gathered according to ancient lore - and at the fortunate time." She squinted at their troubled faces. "But, see ye, Agnes had the potion, so she mun also have the antidote! Many a witch has escaped the gallows by its aid, and lived to tell the tale.''

Bess, her face flushed with excitement at this chance to save her sister, broke in. ''There are lots of different flasks and bottles in the cupboard, perhaps it's amongst them. Can you tell which it is?''

''Yer mother would certainly not have labelled it and it's a long time since *I* made it up, but bring 'em all to me, lass, and I'll see what I can do.''

''Are we not forgetting something?'' asked Arthur. ''Meg, herself, is not here.''

''Damnation!'' Robert's fist hit the table. ''I can't see how we can find her in time. For all we know they might have already buried her in the prison yard.'' He could have bitten off his tongue when he realised what he had said, and hastened to reassure them. ''Of course, even Hopkins dare not do *that*. He has seen Meg before and would know who she is.''

But Bess stood as if carved from stone. Her grey eyes, drowning. ''Oh poor Meg. She may have been buried alive! Oh, it's too horrible to think on.''

''Now, now!'' Again, the finger was wagged in the speaker's direction. ''Witches are no cry babbies! If ye blubber easy, yer no witch!''

Quite taken aback at being spoken to in such a fashion, Bess tossed her fiery tresses and departed to heat some water. Secretly, she knew Polly was right - a witch *must* be strong. She would show the beldam she had plenty of courage!

Bess helped Polly up the stairs and put her to bed in the secret room. She washed her and put salve on her sores. Polly sighed with bliss at the comforts afforded her and stroked the bed-clothes to see if they were real.

Bess left all the bottles with her and muttered a silent prayer for the correct one to be discovered. She kissed Polly on the forehead, then slowly returned downstairs.

Arthur had gone home, promising that discreet enquiries would be made at the prison. So Bess fetched a hot posset for Robert and herself. It would somewhat sooth their jagged nerves.

They discussed the recent happenings in subdued voices; huddling round the embers of the fire. How could they find Meg? Then, without warning, a loud knocking shattered the silence.

"Who the devil can that be at such an hour?" asked Robert, angrily.

"I'll go and see," whispered Bess. "You hide in the larder and listen." She waited a moment, then gathered her courage and unbolted the door. What she saw caused her heart to leap into her throat. Hopkins and Stearne stood on the threshold holding their hats in their hands - deferentially.

"Yes? What do you want?"

"I trust we did not frighten you by calling at such a late hour, but I'm afraid we are the bearers of bad news," Hopkins explained apologetically.

"Bad news?" Bess clutched at her throat. "Don't tell me that my mother has died?"

Hopkins held up a hand and replied, evenly, "Your mother is well, but I'm afraid your sister has taken her own life. We found her body in the river, not two hours ago.

"Drowned?" cried Bess.

"Aye, poor girl. The thought of her mother being a witch must have turned her brain." Hopkins sighed, extravagantly.

"Where is she now?"

"We have her body in the lane - on a cart. Er . . ." he hesitated, "Shall we bring her in?"

"Please do so at once!" said Bess.

The two men carried Meg carefully into the house and Bess lit a candle and led them upstairs, where they laid her on the bed. When Bess saw her sister's white face, she wept.

"Please accept our condolences," said Hopkins. "We will see ourselves out." He beckoned to Stearne and the two men departed, closing the front door quietly behind them.

"We shall soon know - one way or the other," muttered Stearne, as he took up the reins and headed back to Belford.

"Indeed, indeed," agreed the witchfinder.

Robert wondered what kind of trick they were cooking up. As soon as they had gone, he bolted the door and rushed up to the bedroom. "Fetch Polly," he said, "and let's hope she's found the antidote."

Bess dried her eyes and went to the secret room. Polly had fallen asleep, but two bottles stood on the chair at the side of the bed - the rest of them were on the floor. She shook the old woman, gently. "Wake up, Polly, we've got Meg." Bess could not rouse the sleeper so she shook her more vigorously. "Wake up, Polly, do!" There was no response - perhaps she had fainted? Bess peered at her closely and suddenly realised that no one would wake her again. Her terrible troubles were over at last.

"Oh, no!" wailed Bess, sinking to her knees and holding Polly's withered hand. Then, she remembered the witch's words and stood up. 'I must be strong, now,' she thought.

Robert, hearing Bess cry out, was soon at her side.

215

"Polly's dead," she said, quietly. "We cannot save Meg, now." He put his arm round her. "Now, dearest, we must not give up yet. We have so much to do, in so little time."

He examined Polly and confirmed that she had died. After being in prison for so long, the excitement of escaping had been too much for her.

"Let us thank the Gods that she died peacefully in her sleep - and in comfort," he said, as he covered her face with the sheet.

"But - the antidote? What can we do for Meg, now?"

"The Gods have brought her back to us - they will not allow her to die, yet."

"I wish I had *your* faith," whispered his wife.

Robert kissed her. "You have, my dear, but you have borne too much sorrow of late." His eyes rested on the two bottles.

"It looks as if Polly picked out these two, and either could not make up her mind between them, or fell into her last sleep before she was able to select the correct one."

"It makes no difference now," sighed Bess. "We can't decide on our own, and administering the wrong liquid would be fatal for Meg."

"Then we must invoke the Goddess and ask *Her* aid - come on!"

They ran downstairs and Bess placed the two bottles on the table, while Robert brought two candlesticks and two white candles, which he lit - putting a candle behind each of the flasks.

Bess produced her black-handled knife and drew a circle round the table, inscribing the Pentagram of Invocation at each of the Gates. Then, she spoke:

"I invoke Thee O' gentle Goddess - Lady of the Moon - to

216

come to our aid this night and reveal to us the flask which contains the antidote. So that our beloved sister, Meg, may live. If it be Thy will, we beseech Thee to grant this boon. So mote it be!"

They knelt in prayer, one at each end of the table, then Bess stood up and closing her eyes, asked her husband to pick up the flasks and hold one in each hand.

With the blade of her athame pointing across the table, she slowly intoned the secret names, which may be uttered, only, in times of direst need. The silence which followed was broken at last, by a sudden gust of wind which rattled the shutters.

Suddenly, the athame began to tremble. Whether it really moved or merely followed its owner's agitated fingers, they would never know, but it wavered, then pointed to the left. At the same moment, the candle on the left side of the table, fell from its holder; splattering wax on the polished wood.

Stopping only to close the Circle, they rushed to the bedroom, where Meg lay - the wet, shorn locks, clinging to the white forehead - lashes, dark, against the pallor of her skin. To all outward appearances, life was extinct.

Bess lifted Meg's head, while Robert carefully poured a little of the liquid into her mouth. Beads of perspiration stood on his brow as he administered the potion. Then, the two, held hands by the still figure, scarcely daring to breathe - the thudding of their hearts, loud, in their ears.

Nearly half an hour passed, and nothing happened.

"Oh, Robert," said Bess. "Do you think we have used the wrong bottle?"

"No, and I don't think *you* do, either."

"I don't know *what* to believe."

Her husband smiled. "I know it's difficult for you at present, sweetheart, but I still have faith in the Goddess."

"I have, too - you *know* that." She looked up at him, returning his smile.

Robert pressed his wife's small, but capable hand. "Aye. But mayhap she needs a larger dose."

"We can try."

So, again, Robert put the bottle between Meg's cold lips and allowed the liquid to drip into her mouth. Bess wrung her hands - she felt so impotent - but she *could* pray!

"Oh lovely Goddess, I beseech Thee - help us to give Meg the appropriate dosage."

Suddenly, the rush mat beneath Robert's feet, slipped, and he fell across the bed. But the bottle had left Meg's mouth! They looked at each other without speaking, then held hands and waited, concentrating on Meg's recovery.

In spite of themselves, they felt a despair borne of fatigue and began pacing the room. Bess opened the window and leaned out, inhaling the fresh night air, then:

"Come here, I saw her eyelids flutter." Robert grabbed his wife's hand and gripped it until she gasped with pain.

"Do you think . . .?"

"Shush!" The sapphire eyes were riveted on the white features. Again, they waited, then miraculously, Meg's eyes slowly opened and she sighed, deeply.

Bess fell to her knees. "O' thank you, thank you, beloved Goddess," she cried.

Meg, dazed, and still heavy with sleep, stared up at the raftered ceiling. Robert rubbed her slender hands and eventually, Meg turned her head - her vision slowly clearing - and saw her sister's anxious face. "Oh, Bess," she breathed, faintly.

Later that morning, Arthur called, and was delighted to
hear the news of Meg's return, and that although still very
weak, she was on the road to recovery. Polly's death, however, sobered him.
"She did not deserve *that* fate," he said. "She was a very
learned witch and saved many lives with her knowledge of
herbs." Bess squeezed his calloused hand. "For sure! She
saved Meg, too! May her soul dwell in bliss. But, there is
something I would like to show you - something I saw when I
was washing Polly."
She led him to the secret room, and uncovering the body,
pointed to a spot beneath the left breast. "See, that mark. Do
you know what it is?"
Arthur examined it closely. It was a small tattoo. The old
man whistled through his teeth. "Well, well - so she was *that*
important."
Bess chafed, impatiently. "But - you know what it is?"
"Yes, I do," murmured Arthur. "And as you are also a
member of the Craft, I think I may tell you. As I said, Polly
was a High Priestess of the Goddess, but this mark is only
given to those who are entrusted with the most important
secrets of the Craft. Not all witches have this knowledge,
even when they hold high rank." His eyes held a far-away
look. "No, not many are permitted to know them. They are
very well protected. My own mother had such a mark -
which is how I know on it. Our High Priestess also has the
knowledge." He scanned her face - deliberating.
"Oh, do go on, Arthur - tell me more," Bess entreated.
"Well, these are the marks that our persecutors call 'Devil

Marks', or 'Brands of Satan'. Hopkins and the other witch-finders are looking for this kind of thing, but it is only witches who are initiated into the Inner Mysteries, who have them. So, the witchfinders accept any kind of wart or blemish as the same thing.''

"Thank you for telling me, Arthur," said Bess. "I'm sure that you know I would never reveal anything you have said. But, I have something else to show you."

She led him into Meg's room, where her sister was in a deep sleep. Taking care not to disturb her, Bess lowered Meg's nightgown and indicated something under her left arm. "See, she's covered with weals and bruises, poor love, but look at that!"

It was a mark identical to the one on Polly's body, but whereas the former had been made with a needle and dye; the mark on Meg's side had been achieved with a sharp instrument.

"Now! What do you think of that?" asked Bess, her eyes, wide and questioning.

Arthur blinked. "Extraordinary! I'll tell you what I think, downstairs."

They found Robert had come in from the yard. Bess looked at Arthur, and he laughed. "I think I can trust your husband - I'll tell him about it."

Bess prepared a meal and when they had finished eating, Arthur wiped his mouth and took a swig from his tankard.

"Well now, as I have already told you, Polly was a High Priestess, but her arrest and imprisonment prevented her from passing on the secrets. However, when Meg was thrown into her cell, Polly, through her considerable psychic powers, recognised your sister as a member of the Craft. She may even have seen Meg when she was a little girl, because she knew

Agnes. Anyway, she managed to scratch the sign into Meg's skin - probably with her nails - thereby passing on her powers to Meg. It is unfortunate that she did not live long enough to instruct her. But, you know, there have been many cases of witches being unable to die until they have found the right person to inherit their knowledge. It has ever been thus at this level of the Craft, and it bodes well for future times. It seems the proper person is always found - even at the last!

Usually, it is a young person who is thus endowed - an old witch, teaching a budding one. In Polly's case, she must have thought that the heavens had opened when Meg appeared. And you will notice, she died soon afterwards!''

"But, Meg cannot be a High Priestess, yet," said Bess. "She would have to study and earn that degree - as our law states."

"I'm sure *that* can be remedied," replied Arthur, with a knowing wink. "All we have to do is to inform the present High Priestess, Lucina. She has been waiting for an opportunity like this. She is soon to be married and become the mistress of a manor in Cornwall."

Robert frowned. "Will Lucina be able to instruct Meg in these secrets?"

"Aye, I can vouch for that," grinned Arthur, "because it was Polly who taught Lucina!"

"How wonderful!" cried Bess. "It all seems to fit like the pieces of a puzzle."

"Just so!" Arthur lowered his voice. "It is a great honour for your family. And now she carries the mark, all witches - worthy of the name - will accept her as Queen of the Sabbat. If only Agnes knew . . ."

At the mention of her mother's name, Bess clasped her

brow. With Meg's terrible troubles she had hardly thought of her. How could she forget?

Robert took her hands in his own. "Listen, sweet. We have done everything possible to help your mother. No one could have done more. The Gods know that! But, it was not to be. Think on the old idea of Sacrifice. Perhaps it is fate that she should give her life - in order that the other witches might live?"

"That is so," said Arthur, sadly. "I don't see what we can do now. And we still have to thwart that demon, Hopkins. We are not out of the wood yet by any means. We have to dispose of Polly's body - and keep Meg safe, too."

Bess looked up quickly. "Surely, what Arthur has told us, means that Polly should have a proper Craft funeral?" "That is true," agreed Arthur. "Her body will have to be cremated on the sacred hill."

Bess stared. "How *can* we do that? We would never get away with it, again. Hopkins will be watching our every move. I'm sure he had an ulterior motive when he brought Meg home."

"Of course he had," laughed Robert. "That man's motives are as obvious as the nose on his face. He is still not sure if we are witches, so he is trying to find out. That is why he brought Meg home, believing she was dead. Now, if she were to have a Christian funeral, he may leave us alone. But, if we have a cremation at the Nine Maidens, he would follow us and arrest everyone who attended the Passing Rite."

"I'm sure you are right, dear," agreed Bess. "So, what can we do about it?"

Robert began to pace the room. "Meg must be buried - you know what I mean - in the churchyard, and Polly needs

222

be cremated on the hill. Now, do not forget that Hopkins thinks Meg is *dead* and also believes that Polly is *alive* and in hiding. Most likely, his men are searching for her at this very moment."

"I begin to see what you're getting at," grinned Arthur.

"What I'd give to see that rogue foiled again. It should not be too difficult to carry it off, either. As you know, the undertaker is a member of the Craft, although he does not attend many meetings. He will help us - that goes without saying. And there are others I can call upon to help us."

Bess beamed at him. "Oh Arthur, what would we do without you?"

Robert sat down and took a swig of his ale. "Now, this is the idea. We will have the coffin sent here, and anyone who wishes to see Meg laid out, may do so. If we set it up in the kitchen and keep the curtains closed, it should work out. Lighted candles, placed in the corners of the room, will throw shadows on her face. But she will have to keep perfectly still and hold her breath whenever someone approaches the coffin.

If one of us remains with Meg, we can give her a sign when a person comes into the room. We will have to take some risks, it is the only way. And, at the very last moment, Meg will escape and hide in the barn, while the undertaker puts a couple of sacks, filled with earth, in the coffin. We can hide them until they are needed.

Then, while Bess and I go to the funeral, Arthur and the others, can take Polly's body to the hill and give her the last rites." Robert grinned at his listeners' amazed countenances. "I think we can safely assume that Hopkins and his lackies will be spying on us, and, hopefully, they will follow us and leave the way clear for Arthur."

There was silence when he had finished speaking, then Bess said, frowning, "Suppose they watch the house? They will see Polly being taken away."

"Have no fear of that," Arthur reassured her. "We will not leave from here. I intend to collect the corpse tonight, and remove it by way of the orchard gate, to my barn." He congratulated Robert on his excellent plan and picked up his stick. "I better go now. There are a lot of arrangements to make and I must inform the others. It's a good thing that the undertaker and his assistants are on our side."

The day of the funeral arrived, and Meg had recovered sufficiently to play her part. Everything seemed to be going according to plan. The mourners duly arrived to view the body and Bess succeeded in detracting most of their attention from the 'corpse', by relating some of her sister's terrible trials to them.

During one of the lulls, when they were on their own, Robert rashly remarked that his wife's part in the plot - that of chattering to people - was not unlike her day to day behaviour, and resulted in him being on the receiving end of a wet dish-cloth!

But, apart from that small incident, things were going very smoothly, until he appeared while the baker's wife was paying her last respects, and whispered, "Steady! Hopkins and Stearne are coming up the path."

Bess smothered a gasp. "What are we to do?" she breathed. Robert waited until the woman had clucked her way, sympathetically, into the living-room, before answering. "We do nothing," he hissed. "Hopkins has more nerve than I thought, but don't panic now. Leave it to me. We may still pull it off."

He beckoned to the undertaker and told him to put the lid on the coffin, quickly. Then, adjusting his cravat, he opened the door and politely bowed the witchfinders in.

"We have come to pay our last respects to the poor girl," Hopkins said smoothly, doffing his hat. "May we have a look at her?"

Robert spread his hands, apologetically. "I'm afraid the undertaker has just screwed down the lid."

Hopkins' air of deference deserted him. He pushed Robert aside and marched into the kitchen, followed by Stearne.

"Open that at once!" he barked - rapping the coffin with his cane.

The undertaker stood, aghast, "But . . ."

"There are no 'buts'!" Hopkins grated, impatiently. "I said, open it up!"

Robert, a great, dark shadow in the doorway, nodded to the man, but his calm exterior belied the pounding of his heart. The lid was removed and the witchfinder peered inside and encountered Meg's serene features. Not quite knowing what he had expected to find - he stepped back - confused. "Yes, well, fasten it up." Hopkins' voice betrayed his annoyance. "Come on, Stearne."

They made for the front door, but before they reached it, Robert called out, "One moment!" There was something in his tone which made Hopkins hesitate, and he turned, his hand still on the latch.

"Friends," continued Robert, addressing everyone in the room. "This family is indeed honoured that the Witchfinder General has come in person to pay his last respects to our dear sister. Who, I might add, took her own life through her great

225

sorrow." He was beginning to enjoy himself. "Therefore, it is only right and proper that we should ask both Matthew Hopkins and John Stearne to act as pall-bearers."

"Aye, aye!" agreed the mourners, and brimming tankards were pushed into the newcomers' hands.

Hopkins was caught completely off guard, but Stearne's only emotion was a twinge of sadistic pleasure at seeing his master's embarrassment.

For a moment, the witchfinder, stood, gazing down at the mug of ale, which had appeared, as if by magic, in his hand. What to do? He could hardly refuse such a request in the presence of these townsfolk. "It will be a pleasure," he mumbled into the tankard - his thoughts, murderous.

Bess gritted her teeth into the semblance of a smile and offered the two men some sweetmeats. Stearne accepted, but Hopkins waved them away.

Robert allowed them a short time in which to drink their ale - making small talk with the mourners. It would also give the opportunity for the exchange to be made in the kitchen, but Hopkins must not be given too long, or he might become suspicious.

As soon as the visitors had finished their drinks, he intervened. "I think it is time we started. Will the four pall-bearers please come this way?"

The miller's son, and a friend of Robert's, together with the witchfinders, followed him into the kitchen. Robert smiled grimly to himself as he heard the cupboard door squeak on its hinges, behind him. Hopkins was looking for - he knew not what - while Stearne pulled back the curtains and glanced casually out of the window. They were not entirely convinced!

The four men lifted the coffin onto their shoulders and carried it out of the house and down the lane towards the churchyard. Bess and Robert, followed behind it and the rest of the mourners joined in the procession.

As they walked slowly along; two men, pushing a hand-cart full of newly-chopped wood, approached them from the opposite direction. They halted and doffed their hats.

"I can't understand this at all," hissed Hopkins. "It's all too above board. I have a feeling in my bones that they are hoodwinking us, but for the life of me, I just cannot see it."

"You're too suspicious," snapped Stearne, grunting under the weight of the coffin.

They turned right into Stubbins Lane, which led to the church, and folk came to the doors of their cottages to see them go by. Hopkins nearly fell when his foot found a dog's excrement and slithered from under him. Stearne managed to grab his sleeve, while the coffin wobbled precariously on its human trestle. The witchfinder mouthed an oath.

A little way beyond the cottages, a group of children were playing. Their piping voices pierced the hot, still afternoon, as they skipped in a circle: "Deal, Dover and Harwich - the Devil gave to his daughter in marriage. Deal, Dover . . ."

Their voices trailed away and they stood, staring wide-eyed at the solemn crocodile.

A red-haired youth flung a small stone which caught Hopkins on the ear. "God's blood!" he cursed under his breath, but he was forced to continue the journey.

The funeral service proceeded in the usual manner and the mourners stood by the yawning grave as the coffin was lowered into it. "Ashes to ashes - dust to dust," droned the minister as he flung a handful of soil onto the descending

227

casket.

The grave-diggers approached with their shovels, and the people slowly drifted away. Robert and Bess thanked the General and Stearne for all they had done and followed the mourners out of the churchyard. Hopkins and his assistant remained behind, the former, holding a bloody handkerchief to his ear. They watched until the earth had been returned and flattened into a smooth mound, before striding off in the direction of Belford.

"She must have been a Christian, after all," mused Stearne.

"Aye, and we can't arrest any more of that family now. Too many of the locals attended this funeral to believe they are witches. No one would ever stand witness against them. And *we* acted as pall-bearers, too!" growled the witchfinder.

Stearne suddenly halted and pointed across the fields. A great cloud of smoke was rising from the distant tor. "A fire *that* size needs a good deal of wood."

"God's death!" cried Hopkins. "That cart - the one which passed us in the lane! They must have taken the body up there. But, how?"

Stearne took off his hat and scratched his head. "Then whose funeral have we been attending?"

"Jesu knows!" Hopkins' eyes narrowed to slits as he watched the distant smoke. "These damned witches are too clever by half." He turned on his heel. "I'll be happier when the business here is finished, then it's Aldeburgh for us. Mayhap there will be easier pickings there."

Stearne shrugged, then hawked and spat into the hedgerow, but he seemed unable to take his eyes from that great plume of dark-grey smoke, which ribboned upwards to greet the blue vault of heaven.

CHAPTER 12

The Nokes' family were jubilant over the success of their plans, but although the witches knew that Meg still lived; many of their friends, including the people of Belford, believed otherwise, and this was not the right time to tell them the truth of the matter.

It was decided that Meg should go to Greycoats, Robert's farm. It lay four miles north of the forest, so she could remain there in comparative safety.

Robert had been thinking that it might be a good idea to take Bess and live there for good. So many unhappy memories lingered at Elm-tree farm for all of them. Although these were recent happenings, they were so dreadful, that living there in the future could prove well nigh impossible. Better to start afresh. He did not inform Bess or Meg of his plans. There was still the matter of Mistress Nokes to live through - time enough, later.

Under cover of night, Arthur took Meg to see Lucina and left her in Lucina's care for seven days. Wentworth Towers was ten miles away, but his best horses delivered them, safely. It would be many months before her training was complete, and, as Lucina remarked, Meg must be elevated to the rank of High Priestess *before* she was entrusted with the Inner Secrets of the Craft. So, the High Priest was summoned to officiate.

On her return, Meg was jubilant and full of stories about the grand life-style at the Towers. She said she had been asked to return in two moons, for another week.

Now that she had achieved the status of High Priestess, Meg could call a meeting whenever she wished, and began to talk of holding one in the near future.

"But, dear," exclaimed Bess, "you are going to Greycoats tonight, and it's too dangerous to hold a meeting here - I'm sorry, but I cannot allow it."

"Why not hold it at Greycoats, then?" asked Robert. "That would be safe enough."

"Oh, what a good idea," beamed Meg. "You really are a clever old brother-in-law."

"What is the reason for this meeting?" enquired Bess, her arms in a bowl of flour and her face, red, from exertion.

Meg sat down at the kitchen table and looked earnestly at the speaker. "I want to invoke the Goddess for a very special reason . . . it's for Mother, Bess."

Her sister's hands, stilled, in the bowl, and a look of anguish crossed her features. "Oh, what a clod-poll I am! What is she going through all this time? I can hardly bear it when I think on her. How I wish I could take her place."

Robert put his arm round her shoulders. "Now, now, dearest, we have done what we can - and look what our Meg suffered, we nearly lost her. Surely, we can do no more?"

"But, Mother thinks that Meg is dead! Arthur overheard the gaolers talking in an ale-house. Apparently, after Meg had swallowed the poison, she was carried into Mother's cell! Can we not find a way of telling her?"

"What? And risk Hopkins finding out? He thinks Meg is dead - after all, he attended her Christian funeral!"

Meg said, "I wonder if he saw the funeral pyre on the hill? What a lot of awful things have happened to us - and are still happening! I wish I had been more friendly to poor Polly in that dreadful place. No wonder she looked so terrible after all that time."

Robert nodded and walked to the door. "Yes, we must never forget how lucky we have been to escape from Hopkins' clutches, and it's not over yet. Anyway, we'll be off tonight, young Meg." He winked at her as he went out.

That evening saw Meg safely installed at Greycoats, in the care of Robert's aunt, Sophie, and Robert promised her that he would pass word to the Summoner of the coven, who would inform the 'Pentacle' of her desire to hold a meeting. The 'Pentacle' consisted of the five most senior members of the group, whose duty it was, in times of danger, to consider the wisdom of the High Priestess's desires - whatever they happened to be. Not all the members would be present, but enough for her needs.

The Moon was waning to a thin crescent - the sign of the Crone, when the witches gathered at Hangman's Lane, beyond the forest. The West wind held a hint of rain and carried the trace of Autumn, as they greeted one another. Their horses hoofs were swathed in sacking and made little noise as they rode swiftly for the farm.

Once safely inside, they all made much of Meg and congratulated her upon her new, exalted position.

"Polly did well in her choice," said one of the women. "Meg is not only young and beautiful, but also very brave."

"Aye!" exclaimed Diccon, a young lawyer from Belford. "It's a good thing we have her to take Lucina's place. The Gods move in mysterious yet providential ways."

"May I ask what name you have chosen to be known by, in the Circle?" asked Joan.

Meg blushed. "Of course you may. My magical name is to

231

be Amaryllis." Her eyes suddenly filled with tears and she turned away. "I have prepared some mulled wine to refresh you after your journey."

Lucina had suggested many suitable names to Meg, and 'Amaryllis' arrested Meg's attention, because as well as being a name of the Goddess, it also contained within it, the name, 'Mary'! Assuming this, for her magical name, Mary would always be a part of her, and thus, would be represented in the Circle!

After her terrible experiences, Meg was still far from a full recovery, both in mind and body. And at the moment, her thoughts were centred upon her mother and the suffering *she* was enduring.

When all held a brimming goblet, Robert proposed a toast: "To Meg! May the Gods guide her and help her to rule the coven, wisely and well!"

They all shouted, "So mote it be!" Much to Meg's embarrassment.

Presently, Meg said, "It's time we prepared ourselves," and led them away to disrobe. She explained that Aunt Sophie was a sympathiser and had retired early to bed upon hearing about the proposed meeting.

Soon, the witches were sky-clad and standing in the large parlour where a white, chalk circle had been inscribed on the floor. Lighted beeswax candles stood in brass holders at the four quarters of the compass, and just outside the circle. In the centre, a small carved altar faced the North. Upon its surface rested the tools of the Craft, together with another lighted candle, a dish of water, a pot of salt, and some incense, already alight and burning in a chafing dish.

Meg entered the room, last, wearing a black robe and car-

232

rying her athame. She stepped across the barrier and slowly traced the circumference of the ring with her ritual knife.

Moving to the altar, she blessed the salt and the water and blended them. After purifying the Circle with the now consecrated liquid, she welcomed each witch into the sacred enclosure until all were 'Between the Worlds'.

After re-drawing the Circle, Meg called up the Mighty Ones of the Four Elements in the same manner as Lucina had invoked them in the sacred grove. Although this was the first time she had performed the ritual, herself, Meg felt she had executed it many times, before. This inner certainty links with far memory, which in turn, suggests reincarnation, and the recollection, however dim, of a previous life. In Meg's case, one in which she had known the Craft.

She knelt at the altar and remained there in silent prayer for some time. Then rising, she allowed the robe to slip from her shoulders. The others gasped in horror when they saw the white skin covered with scars and bruises. On this night, however, inspired and guided by the Goddess whom she represented, Meg radiated power and confidence.

When all the witches had given the oath of allegiance to their new High Priestess, and had undergone purification at her hands, Meg, spoke to them:

"Brothers and Sisters of the Art, I have called this meeting for a very special reason. I have learned that as soon as the imprisoned women are condemned and put to death, Matthew Hopkins and his men will leave Belford and seek victims, elsewhere. For this, we should rejoice, but we must weep for those who are about to die, because, once convicted of witchcraft - few escape the gallows.

We also know that there is only one true witch amongst

these women, and that is Agnes, my mother. The others are not members of the Craft and know nothing of the arts magical, yet they too will suffer death, simply because someone has denounced them as witches. Like Mother, they have most probably never hurt a living soul in their entire lives. We live in an age of superstition and cruelty, and these women will die, merely to line Hopkins' pockets with silver. Mother, on the other hand, is of the Old Religion, and will die rather than repudiate her beliefs, although to do such a thing would avail her nothing.

We are not evil, yet the Christian Church states we have dealings with the Devil! An entity whom *they* invented! They abhor the female and have brought us to a pretty pass. One has only to read what the saints had to say about women to know how much we are loathed by such men. They fear that the Old Religion may regain a hold on the people's imagination, and if that ever happened, the Church would lose its authority and also the wealth it has come to regard as its due.

They say that magic is against the will of God, yet we know that many churchmen practise it. And what of the magic the witches performed to turn back the Spanish Armada? Did not our ancestors raise great storms which scattered the enemy's ships? The Christians would have called it a miracle! So it is at times of great peril in these islands. Powerful forces are invoked and the magic is wrought!

Today, money is the goal and most men prefer wealth to spiritual advancement. The Gods of the West are frowned upon by those who have accepted the new religion from the East, but we know our land is guarded and watched over by the Great Mother - it is the *Mother* Country! I believe that in the distant future, people will return to the worship of the

Goddess and the Green Man."

She paused. "Now, as you realise, we tried to save Mother from undue agony, and we failed - or at least - *I* failed. But I paid dearly, as the scars on my body show. So, tonight, we must work our magic to give Mother strength to bear the torture and help her to face death, bravely - as a witch should. Let us pray to the Gods."

The witches knelt and Meg faced the altar and raised her arms. "Hear us O' Ancient Ones - be present in the Circle this night. Take our power and grant our wishes to aid Thy child - my mother - Agnes Nokes, in her darkest hour."

Slowly, they began to tread the Mill with Meg leading them in the ancient Dance. Gradually, the pace quickened until they were flying round the Circle, the rhythm of a chant lending them a power of its own.

Now, they were as one, turning with the seasons; a miniature cosmos - a world in its own right.

Then, imperceptibly, the chanting changed to a simple statement in rhyme, expressing the reason for the Rite and bringing it into conscious form:
"Agnes will be strong and true,
To face the torture she'll go through."

After a while, the words seemed to say themselves and became a meaningless stream - an absurd amphigory - but the witches still intoned the chant and the momentum of the spinning 'wheel' never faltered.

It was Meg, herself, who brought it to a halt, by collapsing onto the floor. Robert knelt over her and his deep voice resembled the rumble of distant thunder. "Speak! Tell us what you see."

The High Priestess, deep in trance, spoke slowly, in a voice

235

unlike her own. "Agnes Nokes will suffer unspeakable torture at the hands of the witchfinders, but she will endure all in silence and will not betray any other witches. She will happily depart this earthly life, knowing we are waiting to receive her in the Summerlands. Do not weep for her. She will be far better off than any of you who must remain in this unhappy world. Hopkins may be all powerful, now, but the end of his 'reign' is fast approaching.

Although it will not happen in *your* life-time, the day will dawn when souls will be able to freely worship the Gods of their choice. Perhaps, in those far-off days, you may have achieved rebirth in a new body, and thus lead the people back to the Old Religion. Blessed Be!"

They echoed, "Blessed Be! Thank Hu for coming to us."

It was some little time before Meg recovered, but when they related the message, she said, "That must have been the Goddess speaking, through the vehicle of my body. Now, I am certain that Mother will be aided in her hour of need."

Diccon, the scribe of the coven, had copied the message in its entirety, but such was their training, that some of the witches, although unable to read or write, had memorised the communication.

After partaking of wine from the communal horned Cup, the coven performed more magic to help the other women who would be condemned with Agnes.

The work completed, Meg offered up a prayer of thanks and everyone sat down, tired, but contented. The buzz of conversation which normally attended this part of a meeting, was lacking that night, yet they felt that the coven was more closely knit than ever before. Sometimes, words are unnecessary.

236

When the Cup had circulated and been refilled several times in the process, Meg gave the signs of dismissal and closed the Circle. Kisses and loving embraces followed, and some people exchanged plans and made arrangements to meet on social occasions.

They all complimented Meg on the way she had conducted the meeting, and Arthur took her aside. "You did well," he smiled. "You are no longer our little Meg, you are a responsible and articulate woman and it will be a great honour for me to serve you."

She planted a kiss on the brown cheek. "You have always been a dear friend to our family, Arthur, and I know I can depend upon your wisdom in the future."

The coven dressed and all signs of a meeting were swiftly removed. After some food and a rest, Joan volunteered to make sure the coast was clear, and taking their farewells of Meg, they were soon a-horse and galloping home in the darkness.

That same night, Hopkins and his assistants were busily occupied in attempting to extract confessions from the accused women and finally staggered back to their lodgings in the pale light of dawn, for a few hours sleep.

The day was well advanced when they returned to the gaol, accompanied by Goody Phillips, whom they had had to prise away from her customary seat in the Black Swan - swearing and hiccoughing.

They walked straight into Mistress Nokes' cell and without a word, dragged her into the guard-room. Stearne tied her hands behind her back and tightened the rope until it cut into her flesh. Grunting, he pushed her down onto a chair, while Hopkins leaned against the trestle table, his hands gripping the rough wood.

"Now, woman!" he shouted. "Confess you have had dealings with the Devil."

"I know no one of that name," sighed the old lady, her face puckering with pain.

"Liar! Does he not come to you in the shape of a black cat? Does he not sleep in your bed? Does he not copulate with you?" He spat out the words.

Mistress Nokes was suddenly filled with vigour and gritted her teeth in anger. "No, he does not!" she screamed, stamping her bare foot on the floor.

Goody Phillips ambled forward, rolling up her sleeves, but Hopkins stayed her with an imperious hand. "Is not his member, cold?" he asked. "Other witches have confessed as much."

His victim fixed him with a baleful glance. "I know nothing of other witches."

"Lying sow," growled Stearne. "Let me at her - she'll talk, I'll warrant."

But Hopkins ignored him. "Now, see you, mistress, let us talk sense. Did not the boy, Joseph, perceive you at the Devil's Sabbath?" He examined his finger-nails.

Agnes shouted, "No! No! No! They are all filthy lies."

Goody Phillips chuckled and scratched herself. "Yon's as tetchy as two sticks."

"Silence!" The witchfinder never took his eyes from the old lady's face, but she met his gaze with an equal intensity.

"Filthy lies, is it?" he snarled. "By the faith, I swear, not half so filthy as the way you act with those imps of Hell."

Mistress Nokes straightened her back, as best she could,

and her voice was ice. "Matthew Hopkins! You are a depraved, lecherous villain. Your mind and body are dedicated more to evil than any of your victims could ever be. You are a vile, wicked creature!"

Hopkins froze. He could hardly believe his ears. Could such a stream of condemnation really have issued from the old hag's mouth?

What sounded suspiciously like a snigger made him spin round, and Stearne coughed and cleared his throat. Christ's blood! Was he to be spoken to, thus, in front of his own servants?

He swung back to the seated woman. "I'll not take that kind of talk from a slut like you," he roared, and the next moment had delivered a blow across her cheek with the back of his hand.

Agnes cried out, but returned the attack by spitting on the floor. "Only a dirty coward would strike a defenceless woman," she yelled.

Hopkins brought his face close to hers. "By the Holy Writ you will hang, mistress," he hissed, his features working with emotion. "But not before you know agony as a close friend." He flung away, "Walk her!" he barked, and left the room.

Stearne and Phillips took two-hour turns to keep Mistress Nokes on her feet. The more tired she became, the faster they made her walk, until she tottered and reeled, round and round in that confined space.

When she dropped with fatigue; her breath wheezing in her throat and the sweat running down her haggard face, they dragged her back to the cell and brought her salted herrings and a mug of brine.

Again and again, they walked her, and when her head nodded, they slapped her awake. But as a distant clock chimed the strokes of midnight, the will of Agnes Nokes remained unbroken, even to the hour of noon, on the next day!

Stearne told Hopkins of her reticence outside the prison. "The old sow's not talked yet, Matthew. I'll swear she's the Devil's own."

"Bring her to the guard-room." Hopkins knew that the magistrate would believe Joseph, yet he was a mere child. It would be much easier if the woman confessed. It would show the people that he did not have to rely upon the words of children in order to obtain a verdict of 'guilty'.

By the time he reached the dismal room he was seething with rage. Agnes was propped up in the chair; her face, bruised and swollen - her lips, blue. She seemed not to recognise him at first, as her eyes would not focus properly. Then his figure became clearer and she gripped the arms of the chair, gathering her courage.

"Now, you child of Satan! You dumb bitch! Confess your sins of witchery - reveal your accomplices!"

"I know of no one," came the now weak voice.

Hopkins swallowed hard and gripped his cane. "See, mistress," his tone was smooth and belied the glitter in his eyes. "If you be wise enough to inform me of your fellow fiends, I will allow you some vitals. Hot broth and stewed giblets with perhaps a mug of beer to wash them down."

Agnes turned her face away, and now, the witchfinder's small control on his temper, evaporated.

"You filthy whore! You Devil's wanton! Speak and confess in God's name! Tell me the names of your associates, or by the Holy Rood . . ." He paused - his chest heaving.

"I have told you. There is no one."

240

"This she-wolf is making a complete fool of me," he yelled. "Tie her up!"

Stearne, and a new gaoler, a callow youth who answered to the name of Gill, dragged Agnes to the whipping-post and fastened her arms above her head.

"Fetch me some sulphur and be quick about it."

Gill ran from the room and returned with a tin box. Hopkins tore the dress from her shoulders while Stearne obliged by lighting the substance from one of the tallow dips.

At a nod from his master, he applied the burning sulphur to the victim's armpits and was rewarded by a shriek of agony. Tears streamed down her contorted features but she said nothing.

The witchfinder's rage invoked a stutter. "W - w - will you confess?" he roared.

Agnes moaned, but shook her head.

"I'll break you if it's the last thing I do," he screamed - his face, scarlet.

The whip materialised in John Stearne's hands. He grinned at Hopkins, who uttered a guttural cry, grabbed it, and belaboured Agnes across her back. Again and again, he struck, her shrieks filling the small room, but she still refused to speak and in a short time lost consciousness.

"You've killed her," shouted Stearne.

Gill went over to the limp figure, then halted and blushed up to the roots of his red hair. He had not come into contact with a naked female before - his innate shyness had always prohibited any contact with the opposite sex.

"Out of my way, clod," Hopkins flung the whip down and quickly examined Mistress Nokes. Then, "She's not dead - she's merely fainted." Relief flooded through him. He knew

241

only too well, the methods of torture that were permitted by law, in order to extract confessions, but flogging was not one of them. His belly writhed. He would have to be more careful of his temper in the future, but he could not understand the woman's obstinate silence. How could she remain so obdurate after all her suffering? He cast his mind back - yes, there had been one other like her - that beldam at Chelmsford, Elizabeth Clarke! But even *she* had confessed before the end. He realised that the men were watching him curiously, and pulled his thoughts back to the present.

"This must be witchcraft," he said, shortly. "The others bared their souls easily enough. The Devil must indeed have her's." He turned to Stearne, "Take her back to the cell and see to it that she recovers. Put some balm on her back and give her something to eat - beef broth and bread." They were still staring at him. "Well, get on with it! What do I pay you for?"

At last, they moved towards the pathetic tortured frame, and Hopkins turned on his heel. "She'll appear in court tomorrow. I hope the judge can loosen her tongue." He marched out and banged the door behind him.

The next day, Agnes was conscious but too weak to stand. She had to be carried to the hearing. The court-house was packed with spectators and the boy, Joseph, appeared as witness for the Commonwealth. He repeated his story about the black cat that changed into the Devil, and how Mistress Nokes had bewitched him and made him vomit pins and needles. He described the Sabbath in the forest and the demons which attended it. Then his parents came forward and vouched for the truth of their son's evidence. It was obvious that Hopkins had paid them well.

The magistrate, Sir Peter Seaton, had presided over several trials of witches. He was in his forties and a devout Protestant. His studies had led him to read, and wholly commend, the *Malleous Mallificarum,* or as it became known, *Hammer of the Witches.*

His was a male world in which women rarely entered, and after one or two homosexual encounters, he had settled down in a smart country house outside Belford, with his faithful retainer and servant.

His newly acquired position as Magistrate, satisfied his sadistic tendencies - he enjoyed every minute of the trials, especially the often horrific evidence. During the first few months of his appointment he had sent many women to the gallows.

Agnes was the first of the accused to stand before him, or rather she was held in an upright position by two officers of the court. Sir Peter pointed at her with his quill pen. "So, this woman has been accused of witchcraft. I will not tolerate these daughters of Satan in my province. The evidence against her is very strong. Has she confessed?"

Hopkins stepped forward and bowed to the bench. "She will confess nothing, your honour. She still persists that she is innocent." He raised his arms in a gesture of resignation.

"I *am* innocent," declared Agnes.

There was excited murmurings from the court.

"Silence!" roared Seaton. "*That* is for *me* to decide." He turned to Hopkins and raised his eyebrows. "Have you tried persuasion?"

"Indeed," replied the witchfinder, "but it is useless. Her master, the Devil, has sealed her lips."

"Then we must unseal them - eh?" leered Seaton. "I under-

243

stand, General, that you have an excellent method of discovering 'witch-marks' by pricking - what?''

Hopkins had refrained from this kind of examination since the Reverend John Gaule had exposed him. But, recently, Goody Phillips had obtained a new kind of pin. This was a bodkin with a wooden handle. It was impossible to turn it and use the blunt end, as Mary Summerset had done with the older one. This new instrument *appeared* to be genuine, to those who were not 'in the know'. Yet, the bodkin *was* a fake. By touching a concealed spring, the pin could be drawn up into the handle, but give the illusion that it had indeed entered the flesh of the victim. After a careful examination of this new implement, Hopkins had decided he could begin 'pricking', again.

At the magistrate's words, the General found it difficult to conceal his delight. What an opportunity for re-introducing the method! He informed the bench that this mode of discovering witches was infallible and handed Seaton the bodkin for him to examine.

The man held it in his hands and surveyed it closely. ''A splendid tool,'' he opined, smiling, as he gave it back. ''Have this woman searched for witch-marks at once!''

Hopkins passed the bodkin to Phillips and told her to carry out the order. Goody shuffled over to Agnes; lifted her stained skirts and pushed the pin beneath them. After fumbling and stabbing for several minutes she turned to her master and shook her head.

''See you,'' called Hopkins, ''the woman feels no pain - forsooth she *is* a witch.'' He appealed to the whole court which burst into a hum of animated whisperings. Only one, weatherbeaten face, stared impassively ahead. Arthur leaned heavily on his stick.

Sir Peter's gavel rapped, and he eyed Goody Phillips with disdain. "You are too modest. I always thought it was the custom to strip the victims *before* they were pricked."

"Well . . ." Phillips looked at Hopkins for help.

"There are no 'wells'," Seaton tittered behind a raised hand at his own joke. "I prefer to have it done properly." He gazed round the court-room. "I must see things with my own eyes, do you see?"

The magistrate leaned back in his chair and watched with avid interest while Phillips and Stearne undressed Agnes until she stood naked before the court. Even Hopkins thought this was going a bit too far, but was obliged to remain silent.

Seaton, a voyeur, passed a tongue over fleshy lips as he eyed Agnes up and down. "*Now* prick her," he said.

Agnes cried out when Stearne pushed her to the floor. He held her while Goody stabbed at various parts of her body, and every time the pin entered, it was answered with a scream. Arthur could bear his friend's torment no longer and shouted, "She feels the pain! That woman is no witch!"

Seaton leaned forward and glared angrily in the direction of the voice. "Throw that hooligan out," he yelled.

There was a scuffle, and Arthur, who had dared to express his opinion, was thrown out of the court-room.

The pricking continued and the magistrate watched the proceedings intently, making occasional smacking noises with his lips. Then he pointed a fat finger. "Should you not try lower down? I have heard that the Devil is a very cunning fellow and often marks his followers in their privy parts."

Goody Phillips, panting from the exertion of her efforts, duly rammed the bodkin home in the victim's navel and was

245

rewarded with a scream.

Seaton nodded his approval, "Maybe a little lower?" he suggested, and leaned forward, his burning eyes revealing prurient thoughts.

Goody suddenly tired of pandering to the depraved tastes of 'his lordship' and decided he had had enough entertainment for one day. Pressing the hidden spring, she stabbed once more at the tortured flesh.

The magistrate *believed* that he saw the bodkin enter the victim's body, but this time no sound issued from her lips.

"I was right!" he exclaimed, triumphantly, striking the bench with his fist. "That spot is insensible to pain. The woman *is* a witch!"

Then, his appetite alerted for more of the same entertainment, he delivered a verdict of 'Guilty' and gave orders for Agnes to be taken back to the prison and hanged, publicly, the next day.

CHAPTER 13

The following morning, the sky was overcast with a hint of thunder in the air. Workmen were busy constructing the gallows in the Market Square and tradesmen from all parts of Belford, and beyond, were setting up their stalls. Hangings were always good for business.

Men were positioning empty carts for folk who would pay sixpence to obtain a better view, and a row of chairs was placed in front of the gallows, for the magistracy, the gentry, and their wives. Wide-eyed children watched the proceedings silently, then lost interest and returned to their games.

It was to be Matthew Hopkins' 'farewell' performance and the whole town was expected to be present to give him a good send-off. The majority of people were very relieved that he was going. The fear of being accused of witchcraft was stronger than the fear of witchcraft, itself. After all, a person knew not when *their* turn to be suspected might be at hand. It was a dangerous and frightening time. Yes, the town would be a great deal happier when the witchfinders had gone.

People were slowly trickling into the square and a church bell tolled eleven. It was now only one hour from the time of the executions. Clouds were banking up in the west and there was a rumble of distant thunder as traders began to call their wares.

"Fresh fish! Come and buy . . . fresh fish!"

"Sweet-bread, lovely sweet-bread. Come and try me sugared apples!"

"Here's yer best lace . . . buy a ribbon for yer sweetheart!"

The inns around the square were full, and one landlord had

set some bever-barrels on a trestle outside, to catch more customers.

The humid air held an atmosphere of suppressed excitement. Folk called to one another and there were shrieks of laughter as a puppet show started its performance in a nearby alley. No one gave a thought to the condemned women - witches were for hanging!

The square was rapidly filling with a jostling throng, all determined to secure the best vantage positions. Pedlars passed among the crowd selling pamphlets which described the foul deeds of the witches. Deeds, that some hack writer had visualised in his imagination. The more blood-curdling they were, the better they would sell. "Read all about it for a penny! The stories of the Daughters of Hell!"

Piemen and fruit girls were doing a roaring trade and householders, whose premises overlooked the scene, bartered with the wealthier folk who wanted comfortable seats away from the stench of the masses.

A drum beat in the distance heralded the approach of the militiamen and the swaying wedge of people, broke, as they entered the square. They marched in two lines of twelve and took up their positions round the gallows.

Robert, Bess, Meg and Arthur, pushed their way through the crowd. They wanted to be as near to the gallows as possible, and finally obtained a vantage point just behind the row of chairs.

The officer of the guard moved pompously among the throng. "Make way! Make way, there!" he shouted as he ushered the gentry to their seats.

Bess, white-faced, asked, "Have we no chance of rescuing Mother?"

248

"Not the slightest," replied Robert, shortly. "And please keep your voices down. This mob would tear us limb from limb if we attempted anything. You know how they enjoy hangings."

"Inhuman beasts!" hissed Meg.

Bess pointed to the upper room of one of the houses. "Look over there." A boy was climbing up onto the edge of a balcony and finally stood, swaying, on the top.

"It's that villain, Joseph," cried Meg. "I should have thought his parents would have had the decency to keep him away - after all *he's* done."

"He does not intend to miss any of it, either," growled Arthur. "He wants a bird's eye view."

"I wish he would fall," gritted Meg. "It would serve him right!"

As if in answer to her wish, Joseph's parents came out onto the balcony and their son turned to look at them. That was his undoing. His foot slipped, and, unable to keep his balance, he tumbled, screaming, into the street below.

"God!" cried a woman. "He's fell on them spikes!"

People moved in the direction of the accident and obliterated their view, but eventually, they saw Joseph being lifted over the heads of the crowd and carried back into the house.

"He'll be dead right enough," said a man behind them. "Those spiked railings went right through him."

The Nokes family said nothing, but each of them knew what the others were thinking. If what the man said was true, the boy had paid dearly for his crimes. Those nearest the accident, chattered about it for a few minutes, then turned their attention back to the main event.

At fifteen minutes to twelve, the humming of the crowd

249

was stilled as the hangman and his assistants made their entrance and walked over to the gallows. The executioner wore the customary black mask, and folded sinewy arms over a broad, hirsute chest. The lower half of his body was clad in leather breeches, held in place by a spiked belt - as befitted his profession.

The gallows, itself, comprised of two uprights; a horizontal bar (from which four noosed ropes dangled), and a plank for the condemned women to stand upon.

A cheer went up as Hopkins and Stearne emerged from the Black Swan and walked into the centre of the square. The Witchfinder General acknowledged the ovation by raising his broad-brimmed Puritan's hat. He gazed at the sea of upturned faces from a small platform near the gallows, and his eyes finally rested upon Meg. He started and paled, visibly.

"What ails thee, Matthew?" enquired his companion.

"I've just seen a dead woman."

"Oh . . . someone collapsed in the heat, eh?"

"Idiot! I do not mean that! They can all be crushed to death for aught I care. No, it's the girl whose funeral we attended."

"What?"

"I tell you she's alive, man."

Stearne pulled at his beard, his eyes on the crowd. "But, we know she's dead! Didn't we deliver the body to her sister? It must be a lass who looks like her. Where is she?"

Hopkins thought he must have been mistaken and glanced again in Meg's direction. It must be the same girl!

"See you. Behind that thin woman with the raddled cheeks - one of the gentry - yes, Sir Latimer Congreave's wife."

"Christ! That's her . . . I can't understand it. She was stone cold when I dressed her in that cell. How could she be

250

alive?"

"I don't know, but you'll notice she's with her sister and Maxwell."

Stearne nodded. "Aye! How in God's name can it happen? Mayhap there *is* something in witchcraft after all."

Hopkins turned away. "Well, I like it not. I'll be very pleased to put several leagues between myself and this town."

"Well, you won't have long to wait," Stearne grinned without humour, "Here come the witches."

There was a murmur of anticipation from the mob as the four condemned women arrived in a horse-drawn cart. The people swayed and strained their necks to obtain a better view of these human beings who were about to die.

The women were pulled roughly from the cart by their guards, and hustled on towards the gallows, the crowd melting away before them.

One or two voices cried out. "Look at the Daughters of Satan - they'll soon be kicking the wind!"

"Satan's vessels they be - good riddance! We don't want witchcraft in Belford."

A black-garbed chaplain appeared out of nowhere and began muttering from his bible. Three of the women were in tears and cried out to anyone who would listen, that they were innocent. But, Mistress Nokes, despite all that she had been through, stood erect and carried herself with a calm dignity.

Bess began to cry again when she saw her mother, but Meg gently touched her arm, "The Goddess is good," she whispered. "She has granted our wishes. See how brave Mother is . . . look!"

As they watched, Agnes glanced in their direction and saw Meg. Her pain-wracked eyes lit up with joy and the ghost of

251

a smile crossed her haggard features. "It is true! My daughter lives! Now, I can die happily," she whispered.

As Mistress Nokes looked upon her family for the last time, the square was lit by a huge flash of lightning, followed almost immediately, by a deafening roll of thunder. For a moment, it seemed as if the participants in that awful drama had become immobilised by the elements. The only sound was that of a child, crying, somewhere in the crowd.

As the first large drops of rain fell from a darkening sky, the hangman leaned the ladders against the gallows and pushed each woman onto one of them. The spectators moved forward - faces lit with a morbid curiosity. Only the guards prevented them from encroaching further - their pikes at the ready - protecting the place of death.

As each woman climbed a ladder, their hands were tied behind them and a noose was placed over each of their heads. The ropes were tightened around their necks as the chaplain held up a cross before their eyes. Agnes stood quietly, but the other women howled and blasphemed, screaming for mercy and still protesting their innocence.

The hangman turned to Hopkins, waiting for the signal, and the witchfinder raised his hand, then:
"Wait!" cried Mistress Nokes.
A second later, a streak of lightning, directly overhead, illumined the macabre scene then spoke with an ear-splitting roar.

The voice of the heavens, coming at so spectacular a moment in the proceedings, created a minor havoc. People stirred uneasily, looking up at the menacing darkness, their faces resembling a crop of monstrous pallid fungi - welcoming the torrential downpour.

Children started to cry, dogs barked, while horses whinnied, tossing their manes and showing the whites of their eyes. One broke loose and cantered off down a lane; the sound of its hoof-beats echoing strangely in the sudden silence.

Gradually, the attention of the crowd became riveted upon Agnes. Hopkins, too, gazed up at her - shocked by the untimely interruption.

"Well?" he asked.

"I claim one last privilege. I wish to speak to the people of Belford."

Her voice, strong and clear, seemed not to come from that pathetic figure - the grey hair, wet, and clinging to the lined forehead. Her companions, too, were effectively silenced by this unexpected and defiant intervention.

"It is not customary for witches to make speeches from the gallows," sneered Hopkins.

But the townsfolk thought otherwise.

"Let her speak!" they yelled. "Give her a chance!"

The mood of a crowd is ever fickle and now appeared to be turning in the condemned women's favour. Hopkins knew he would have to accede to the demands of the people. His cold eyes flickered over the sea of faces and a knot of fear tightened in his belly. He addressed Agnes:

"I cannot deny your last request, woman, speak!"

Mistress Nokes gazed over the throng. The storm vividly recalled that afternoon when she had hurried home through the field, starred with white flowers, and Joan's prophesy suddenly flashed through her mind.

Gathering her now failing strength and finding comfort through the presence of her children, Robert and Arthur, the people who meant the most to her, she moistened cracked lips:

"I am a witch, yet I have committed no evil! I die innocent because I have been convicted on the evidence of lies! I only wished to live and worship the ancient Gods, whom I dearly love. Any one of you, standing here today, may yet be in my position, unless we rid our country of this vermin - the witch-finders.

These women who are to die with me, are not witches, and are here merely because their neighbours had some grievance against them - they too are innocent."

At these words, the other women nodded and seemed to take courage from Agnes - glancing sideways at her - momentarily forgetful of their plight.

And now, Agnes looked directly at the General:

"As for you, Matthew Hopkins, your days are numbered. People will begin to suspect your integrity. Judges will query the confessions you extract by torture, and the fees you receive from the blood of innocent souls. You will go to the Devil! Your name will stink in men's nostrils as the foulest of foul parasites - an obscene bird of prey! The Old Gods are not dead - they are only waiting, and will rise again to bring peace and contentment to our down-trodden people!"

Amazingly, a faint cheer went up from the listening multitude, but Hopkins was shaking with a mixture of rage and fear, unable to believe what he had heard. He glanced at Stearne, who was intently studying his wet boots and wishing he was miles away.

Mechanically, Hopkins motioned to the hangman who spoke to each of the women in the usual manner, asking their forgiveness for the act he was about to commit.

254

They all gave him absolution, calmly, which infuriated the witchfinder even more. How dare *they*, on the brink of eternity, behave so decorously?

Once more he raised his hand, and once more the chaplain lifted his cross on high. The hangman moved behind the women, pushing each one off the plank on which they stood. As they trod air, choking and kicking, he and his assistants sprang onto the threshing bodies and grabbing them around the waist, lifted their feet from the plank, thus adding their own weight to the rope and hastening the end.

Bess and Meg hid their faces on Robert's wet jerkin. His arms gripped them tightly as he watched the executions. If it had not been for the girls, he would have killed Hopkins there and then with his own hands. Arthur stared grimly at the barbaric end of his life-long friend, the tears coursing down his cheeks.

The people viewed the hangings in silence - an occurrence hitherto unknown. Usually, there was much excitement with jeers, cat-calls and obscene remarks. But, both the words of Mistress Nokes and the steady downpour had taken effect and there was even the sound of quiet sobbing from some in that vast assembly.

Everyone was soaked to the skin and the victims hung, like limp marionettes - sodden and lifeless. Even the storm was passing away from Belford, its rumbles, echoing in the distance. It was over!

Meg and Bess waited quietly to take possession of their mother's body, while Robert and Arthur fetched the horse and cart from a friend's yard.

Hopkins was still thinking of Mistress Nokes' last words. What if the mob turned on *him*? He pulled nervously at

Stearne's sleeve and they made their way through the now rapidly thinning crowd, to the Black Swan.

The witchfinders hastily packed their possessions, peering continually through the thick bottle-glass windows of the inn. The sight of Meg, followed by Mistress Nokes' prophesy, had put the fear of God into both men.

They paid their bills and left by the rear entrance, leaving Goody Phillips to follow as best she might. A stable-lad waited in the yard holding two saddled horses. Without a word, Hopkins threw him a purse of silver and the two men mounted and wheeled out of the inn.

They spurred for Suffolk in an almost headlong flight, their breath rasping - hearts, thudding, as they hurtled onward, the hedgerows flashing past unheeding eyes.

A mile further, the road curved upwards round a wooded knoll and they reined in their mounts and looked back. Belford's distant spires were etched against the receding storm clouds, but no other traveller disturbed the quiet of the countryside. The air smelt fresh and sweet and birds in the nearby copse twittered and preened sodden plumage in the afternoon sun.

Hopkins grunted, his gloved hands, taut, on the reins. Stearne swore softly and wiped the sweat from his eyes. "By the bowels of Christ, I'm glad to see the last of yon town," he muttered, squinting in the new brightness.

"Yes, we'll have to be more careful in the future," agreed Hopkins.

The two men turned their horses and set off again at a brisk canter.

An hour later, they were approaching a hamlet which clustered near the banks of the river Stour. A mill dominated the scene; its great wheel creaking and spewing tiny globules of water into the sunlight.

They crossed by the bridge - hooves clattering noisily. "We can't be more than a few miles from Ipswich," offered Stearne. "I've a mind to visit a certain doxy in those parts. What say you, Matthew?"

"I'll not go further this night," returned Hopkins, brusquely. "There's an inn sign yonder. A meal and a bed is all *I* need - the sooner the better."

Stearne grinned. "No doubt I'll get *them* and a lusty wench twixst the sheets, too. It will be worth the extra miles."

They arranged to meet in Ipswich, the following day, and Hopkins watched his companion ride jauntily away, a hand raised in farewell, before he dismounted outside the Green Man inn.

He obtained a room easily enough. Travellers usually pressed on to Ipswich town and a more varied choice of hostelry. A pot boy stabled his horse and after a plain but substantial meal of mutton followed by an excellent apple and blackberry pie, Hopkins retired to his room and fell into a fitful sleep.

He awoke from the nightmare with a shrill cry and it was some minutes before he realised where he was. With shaking fingers he lit the solitary candle then lurched over to the tiny window.

The night air felt good and his racing heart gradually steadied. He wished he had gone on to Ipswich with Stearne; this place was damnably quiet. Still, in a few hours he would be on his way. With a sigh, he climbed back into bed; the candle flame casting a comforting glow. He was just dozing off when a tap on the door, jolted his head from the pillows. "Who's there?"

The inn-keeper's voice came muted and apologetic. "Is all

257

well with ye, master? I heard ye cry out."

"Yes, yes," replied Hopkins, irritably. "I merely stubbed a toe on the chamber-pot." He muttered a curse for drawing unnecessary attention to himself.

The voice came again. "I've brought ye a mug of ale - to help ye sleep, like."

Unaccountably, a lump rose in the witchfinder's throat and his eyes pricked with moisture. This unexpected concern, from a stranger, and following so soon upon the nightmare, in which his victims returned from the dead and took their revenge on his person with unspeakable torture, had left him almost sick with self-pity.

He flung the covers aside and swung skinny legs to the floor. A moment later and he had unlocked the door, his hand held out for the promised refreshment. But his hand remained empty and he suddenly realised that something was very wrong.

His reaction came a second too late. The door crashed back and a huge, gloved hand reached out, took him by the throat, and threw him to the ground. Hopkins yelped and lay on the boards gasping like a landed fish. Pain from the impact flooding through his body. When he finally looked up he beheld the face of Robert Maxwell.

The witchfinder scrambled away and pulled his nightgown over his knees. This pathetic attempt at modesty caused the second intruder to smile, grimly. "We must have come to the wrong place, Robert. Yon bundle of sticks can ne'er be the Witchfinder General."

"Well, now, you should know better, David," replied Maxwell, his eyes never leaving the cowering figure. "Take a look in his saddlebag, I'll wager it's full of blood-money."

258

His friend bent down and dragged the satchel from its hiding-place beneath the bed. The silver fell in a shower onto the counterpane.

"Huh, a goodly haul, wouldn't you say, Robert?"

Hopkins sprang to his feet and at last found his voice.

"That money has been earned by doing God's work. I'll caution you, the law of the land is on my side. My work is also approved by the magistracy."

"Save your breath, lawyer," snarled David. "I'll wager you'll need it 'afore this night's out."

The witchfinder's heart leapt at the threat. "You'll find there are penalties to be paid for false accusations. If you have a complaint - take it to the courts," he blustered.

Robert's fist struck Hopkins on the mouth. "You murdering swine. You *dare* to speak of false accusations to us?"

The lawyer reeled back, a hand to his bleeding lips. "It was God's work, I tell you, and I warn you . . ." he stopped, and stared at the faces before him, aware that his protests were availing him nothing. "See you, take the silver and have done." He raised his arms, "Take it all!"

"Think you we would touch such money, witchfinder?" snorted David. "We would not besmirch our souls with such corruption."

"Enough of this pretence," snapped Robert. "Bring him out."

"Wait!" yelled Hopkins. "I'll not be taken, I have my rights . . . innkeeper!" he screamed, as Robert thrust him back to the wall.

"Listen, you . . ." he almost choked on his words. "Call not for the innkeeper. His loyalty lies with us. It was *he* who sent word as to your whereabouts." Robert's lip curled in

259

derision. "When you have hung a man's own mother for a witch, ask not for *his* aid."

Hopkins bellowed and made for the door, but David's outthrust foot sent him sprawling. They dragged him, struggling and moaning, down the stairs and out into the night.

Silently they bore him, smothering his cries. His flimsy nightgown flapping round bare knees. When they reached the Mill they flung him onto the dew-wet grass.

"In God's name, what infamy have you planned?" he croaked. But they ignored him and proceeded to bind his wrists and ankles, their heavy breathing, loud, in his ears.

"Christ Jesu - have mercy!" he shrieked, writhing against his bonds.

The two witches stared down at him for a moment, then hauled him up, and wading into the knee-high water of the pool, they bound his spare frame to the great wheel.

Hopkins moaned, drooling saliva, "Christ! Have mercy!" His desperate plea hung on the still air and the only answer he received, was the sudden screech of a startled water-fowl.

He shivered and sobbed, his body drenched in the sweat of fear, the ropes cutting into his flesh. Dear God, they are going to kill me, his thoughts screamed. Dear God - I am going to die!

They had released the sluice-gate and the water was pouring onto the wooden paddles. The wheel shuddered and began to turn. The witchfinder gave a despairing cry as he felt the movement and saw the trees move out of his vision. A dawn-streaked sky followed, and as suddenly, disappeared. Then, the falling water hit him and drew him under. It filled his gaping mouth and stung his eyes; its iciness numbing his already cold limbs.

A moment later, he emerged, gasping and retching, only to witness the earth and the sky swinging crazily past. He caught a glimpse of his executioners - dark forms against a brightening horizon. He tried to cry out but his throat was fast closing and the air came whistling from bursting lungs. This was indeed, death.

The great wheel gathered momentum and thrust him into the water again and again, until at last, the darkness crowded in . . .

THE END

Historical Note

Although most of the characters in this novel are fictitious, Matthew Hopkins, John Stearne, Goody Phillips and The Rev., John Gaule, were real people. Hopkins was responsible for the arrest of at least two hundred people on the charge of witchcraft. Most of them were hanged.

In 1646, he encountered a set-back which finally led to the termination of his career. A Parliamentary news magazine, *The Moderate Intelligencer*, commented upon the hangings. It stated - "Divers are condemned and some are executed and more likely to be. Life is precious and there is need of great enquiry before it is taken away."

Then, The Reverend John Gaule began preaching against the witchfinder. Hopkins threatened him, hoping the cleric would recant, but it only served to elicit a publication, *Select Cases of Conscience touching Witches and Witchcrafts,* by Gaule, in which he exposed Hopkins' methods of torture. The General replied in a little pamphlet entitled, "Discovery of Witches", to prove his case, but it was a lame answer to his critic.

Gradually, enthusiasm and respect for Matthew Hopkins started to wane. He had overshot his mark and accused too many people. As the character of Mistress Nokes prophesied, judges did indeed query his methods of torture and his fees.

The witchfinder's health deteriorated rapidly and he retired from public life. One source states that Hopkins, himself, was subjected to the ordeal of 'swimming' and that he floated! Another version of the same story says that he was drowned on this occasion. But, his partner in crime, John Stearne, wrote that Hopkins expired "After a long sickness of a Consumption . . . without any trouble or conscience for what he had done, as was falsely reported of him." Certainly, an entry in the parish register of Mistley-cum-Manningtree, states that 'Matthew Hopkins, son of Mr. James Hopkins, Minister of Wenham, was buried at Mistley, on 12th August, 1647'. The author, however, preferred the former rumour of a 'watery' end, and one, moreover, which would not have prohibited his body from being buried - as stated, above.

It seems that John Stearne lived out his days, peaceably, but nothing is known concerning the fate of Goody Phillips.

Throughout the three centuries of the persecutions in Western Europe, whole families, including children, were burnt alive on a daily basis. In England, the penalty was that of hanging or disembowelling. The estimated number of executions has been given as nine million.

Printed in the United States
93271LV00003B/1-18/A

9 780979 140259